Oldness;
or, the Last-Ditch
Efforts of Marcus O

Oldness;
or, the Last-Ditch Efforts of Marcus O

A Novel

Brett Josef Grubisic

| N₁ | O₂ | N₁ |

CANADA

*Publisher's note: This book is a work of fiction. Names, characters, places and
incidents are either the product of the author's imagination or are used
fictitiously, and any resemblance to actual persons living or dead
is entirely coincidental.*

Library and Archives Canada Cataloguing in Publication

Grubisic, Brett Josef, author
Oldness; or, The last-ditch efforts of Marcus O / Brett Josef Grubisic.

ISBN 978-1-988098-63-0 (softcover)

I. Title. II. Title: Last-ditch efforts of Marcus O.

PS8613.R82O43 2018   C813'.6   C2018-904206-0

Printed and bound in Canada on 100% recycled paper.

Now Or Never Publishing
901, 163 Street
Surrey, British Columbia
Canada V4A 9T8

nonpublishing.com
Fighting Words.

We gratefully acknowledge the support of the Canada Council for the Arts
and the British Columbia Arts Council for our publishing program.

Institution, employees, undergraduates: continuous inspirations.

Contents

2023

(On an early afternoon between mid-October lectures)

Now, a man is praised for being angry
under the right circumstances,
and with the right people,
and also in the right manner,
at the right time,
and for the right length of time.
—Aristotle*

*_Nicomachean Ethics_, trans. Martin Ostwald

B efore crossing to a shaded bench Marcus O roasted under the sun for five long minutes. Briny moisture beaded under his professorial attire, trickles bloomed. Tenting the front of Wednesday's maroon wool pullover, he kept watch on the concrete tower's longer clock hand and muttered a wish for accuracy from the mechanical drivers within.

Marcus peered at depthless blue above full boughs of yellowed leaves and wondered about Vitamin D, that regulatory godsend. More particularly, he wanted data: the exposure patches of skin (two size L hands, one largish head) require to churn out a useful dose. *On-the-cusp-of-old skin*, he corrected, curious too if dermal efficiency slips decade after decade.

Any passerby could ask their gadget assistant of choice—a veritable UN of languages with accent submenus, all housed within lucrative products globally monitored every second by patent lawyer armies—and solve the mysteries in a trice.

For the moment Marcus preferred the respite of silence. He'd settle for grasped-straw answers: "A half hour" and "Yes, it does. Of course efficiency slips, why wouldn't it?"

If the matter had staying power, he'd ask Syb, standing sentinel on his office desk and currently set at *British (Female)*. She'd know.

Syb™, a naming agency's brainchild. The zeitgeist embodied, on flat surfaces everywhere.

"Incidentally, Syb . . ." With that activation prompt the everready assistant replied with "What's on the agenda, Marcus?" Though almost flawless, the artifice of bygone Speak & Spell could still be heard in sporadic affectless syllables of Syb's voice. To trained ears, she bumbled with diphthongs and triphthongs.

An indispensable Miss Moneypenny at the filing cabinet in the guise of a tubby aluminum cylinder, the machine—not a gear to be found, but essentially that—gladdened him. He welcomed

Space Age faith in ingenuity. ENIAC, the Thames Flood Barrier, Telstar 1. Utopianism in the Atomsville U.S.A. mould inspired the hoarding of hope. And counterpoint relief to screen news in ominous streams, feeds, banners, and broadcasts. Whenever possible Marcus kept undiluted promise and the big picture in mind, the aftermath sequestered. True, *World's Fair* and *money pit* fell under the same column. And, okay, a scrap metal dealer had bought Expo 75's Aquapolis for a steal, towed the oxidized pile to Shanghai, and auctioned off the useful remnants to a soup can manufacturer. Still, the dreamy impulse—the vision, the wonderment—couldn't be dismissed outright. Better that than forecasting eras of diminishment, hard going, or outright apocalypse just past the horizon.

Marcus pictured a timeline and his era on it. Bland, an inbox overrun by unsolicited—undesired, unneeded—ads for compression technology hosiery and outreach from fictional rich ladies in otherwise destitute nations whose vaults of cash could be unlocked and shared if only he'd reply with credit card details.

2023. Just a loitering interregnum of bot companions, software vulnerabilities, drought alerts, geopolitical skirmishes, data breaches, and anti-obesity campaigns before the next regime, or the postpeak origin on a cartoon sales chart where the black arrow would soon tumble down, down, down, and right off the page?

The easy bet: he'd shuffle off permanently—bagged greywhite residue in a funeral home's discreet gift box—without ever witnessing the answer.

Uncomfortable and shifting, Marcus flattened his palms against the baked wooden slats. For oblivious walkers, the hands modelled visible blood vessels and tendons wrapped by creased papery skin. Another of carpe diem's living PSAs.

His mind leapt from visible fact to foreseeable near future. Porous, dried-twig bones and handicapped immune function loomed without regular activity and influxes of Vitamin D, declared medical authorities. Hello aches and stiffness, osteoarthritis and hip fractures. Livid staph infections, pleased to finally meet you!

All that was common knowledge, thanks also to dairy marketers and never-ending infomercials for medical alert pendants. "Help, I've fallen": one jest in an elongated series launched with the sluggish metabolism and bread dough waist. Anemic, couch potato muscles. The late-onset A-cup made of flab. Bristle-sprouting ears that obeyed deranged genetic instructions to enlarge. These proliferating indignities—weekly pill holders as big as tackle boxes, hardy har har—rich material for stand-up routines wherever stooped, pot-bellied snowbirds roosted.

And, naturally, for web snark: "a old mans face has more crack than a hooker on a good night." Marcus had run across that, mentally corrected the kindergarten grammar, and wanted to—. He couldn't decide. Accept every bit of it with all-turn-to-dust-again resignation? Rage, rage, but to what end?

Sans teeth, sans eyes, sans taste, sans everything, Marcus recalled. Old dead William had reserved some of his caustic best for the sunset years' cankered minds and shrunk shanks; OzSteve-o, the online contributor of supposed wit about addict prostitutes and geriatric male faces, dug from the same soil, fertile now for centuries.

Still. Cracks about cracks from now on? Twenty-one days and some hours away, his sixtieth increasingly felt equivalent to a futile, slow-motion bracing for impact. Back slaps, loud cards with glitter exclamation points, and musty zingers about heartless gravity, erectile dysfunction, or a gold watch: oh, boy. He couldn't wait to attend his first Honk to Support Seniors rally. *Notice us, please. We've survived.*

Self-pity, party of one, Marcus thought, what's with this sourness? He craned his neck, swapping a downcast view of a grey woollen lap for a vista where the tower stood at dead centre. Springing to life in the same decade as me, he remembered. All the clock requires for social usefulness is basic functionality. And, admittedly, a maintenance crew.

Happily at least, Marcus decided, he could count on a bus seat with near certainty. He'd turned grey early.

His first solar lentigine, or at least the first he'd noticed, had appeared on the top middle of his left hand soon after the big five-oh. Mottled, a geezer, just like that. A "common condition," he'd read, "aka liver spots, age spots." A *condition*? Pesky but treatable à la dandruff, or that perpetual human one troubling sages since *The Dialogue of Pessimism*?

Science pooh-poohed the ominous reputation of these common condition blemishes as a telltale for organ dysfunction and impending decline. Baseless, medical web truth-tellers decreed. Folklore.

Commerce preferred the unsettling myth. C'est la vie contentment didn't serve business interests. But consumer gut pangs, frown lines, and lung gasps at mirrors transmuted into annual executive bonuses.

Skipping over ad copy with gaze-conscious female targets and that whole virtual civilization of corporation-funded makeup tutorials, Marcus had found independent product testing sites. He learned about a "tunable polysiloxane-based material that can be engineered with specific elasticity, contractility, adhesion, tensile strength, and occlusivity."

(Although impressively scientific in tone, the last word had stumped him. Searching led to blind alleys: "The condition of being occlusive." → "Occluding or tending to occlude." → "Occlude is defined as to hide, block or close. Chem.: to retain or absorb (a gas, liquid, or solid). Dentistry: to meet with the cusps fitting close together, said of the upper and lower teeth." Remaining stumped, he'd returned to the ad's triumph-over-adversity narrative.)

Evidently, the micro-film would stick like wallpaper, a literal second skin for ten hours. Enviable age-defying results, a temporary new you. In appearance, anyhow. And from not too close up, thank you very much.

A world of wonders, courtesy of Twelve Oaks Pharm, LLC—

"Okay, Helena, you spill it now, what's your secret?!?"
"Oh, you know. Dark green vegetables, plenty of rest and exercise . . . and I trowel on that tunable polysiloxane-based material before I arrive at the office! Its specific occlusivity is out of sight!"

Per diem mummification and demummification, though, the upkeep.

For his own dermatological misfortune Marcus had discovered cryotherapy and enzyme inhibitors, profiteer margins, and distressing side-effects. Word was, judicious application of blemish-fading biological extracts—from foraged licorice root, bird of paradise, and sweet chestnut rose—could forestall a "hyperpigmentation intervention."

He'd chuckled at the notion. Daily moisturized friends and family (shade dwellers all) hosting the locked-door event, slathering pricey goo on the offender's peppered skin and waiting for the answered prayer of melanin loss. Inevitably, a later relapse. Barking "What I do with my skin is my own business!" the sun junkie would secretly book a seat on a Los Cabos-bound charter and pack tanning butter. A lost weekend with slippery bottles of O SPF.

Skeptically wandering an all-night pharmacy, Marcus had nevertheless tapped away a c-note on Japanese serum inside a minute green glass container—an *alabastron*, its glossy white box whispered. Grabbing surplus items as misdirection—discount bin shampoo, shaving cream, and deodorant—he recalled doing the same decades before to distract cashiers from *Penthouse* and condoms in optimistic twelve-packs. Who wouldn't avoid embarrassment if they could?

Once home, Marcus scrutinized Lucent Blanc's small print with a magnifying glass. Finger/dyke, basically. And a soul owed to the company store: *Continued usage of the product will assure optimal results.* Surrendering to the instructions, he'd dabbed and rubbed. Halfheartedly, since web medical sites let him know the actual requirement—an impossible gizmo opening a time tunnel to the summer of *Grease*. He'd step through, warn his adolescent self about the inspiration to grab a ladder for rooftop marathons of coconut-scented tanning in gym shorts on August afternoons.

He read that the serum's parent company, a multinational based in the Netherlands, also held oven cleaner, meat snack, and spreadables divisions. Though one of its marketing tentacles had conjured Lucent Blanc as arcane wisdom retrieved from the very depths of ancient history, for all Marcus knew (Syb being little help) workers vat-grew the ointment in one of the conglomerate's margarine units. Substitute butter flavouring for tuberose and replace pearly white with beta carotene and he could swipe the stuff over toast.

Dotage, downturn, decrepitude, debility, diminution, dementia, the dyspeptic declining years: the late autumn of life, a shadowy thicket of maladies, could scarcely be labelled a vacation destination.

Faced with the handicap of tough-sell facts, the retirement industry counteracted with seductive paper and pixel images of golf club backswings and an eternity of placid waterways for sleepy cruises; at home, apparently, an adorable litter of grandkids softened the frosty bite.

So what if you'd packed a king's ransom of pharmacological brand names and snuck on absorbent disposable underwear lined with proprietary Acti-V-Smartgel before a starry night on the Lido deck?

With his back to the clock, Marcus relished the cooler air. He'd welcome a few melancholic hours of mist—grey Highlands weather in moody squalls, foghorns switched on, foreshortened views, the tonic of quiet light. Better socked-in gloom than melting flip flops under static SoCal glare and pupils squeezed to pinholes. Nordic melancholy instead of go, go, go with sea-sprayed, breeze-tossed manes.

He watched student herds of twos and threes skitter by. Not quite carefree but close. Hacky sacks: a resurrected trend or an ongoing one? The birth and death of youth culture's sudden fascinations, he couldn't—didn't bother to—keep track. Greek system pledging, skateboards, boycotting manias, candlelight vigils, piercings, public chastity vows, trucker hats, phone games, frat mixers, hula hoops, raves, silent marches, rainbow dyes, beer pong, VR headsets, conspicuous charity work, pin-pimpled backpacks announcing causes and allegiances? Small wonder Enlightenment honchos had preached against the anarchy of religious Enthusiasts.

Still, he'd gladly siphon off an ounce of that brimming sense of limitlessness, as myopic as it might be.

Distempered mood aside, Marcus had come outside to bask, enjoy the balm of a fine day in and of itself. Minus implications, free of undercurrents.

Formerly, searing October weather would have inspired meandering walks and rhapsodic pronouncements about the blessed gift called an Indian Summer. Now anyone of Marcus' acquaintance dodged the I-word. And First Nations Summer had never caught on. "An unseasonably warm autumn" lacked in poetry, but caused no offence.

Worse than an accusation of insensitivity, blazing months late in the year summoned an everyday dread related to business-as-usual emissions, greenhouse gasses, and shrinking habitability. Blue-skied woe: real-time global maps where sun-hued colours (corona yellow through thermometer red) steadily annexed the reassuring edenic green, and where newish concepts ending with -ation—desertific, salinific, deforest—raced ahead of nuclear pro-lifer, the Cold War's bogeyman. The pulses of misgiving in turn inspired decisions to don facekinis or rub on coatings of broad-spectrum salve and shake fists at Henry Ford and Co. Or to scur-ry back indoors and stare at trees and lawns through polarized glass while cursing the human appetite for gassy livestock num-bering in the billions.

Younger generations still consumed entire afternoons at beach volleyball, Marcus understood. And he'd overheard quips about melanoma lobbed around with "Duuude!" from bleached-tooth mouths. Despite the public displays, he imagined the caramel-tanned players alone afterwards and positioning them-selves, necks wrenched, at mirrors. They'd scrutinize irregular freckles and moles, comparing what they saw to gruesome documentary images on clinical websites probably funded by a skincare and oven cleaner conglomerate. On the following after-noon, an identical, practically Sisyphean if self-inflicted, routine.

Caution thrown to the wind: a species trait with divided out-comes.

Besides autumn's dappled semi-pleasures, Marcus had headed outdoors on impulse, needing to calm down.

The dangerous atoms to avoid: office walls in solitude and vitreous passageways chock-a-block with faces of querying students, colleagues, or staff.

You'd better simmer down, he'd instructed himself three flights up and fifteen minutes earlier. Attached to an obsolete usage of simmer that had nothing to do with cooking, that phrase had entered circulation before the Gilded Age, waned, and gone extinct. He hadn't heard the expression forever. When they weren't spitting "Get turft, hombre" and "That's so tranked," students now passed around "Mellow out, man" as though they'd coined it. Shortly before that, "Chill, bro," yet somehow altogether unaware of Haight-Asbury and Timothy Leary. Never mind *The Doors of Perception* and *S.C.U.M. Manifesto*. Marcus wondered if all knowledge amounted to heaped trivia.

He'd *reacted* earlier, true, the bolting for the stairwell and outside air as immediate as panic. No wonder people stormed from rooms and set out on long solitary ambles. Clear the head, vent some steam, etc, etc. Let the *mal aria* dispel.

As expected, the unadulterated ire—fiery, a compassionless void—had begun to subside. Breathing consciously slowed, jaw muscles kneaded into submission, and hand shape changed from Rock to Paper had helped too.

Outbursts, fists, and the myriad subtle human forms of pilo-erection had no respectable place, no demonstrable history in a deliberative environment with such a temperate composition, where even-keeled amounted to orthodoxy, a primary operating principle. And where *measured* represented a communal standard and cool heads filled with starchy abstemiousness prevailed.

Paintball battle simulations, faculty *Fight Club* combatants jacked on performance enhancers, arm wrestling, escalating shouting matches, the first- or second-degree inflicting of physical harm, or slaps, punches, and shoves. Here? Never. Grand Guignol's arterial sprays? Absurd. Bellowing and brawls? As probable as chimps in jetpacks. All that had gone deep underground. As much as possible, faculty had perfected the art of sublimation.

Scripts and mystery novels might traffic in the two-faced professor trope—a frigid or slack-muscled bookishness disguising the criminal mastermind's ferocity—but Marcus didn't need to query Syb for an answer about literally murderous professions. His wasn't and hadn't ever been.

Rocking slightly on the weathered bench Marcus felt flabbergasted still, though less so with each passing moment. Also, less smarting and raw because stung. Plus: less maligned, ridiculed without obvious recourse, and Klieg lit as the recipient of excoriating gossip. Less outraged too. He hadn't thought *How dare she!* for a minute at least.

Marcus, a complex system gaining equilibrium, sensed a neuronal cluster that throbbed with sobering perspective. It said its piece ("Whatever, guy, big fucking whoop. Get over yourself and grow a pair") in the voice of a playground tough.

Until the incident Marcus had assessed Judaea without much kindness or generosity. He wouldn't have claimed to *actively* dislike her clenched demeanour, not aloud. Nor to have brightened at the sight of her brisk, wound-up movements. Thrumming at the woman's intellectual prowess? No dice.

Even though their antipathy grew and shrank at unpredictable intervals, he'd adopted congenial indifference as a general policy. And watered-down scorn, that regular insincerity. Another communal practice.

Ordinarily he directed polite nods and nanosecond quarter-smiles toward the woman in elevators and corridors and noted their return. Keeping to himself, he contributed only silence or shrugs when closed-door air-clearing at the ends of semesters commenced. To the "What's up with that" pinpointing Judaea's unabashed careerism, he responded with changes of subject. Usually, anyhow.

Now, she'd pushed him into devising a new policy.

As for the quality of Judaea's thought: meh. At best, humdrum decorated with sprinklings of on-trend jargon and names with cachet. Consumeristic, a follower of passing fashions. Third-string otherwise, parasitical. Never mind that galling politicized gesturing—a late model storm-the-barricades prof—that x'ed out the tenure, sabbaticals, pension benefits, travel funds, and Volvo coupe. That pretended the securely fastened and pristine white collar did not exist and bi-annual publication shared ground with the Salt March. 250 footnoted sentences about gendered ware-house worker precarity or post-image economy capitalism appearing in university-funded journals sweated over by graduate students and comfortable peers had less political effect, he'd swear, than battery recycling. Such postures were, however, boons for a fast-track career.

On any given day Marcus viewed Judaea as dull, then pre-tentious, then dull again. A thorn in his side, her mannerisms grated, though less than that whooping laugh the kindest of eulo-gists would call distinctive.

He'd imagined she regarded him with equal sangfroid. She'd list different reasons, of course. His unthinkingly typical overcon-sumption of social space. Conventional Heteromasculinity's Lebensraum Imperative: he'd listened to a minute of that sermon on her vlog channel. Yes, yes, the Himmlers and Hitlers casting shadows over every woman.

The banality of SWM privilege: he was stuck with those traits, the polar opposite of disadvantaged.

In any case, she'd surely made no effort to ingratiate herself in any way or seek his friendship. Marcus had seen that her cam-pus kinship pattern favoured same-generation women in tight, exclusive triads in belted trench coats of black canvas and fuzzy beet-hued scarves knitted in artisan cooperatives.

If no friendship or genuine collegial professional courtesy developed they'd agreed—informally, having never discussed or even hinted at any need for a border-defining conversation—to abide by the philosophy of leave well enough alone.

Even so, at unit meetings he'd noticed how they always wound up in diametrical seating.

In groups of all sizes incompatibility and mutual ill will developed as a matter of course. Why would a competitive society composed of former A+-or-bust students and current never not evaluative PhDs accustomed to taking the room's leadership in documented book smarts act any differently?

Minutes ago Judaea had arbitrarily totalled the equilibrium: lowered the façade, presumed to alter the implied contractual terms. Unilaterally, just like that.

He could swallow the taunt, true, feign indifference and carry on as before with a turned cheek. But should he?

Already a memory in the process of capitalization, the Incident—merely one cycle of blood circulation, a few syllables and pauses, a flurry of nonverbal communication cues—had shocked him, much in the same way student evaluations of his likability and the class content he'd muscled into existence had once surprised, then peeved, infuriated, or pained him. Anonymity bred a peculiar species of viciousness and brutality. Punitiveness too. In turn, he'd begun a tradition: delete any email announcing the latest batch of class evals. Thanks but no thanks, galling pipsqueaks, until you're prepared for choice anonymous phrases from us that are posted for all the world to see.

At 1:35 he'd rounded an out-of-the-way corner and faced startled peers tête-à-tête, the privacy of their conversation instantly spotlit.

Verbal information: "Oh. Marcus. Hi. Well, we were just—."

Corporeal cues: shifted feet and glances dropped to the flooring, the universal tells for guiltiness.

Marcus hadn't recognized Judaea's friend. Charcoal-haired with a Susan Sontag white swath, the stranger had immediately checked her watch for time, messages, weather, heart rate, feeds, notifications, calorie usage, horoscope, and pending appointments.

Steps before that inauspicious corner, he'd registered Judaea's poor approximation of a stage whisper, complete with relentless italicizing she'd picked up who knew where. "*Come* on, that *fossil?!? It* hasn't published a worthwhile *idea* in, well, *really*, a case could be made for *never*. As in *ever*." He'd heard that, a happy fluke of acoustics and unwanted publicity for some poor soul nonetheless, from a dozen paces. Acoustic baffling soaked up titters and syllables as he drew closer. Murmuring, garbled words, and then the barb of Judaea's retort: "*Relevance*? In. What. Multiverse?"

The worthless fossil under attack might be faculty anywhere, Marcus had decided. Everyone compiled their own list. If pressed, Marcus could name a half dozen husks on the same floor whose blathering sound waves some cortex or another had processed for years. Double that for those whose estimation of their capabilities in no way matched peer consensus.

He'd stridden into view.

Recovering from the verbal stumble, Judaea had raised a hand to cover her mouth. Acting dumbfounded, she pitched her torso back a few degrees. The hand dropped and came to rest over a jade pendant: *Oh my!*

The smirking coyness suggested a pretence of shock suitable for a dastardly soap opera villain: *Could such caustic words really have come from this minty-fresh mouth?*

Centimetres above, another message. Hazel-flecked green eyes with balefulness switched on: *I meant you, fossil.*

Reptilian-minded, he'd nodded at Judaea's challenge. The audacity, he thought. You cunt. I will pulverize you.

What this unmasked foe discerned in his gaze, Marcus couldn't guess. Nothing dangerous, certainly. Save for their stony weight, fossils do not pose much of a threat.

As though propelled by urgent business at the main office, Marcus steered past the conspirators.

Months earlier he'd locked away a morsel of did-you-know? from a colleague whose wife worked across campus in Neuroscience. She'd told Marcus that anger, like all emotions, has psychological but also physiological components. Joy, rage, bliss, love: each a neuronal torrent of a differing size, consistency, magnitude, and duration. And that anger, a hormonal flash flood, took hours to chemically wane, dependent on body weight and, oddly, sex. A cocktail that incited primitive self-preserving thoughts and prompted immediate actions, its tart ingredients would gradually dissolve into utter harmlessness: sugars, proteins, water, salts, acetic acid. Marcus had understood that the basic concept, not molecular specifics, mattered.

Would that same process recur the next time he and Judaea crossed paths? And the instance after that—the automatic coalescing of microscopic components into a stew of chemicals felt as hot, red-eyed fury?

Even as the questions fired, he told himself to give the subject a rest.

Muttering, alone, on a wooden bench. Terrific. Another feature display at the Museum of Geriatrics. Marcus pushed against the wood, his right arm a lever for uprightness.

In the meantime, then, there was no fighting ancient built-in systems of biology. He'd wait until the chemical deluge eased, broke down into manageable everyday civility. Normal-range sanity restored. By dinner, maybe.

That routine organic miracle accomplished, he'd revisit the Judaea question, perhaps select the right tools for the job. Or, anger atomizing quickly, he'd give the preliminary selection process a shot on the bus. He could stand the novelty. He'd already pondered every aspect of the ads for Occupational Constipation (hands deep in the front pockets of his chinos, a white clean-cut middle-age, middle-management type eyes a toilet stall dubiously, a captive in the purgatory of a grey-tiled public washroom) and HPV Spectrum Disorders (a recent, out-of-frame medical discovery causes a towel-wrapped cross-armed white woman at the steel-framed mirror of a white-tiled gym bathroom to ponder her woeful fate and a reluctant date-night disclosure). Judaea could displace those other worries.

Best served cold, he thought. But exactly how? Like psychics, proverbs traded on vagueness.

Marcus inhaled crisp air that smelled uniquely of October—nature's industrious last-chance flowering before a transformative rotting into nutritious sludge.

Continuance

(Mornings, afternoons, evenings [2023-28])

So many people say that beauty will save the world,
but I don't believe so.
The world will be saved by intelligence and humanity
and generosity—and possibly love.
But of course the aesthetic world helps, a little.*

*Miuccia Prada, 14 March 2018

Pedagogy

Monday 1:00–1:15 PM

Marcus awaited the girl's outburst of revelation. A sluggish volcano and currently slump incarnate, the waifish body beneath the riot of preposterous clothing trends appeared to be building up to . . . something. A subspecies of complaint, likely. Negotiation, pleading, accusation, a furious howl, plaintive apology with an ulterior motive. Who could say?

If nothing else, Marcus had learned to never confuse paper accomplishments—year after year, that standard run of A-equivalents since pre-kindergarten—with the tremendous coruscation found in students' innermost selves. As reflected in frosh think piece essays, anyhow. The surface decoration of current season mall clothes laundered by maternal figures? The late-adolescent classroom behavioural modes characterized by self-absorption, screen fixations, and a never not astonishing speaking pattern noteworthy for its addiction to "like," that forty-year old crutch? Sometimes just an onion's outermost layers. Such melancholy in their paragraphs. An almost Romantic sensibility! The woebegone alphabet began with Alienation, Anger, and Anguish. It could grow practically morbid. Now and then, at least.

The rest? As banal and unreflective as pieces of toast.

The meek student quietly hyperventilating in the adjacent chair felt bewildered, he supposed. In the thick of it. Out of her depth, despite having served juvenile hard time inside windowless, dictatorial cram school rooms in some high-density, sepia-hazed overseas city. And despite passing countless dreamy hours watching online clips while mouthing the words—"For the love of all that's holy, Aurora, not *that* skirt with *those* shoes"—of American television programming aimed at teenage consumers. Evidently, she'd mistaken those empty calories for nourishment.

As the girl rummaged for backbone, Marcus nudged away workaday thoughts. Meetings with posted agendas, low volume exchanges (budgets, funding, enrolment figures) before and after. As always, a puritan undercurrent of fretful dourness. Or cluck, cluck, cluck and Chicken Little's scatterbrained panic. The sky had been falling for the duration of his Methuselah of a career.

The girl's noises, the decibel level of a kitten's sneeze, now swelled. Any moment he expected tearful jury box testimony or an appeal for mercy of the "Please, sir, I want some more" strain. For a moment she snivelled. Grasping for composure, the student resumed with tiny exhalations of anxiety.

An inactive volcano for this visit's remaining 720 seconds in all likelihood, Marcus decided. And too bad too. Lava bomb pyrotechnics might really kickstart his afternoon.

Until the girl found the correct state of mind, Marcus would wait. Though picturing a crocodile with its gaze locked on an oblivious bird, he'd paste on one of his profession's looks with high approval ratings. Lifted brow, wide eyes, the mouth's edges tugged slightly upward: that combination beamed *I'm here for you* while obscuring truer sentiments.

The underperforming pupil remembered the policy. She had to. On every syllabus: *Students must take responsibility and direct office hour conversations.* Marcus made sure everyone in all his classes absorbed that. As for "Okay now, what's the problem, and how may I help?" or Twenty Questions, he left those to psychoanalysts, kindergarten teachers, and Walmart Supercenter greeters.

To the rhythm of the student's barely there huffs, Marcus free-associated.

He pictured long-ago spice route explorers. Queasy from ocean heaves and brined pork the parched travellers held firm expectations about a fearsome unknown, a New World where monsters of legend roamed. Nearing tranquil shorelines their eyes instead settled on conifers towering above stony ribbons of beach littered with kelp. The faint slap of waves. Scattering deer and a curious seal colony with bobbing heads. No Hydra, no Polyphemus. Nary a Siren on any rock. Ho hum.

What foreign exoticism had the student anticipated before her flight touched down on continental North America and she'd taxied by the discount outlet village? Using up an ample portion of a privileged adolescence to piece together a map based on screen images of what her essay—a 58, pure kindness on his part—had called "the nowadays modern Western lifestyle," what fantastic everyday had she spun? Paparazzi chasing black-windowed limousines that housed leggy catwalk models? Chart-topper of the moment pop stars and in-crowd alcohol brands rippled by a trunkful of subwoofers? Treed metropolitan avenues where audacious heists, mechanical creatures, super-powered beings (the earnest good vs the scheming bad, in perpetuity), and slow-motion explosive gunfire couldn't be avoided? Parcels of secluded landscape sheltering trainee magicians, vampires, and metahumans? A cornucopia of luxury brand bargains in daily marathons? Sorority Row pledging?

How prosaic, how utterly disappointing jammed traffic, regulation coastal weather, and exacting professors with tough assignments in tidal barrages must have felt. After so much build-up, how cruel.

Seated chin to chest, the girl struggled to formulate a winning combination of words.

Twelve hours away over in Smog City, the instructor of the student's Contemporary English: Idiomatic Expressions section (the autocratic type, Marcus hazarded, devoid of generosity but a whiz with a ruler and rules) had evidently skipped over *C'mon, man, cut me some slack, will you, I'm totally giving it my all* as too advanced. As suitable for a class further up the rung.

Marcus' mouth pursed with impatience, fingers tapped. *Get the lead out, get a move on, get it in gear.* other useful idioms. *Get a grip, get going, get your act together, get your head out of your ass.*

Stealthy left hand sliding past Syb's bulbous silhouette, he touched the pad and found the class list and student's headshot. Zhang, Haoyu. BCom, Year 2. Preferred name: L'Oréal.

She'll regret that, Marcus thought. Perhaps her cohort had assumed complementary personae for their four years abroad: audacious Revlon, buttoned-up Clinique, affable but slow-witted Maybelline. All led by worldly L'Oréal. In the campus-set movie franchise they'd conjure—*G.L.A.M. Squad!* or such—the quartet would solve crimes or cast spells or rule Delta Gamma while strutting by envious girls and gulping boys mesmerized by the leggy, bewitching glamour.

L'Oréal must see herself at a cliff's edge, Marcus guessed. After all, the business school required a grade far higher than the letters (C+, C+, C-) she'd accrued to date. As for his role in the script: obstacular, the giant tending a rope bridge who'd demand gold coins. Maybe. Or, a warted brook troll quick to pose a mystifying riddle.

In case of emergency—no cash, a bad guess—tears might work.

Each semester Marcus met, taught, and promptly forgot iterations of this student demographic. Career-wise: a cumulative class list of nameless thousands, an essay stack to rival Babel. A drinking game hinged on him asking "But where's the thesis?" would hospitalize several generations of Fraternity Row.

The girl. Absentee but technologically-tethered and sternly expectant parents—with one other publicly-defined characteristic: "they are working very hard"—had invested a fortune in yuan, won, or rupiah to assure their dutiful golden child and eventual palliative caregiver of business-sector advantages once she returned home with a degree in Commerce from the world-class brand name they could afford.

She'd been coached to perform since nursery classes, the spectre of shame always at the periphery.

If she or another from the Classes of 2004 onward had rebelled and messaged her stern overlords in the mother country about an unsanctioned plan to set up a taco stand in Tulum with a 30-hour work week, he'd never caught wind of it. Not once.

"Turn on, tune in, drop out" would sound nonsensical to the girl, as empty as a lecture about the importance of time management.

Marcus graded and forgot these creatures and their surface acquiescence by the gross, in truth, and had for decades. An occupational reality, despite that occupation's pretence.

Could the labourer in Adam Smith's factory assembly line—that chestnut, a teachable Econ moment trotted out since 1776—remember a single specific pin from twenty seconds or an hour before? An entire day? Unless mangled and discarded, Marcus doubted it. Otherwise the units all looked identically sharpened and straight. So uniform and so numerous. Ongoing items to be sorted, the properly wrought ones passed inspection and moved on to packaging and outside-world usefulness.

Materials aside, he wouldn't bother making a plea for categorical differences between that bygone factory floor and his own.

He'd grown accustomed to not mentioning such patterns of near total forgetfulness with colleagues. When tied to national origins, gender, or ethnicity, all discussion of student types or characteristics amounted to a soft but anxiously regulated taboo measurable by cleared throats, telling silences, fret lines, and changes of topic. The semi-official stance: while each student is a uniquely awesome snowflake, every single specimen has equal opportunity, ability, and access to resources. In the interests of productive pedagogical outcomes, blindness to perspectives and behaviours related to cultural contexts must be practiced. A student is a student is a student, in other words.

The surprise at 1 PM had been seeing the girl at all. Asserting just a peep of opinion in that section of WCL 100 and responding to that of others—and indeed vocalizing above a whisper—seemed well beyond her ability. Or, maybe, outside the girl's scope of interests. Despite a clotheshorse wardrobe splattered with evidently significant logos she willed herself into virtual invisibility with that silence. Save for split ends and cuticle health, nothing animated her. Vocalized as he paced or gripped the lectern, the fundamentals of intelligent existence—"How shall we live and why?" and its cognates—only drew her blasé eye toward material trifles: watch or tablet screen, sculpted nail edge, blouse cuff. Today's rumpled T-shirt—"Hi I Don't Care THANKS." Her motto, the summa of her seventeen-year old's outlook?

Marcus spared the girl, respecting her palpable wish and blood from a stone posture, and queried left, right, or behind to keener competitors. Addled by nootropic compounds or not, their trained thoroughbred avidity could be counted on, numeric success the principal carrot urging their minds to gallop.

He'd caught L'Oréal's mousy routine again moments earlier as the student scurried from the waiting area's glossy but hard penitent's bench to an orange fabric office chair he kept for student negotiations. Head bowed, of course.

For what manner of response from him did her heart pitter-patter? He couldn't say.

Watching the girl procrastinate by shuffling through backpack contents, Marcus thought, Alright, I'll let you stew in your juices for awhile.

The phrase brought him the wannest of grins. He'd first discovered its medieval roots—"in his owene grece I made him fry"—a lifetime ago, a surprise factoid from an otherwise frantic undergraduate Chaucer class MC'd by a hyper prof with spangled Renaissance Faire props, thermoses of Earl Grey, hair in a sexless Friar Tuck cut, two-tone riding boots, and dollop breasts under unvarying wool sweaters of a heathery white. The woman's endless war-cries about the perennial relevance of Middle English (which students translated as a trumpeting of the value of her own tenure) had only sponsored helium-voiced, Pinocchio-armed mockery in the murkily lit campus pub followed by banter about the dandelion root-length of delusions and the difficulty of measuring an exact dosage for Valium.

"If only I'd known," Marcus had half-joked a few years after. He'd have secured a part-time job and invested all of his student loan leftovers into the diazepam and SSRI industries then poised for take-off.

That Wife of Bath medievalism had badgered Marcus' unknowing ears often enough still earlier.

Coming across mildewed advice in a child-management article his parents had wielded the updated phrase as a dubious punishment. They'd found the all-purpose application irresistible: "Maybe this time stewing in your juices for an hour will make you two realize. . . ."

Creative, faddish disciplining hadn't ever caught on with Agatha and Henry. Stewing, grounding, extra chores, allowance suspension, "What were you two *thinking*?"—they'd stuck with the classics.

None carried much force or changed the course of history. Even the occasional threat to send Haystack to the Glue Factory—located, by the sound of it, across the road from Reform School—sounded unconvincing. Though Agatha had adopted the pug to teach the boys the value of cooperation, the family recognized the wheezy pet as hers in spirit.

Recalcitrant in twin bedrooms with a shared wall, the boys had schemed instead. Self-taught and keen, they apprenticed as junior architects of revenge—Benjamin sneaky, courtly, and Machiavellian; Marcus happy to risk further parental censure for chances at wallops, shoves, or martial arts kick-chop combos. Marcus wouldn't turn down a prank, either, especially when novel applications for water and ballpoint ink dawned on him.

Stewing? As if.

Fed by an enmity that pulsed steadily, techniques mutated into mutual avoidance in school hallways and slouched mealtime silences. Later pooh-poohing family therapy and life coach exercises, Marcus explained away the routine and perpetual clashes as fate, a genetic quirk, or just one of those things. "That's life" or "It happens" and an oh-well shrug.

A phase of sibling rivalry, the platitudinous diagnosis foisted on them by others, didn't apply. On that the brothers agreed. The bad blood felt constitutional, as real as gravity.

Outsmarting it? Pipe-dream stuff. An arduous wilderness outing together, where in the screenplay version a male-bonding misadventure culminates in a meaningful, relationship-altering epiphany and "Bro, let's hug it out"? No and never.

Marcus understood that in spite of the shelf of dog-eared guidebooks and erratic schedule of kitchen table huddles, his parents had remained perpetually divided about fixing two sons demonstrably born to trade jabs and stand united about nothing consequential, save for an early conviction regarding a maternity ward's clerical error.

The switched-at-birth theory, followed of course by facetious suspicions of their mother's top-secret affair, could never be proven, nor brought up as dinner table conversation. In turn, the elder O's kept mum about the surprise burden of offspring enacting a Cain-and-Abel-as-teens dynamic well past the sell-by date. More or less, that is. Marcus had caught sighs of frustrating defeat and wistful glances at mirages—*if only*—seeping out.

Marcus' hadn't been a household of confrontations. Or adrenalized scenes that culminated in settled dust and placid resolutions. The family system adjusted to quietly accommodate the circumstance.

And workaday solutions emerged as a matter of course. One-son-per-visit invitations, parental vacations for exactly two over Christmas, and phone conversations that might have been set in an alternate timeline where the Os were a single-child family.

For a policy position, Marcus usually turned to metaphors of subsiding. Let the relationship with its fiery perpetual ire wither. To every thing there is a season. Let it die out, end with a whimper, waste away. Dwindle.

Ever since a spat over the memorial service's proper atmosphere—"a Celebration of Mother's Light, Love, and Life" vying with "bloody sad and wear a tie, it's a fucking funeral"—that segued into insinuation and snideness during his brother's eulogy, Marcus reminded himself of gladdening convenient facts. As excuses, a lapsed driver's license, geographic distance, and border crossings with fluctuating levels of militance had the persuasive weight and merit of truth.

Mercurial Benjamin, the bane. Not quite a year younger and yet in Marcus' eyes a creature of willful, combative sequences—queer activist (thick soled oxblood boots, earrings, T-shirts with slogans calculated to offend), manly (lumberjack-style beard, plaid flannel shirts, select lines from Whitman), Radical Faerie (eye shadow slapped on with Technicolor intensity, stiletto heels in the bush, wearying mealtime lectures about "gender system oppression"), hyper-fit (pearlescent fabrics webbed with circuitry, scrawny meals of steamed greens and poached salmon chased by exotic supplements and fitness magazine advice), married in the 'burbs (beer belly pride, weekend recycling errands, ten-day, all-male cruises to Alaska or Cancun), still others never known or since forgotten. A fat catalogue of hair dyes and cuts. Steel jewelry well below the neck.

How many selves to try out could there possibly be? Once Marcus tracked down a sweater with sleeves knitted for his basketball player's reach, he purchased a half-dozen and found sartorial contentment for a decade.

Marcus had come to dread calls, never frequent in the first place. Finger nearing a screen, he'd pause: how might his brother be decked out in this incarnation and what persona would he have devised? Goaded and antagonized by "Notice anything new . . . ?" Marcus swatted back goading and antagonizing guesses. Neck craning, he'd peer right past Benjamin's shoulders and ask about fresh wallpaper, newly changed lightbulbs. The screen's sudden blackness a relief to them both, no doubt.

Portland, the house-proud capital of what Benjamin prophesied as "California's second chance," could clasp a Canadian ex-pat in its shaggy Cascadian embrace; with such ludicrously self-righteous uniqueness worn as badges the two had to be made for each other.

The day for a reunion had to dawn, Marcus conceded. In Seattle, perhaps, they'd have to iron out a selling date and price for the Warfield Apartments, his residence and obligation for decades. Once picked over by salvagers, trucked to a landfill, and turned into a pit for workers to spray with concrete, the address could sprout a condo, the city pushing on with its determined march from an industrial past. Marcus' lawyer could then transfer half the windfall to Benjamin and snip the last cord.

Marcus squeezed his eyes into a display of balefulness for the damned girl, now the unwitting catalyst of his curdling mood. With that head at 45 degrees, he supposed L'Oréal sensed nothing in the air, imagined that girlishness or paltriness or youth granted her the superpower of having zero effect. Dismal and solipsistic, she heard only one panicked exclamation Morse-coding through her consciousness: "58 – ?! – shame – !? – disgrace – !! – despair! 58 – ??!!"

Welcome to the adult world, Marcus thought.

"I'm afraid we've run out of time for your appointment, L'Oréal." Marcus gestured toward milling backpacks and whisperings just past the door frame. "Sign up for another if you'd like. There's room this week. And before you arrive, prepare a list of points to go over with me, alright?"

He looked up to glimpse the retreating streak of camouflage fabric on L'Oréal's back. Should he read that stealthy exit as disdain or defeat? Relief? Hurtling steps into oblivion?

MTL—MoL*

Revenge, counterblow, even-steven. Puh-leeze. Temper your expectations, lower them by three-quarters, by seven-eighths.

No, a dour tough guy isn't about to spring from alleyway twilight with heart chambers tim-tim-timpaning out the primal beat of payback. Lurking nowhere in the vicinity: a grizzled, psychically-scarred manly man gunning for a redemptive arc while *taking out the trash*. Not for a million square miles will you find any coolheaded mastermind fine-tuning his retaliatory, 195 IQ-authorized coup de grâce. Think again if your comic books-nurtured, news cycle-fed, bestseller rack-edified, and Hollywood-trained mind has already conjured a weighty arsenal (firearms, knives, grenades, a nylon bag of C4 loaves) clamped to the revenger's toughened body. "Lock and load" and its martial analogues belong somewhere else.

Really, though, what can you reasonably expect from a sexagenarian prof with soft pinkish fingertips infrequently and microscopically scarred over the span of a career by paper cuts, a man slightly winded after a flight of eight stairs? Prescription sedatives dissolved in a pot of Darjeeling? A stabbing courtesy of a Regency paper knife? Arsenic? A contract killer's silencer peeping over a rooftop? A car bomb? An opportune elevator shaft and an unsuspecting body hurled into its fathomless maw? Something with clockwork intricacy that goes off without a hitch? Get real. You're under the spell of screenplay writers; and they take their

---

* Marcus' Twelve Labours—More or Less.
During which: an insulted, angered, petty, thin-skinned, and retaliatory geezer solves the problem of a bruised ego with an elongated series of actions befitting his temperament, ability, social standing, and fluctuating sense of morality.

cues from crime lit authors, who since Arthur Conan Doyle at least have occupied their days with hatching red herrings and dreaming up murder plots with enough complex steps to spark envy in a Byzantine chess grandmaster.

You'd think a people characterized by graduate degrees, polysyllabic articulation, and salaried analytic bookishness could realize a tortuous scheme in a tick-tock, a book-blurb scenario with a 'chilling atmosphere of shuddering suspense' etc, etc, and yet elegant, voluble, and tweedy, an ideal fit for Masterpiece Theatre. If not for those cool, deliberating temperaments that reserve premeditation for next season's conference papers, course plans, grant applications, and book chapters, they just might. Technical ability? Not the hurtle.

In truth, at those moments when push came to shove (ha ha) and the thorn-in-the-side Judaea problem felt nearer to a knife-in-the-back Judaea problem, Marcus relished but quickly brushed aside the theatrical daydreams with the emotional climaxes that snuck in.

You can imagine the kinds of scenario, those self-rewarding hiccough-free schemes enacted with excimer laser precision that culminate twice: in the there's-no-turning-back action (adulterated Darjeeling served, AS50 trigger pulled by the hired index finger, gloved hands launching the startled abhorrent body over a handy precipice), and the bereaved yet shocked aftermath performance—"Ah, such tremendous promise!" and "O, is nothing sacred?"—for the benefit of unit faculty and staff.

Ludicrous, he'd think. Though Marcus wouldn't actually roll his eyes he'd sense the mental equivalent.

Naturally, practicalities punctured the fantasies. Laurel shrub cyanide: how many leaves steeped for how long, and how administered? Where might anyone stumble upon a gaping elevator shaft? And, really, how does one disable security cameras, source untraceable arsenic, outsmart surveillance satellites, access reliably dark darknet operatives, or acquire a contract without leaving any traces? How could he manipulate Judaea, that shark, so that she'd agree to meet him at this deadly but conveniently depopulated mystery location and stand precisely where he wanted as he barrelled forward, forced her backwards suddenly, and terminated the pestilential lifeform that had grown such a venomous larynx?

With each dreamed possibility disastrous complications replicated with super-viral speed.

Besides, murder? At most, he'd settled on *quid pro quo* and *equal and opposite reaction*. The sinister woman had gossiped. To an audience of exactly one (so far as he'd determined), her insults had dismissed his core being, maligned his CV, tarnished a name he'd laboured to attain and retain. In a semi-public corridor Judaea had assigned him to the waste-of-space and as-good-as-buried categories. As ineligible for the lifeboat. She'd characterized him—caricatured him!—as a so-so at best; mind on a dimmer switch winding down its remaining insipid weeks inside a decelerating body already yearning for slippers, a comfy cardigan, and getting caught up on six decades of *Coronation Street*. Incensed for a lingering period, he'd also questioned himself. Harmless? Irrelevant? Out of touch? He'd show her.

With luck she hadn't turned one conversation into a slander campaign. Shit-talking happened and always would, Marcus believed, with each cultural stratum inventing its unique means and vocabulary. As did reprisal. Such had humanity behaved, since forever.

Here (the corner store for snacks) and there (scrubbing the toilet), Marcus wondered, what fit? What eye, what tooth matched the one she'd snatched? Should he instead contact an Arbitration Officer at HR, initiate an *amelioratory process* aiming for a *productive resolution*? Hell no.

In a spree of professorial jocularity he ran with What Would Hammurabi Do?

He pictured the imposing figure—resolute, beard in neat braids, crushing a lion with a headlock. The ancient world's go-to masculine rite of passage, Marcus supposed, millennia before endangered species lists updated in real time. Hercules had skinned the lion he'd defeated and worn its fur.

Marcus asked Syb about Hammurabian decrees on egregious badmouthing.

For the times, the Code treated slander with a relatively light slap. The closest, #127, ended with "this man shall be taken before the judges and his brow shall be marked (by cutting the skin, or perhaps cutting off half his hair)."

On the home monitor, Syb brought up #127's original placement: about seven inches below the sun god's feet, all chiselled on a glossy basalt finger over seven feet tall. *J'accuse* writ large, no blind woman holding impartial scales anywhere within eyeshot.

Funny, he'd imagined the Code's 282 decrees as being not quite so hot-tempered. More as wise cuneiform marks scratched onto papyrus scrolls using a reed and stored in clay urns wedged in sand with a view of the Hanging Gardens. Prosecutorial Babylonian passersby—in togas?—could refer to the judgements easily, making the carving a handy Wikipedia page for the long since deforested Fertile Crescent.

With her factory-set factuality, Syb explained no and quite unlikely.

Incising a mark on Judaea's forehead did register as harsh, though. Miles past a bit much. Plus, a fine calligraphic pattern or a sociopath's jagged symbol? As a guideline, "cutting the skin" left ample room for interpretation.

Aside from the Ancient World-style extremity, scissoring off half her hair struck him as pointless as well.

Even granting the possibility (a chloroformed rag, insomnia meds?), what then? She'd awaken disoriented on a conference room carpet, scurry to a mirror, and learn that a Central Casting psychopath had hacked away 50%. (And which half: the left part scythed to zilch and the right left intact, or just the length lopped in two, which might only create the impression that she'd taken a chance and mouthed "Let's go for it" to an erroneously trusted hairstylist?)

Without a doubt Judaea would freak out and alert Security. From there, a psychiatric consultant spat from Incident Management would speculate about the assailant's evident motive and point investigators in the direction of a surly troubled student who doodled angrily and ordered monotone apparel from the Teen Loner On The Verge catalogue.

Would Judaea grow pensive as a result and decide in favour of good works, or realize how sunk ships resulted from loose lips? Doubtful. In any case, she'd never peruse the Code, spot #127, and see the light: "Yes, yes, let the punishment fit the crime!"

As a nudge, he might leave a clarifying note at the scene. Beeswax-sealed for effect and tucked into a pocket, maybe. Something camouflaged, anonymous, and broadly threatening printed on the front: "Consider Urself Lucky" or "Woe Betide the Doer of the Deed." Junk mail flyers could provide the letters. Or discarded bestsellers.

He'd prepare the communique in a place with a stream of human traffic, a library carrel perhaps, slip on gloves, keep himself—spittle, skin cells, tell-tale grey strands—away from investigatory eyes and, according to TV, their owners' specialized handheld technology.

The message? Maybe an Old Testament nugget from Job rendered with that emphatic madman-style capitalization. Over the top, sure, but translated passages composed by long-dead, bearded Mediterranean guys in linen robes seemed quite popular with the new century's vindictive, fire-breathing loonies:

> My Experience Shows that those who
> PLANT TROUBLE and CULTIVATE EVIL
> will Harvest the Same.
> A Breath from God DESTROYS them.
> They VANISH in a BLAST of his ANGER.

Cutting out and pasting all those letters, though. He was bound to leave behind damning evidence.

Inside the note, further aggressive lunacy—brand, cut, flog—alongside a contextual explanation:

> #127
> "If a man point the finger at a priestess or the wife of another and cannot justify it, they shall drag that man before the judges and they *shall brand his forehead*."
> (Harper translation)

"If any one 'point the finger' [slander] at a sister of a god
or the wife of any one, and cannot prove it, this man shall
be taken before the judges and his brow shall *be marked
(by cutting the skin, or perhaps hair).*" (King translation)

"If a free person accuses a priestess or a married woman
of illicit sexual relations but cannot prove the charge,
that free person shall be *publicly flogged and half of that free
person's head shall be shaved.*" (Rummel translation)

Risky, improbable, an ordeal to orchestrate. Also, that reflex-
ive scholarly touch, the dutiful acknowledgement of translators.
Dead giveaway. For misdirection maybe thrown-in misspelled
words, a coil of anonymous hair plucked from carpeting.

No note, then. Less consequence.

Not any of it in this lifetime, he saw. Aside from possessing
what he imagined as a statistically normal—which is to say low—
appetite for murder (not to mention torture), Marcus had no taste
for high stakes gambling or assembling the nuts and bolts of the
grand gesture. He'd never go wingsuit flying or cave diving
either. Even his banker, a dapper young fellow serious about floral pink-spectrum ties with matching pocket squares, lobbed
client-suitable jests about the conservative nature of Marcus'
investments: "Let 'er rip a little, Dr. O, jeez."

Orchestrating a plot? A de-evolutionary leap.

Crossing to the transit loop, Marcus brooded on whats and
hows but not whys.

Seated in droning unit meetings and standing-room-only
accordion busses, he ruminated on *death by a thousand cuts.* He
had to admit that, historical veracity aside, the prickling torment
did possess a certain B-movie poetry, especially if death equalled
real contrition caused by deeply-felt—foot in ass—humiliation.

Was that too much to ask for?

As far as flora went, he decided, forgiveness (assuming it
existed) blossomed well after reparation.

ThyssenKrupp (Elevator)

There's the genuine mistake. We've all been there.

It's early morning and you're inside the elevator and have already pressed the button to the floor of your productivity quad. Just as the panel doors begin to slide close you catch the blur of a body approaching at a fast clip, or else an imploring voice: "Hold the doors!" Half-asleep, maybe, or rehearsing the day ahead, you're faced with a tall rectangular grid of lozenge-shaped buttons, numbers, and symbols. At the very bottom of those shapes, two relevant options side by side: << >> and >> <<, never OPEN and CLOSE. While the Law of Probability as you understand it leads you to expect the right choice as often as not, for whatever reasons—a think tank of neurobiologists could-n't adequately explain it—you reach down, fully intent on letting "Hold the doors!" share the ride. Yet you press >> << with a steady lack of variance. Doubting your intelligence or wondering about dyslexia, you also wonder about optical illusions and fight-or-flight, if only for an instant.

During the ascent you think, "Hold the doors!," now snorting out impatience or ire in the lobby, will decide that you're petty. Or yet another selfish city-living, rat-racing asshole. You hope you won't cross paths with "Hold the doors!" over the next few hours. The entire episode will slip "Hold the doors!"'s mind after that, with luck.

In a reversed situation, you'd forget. Mostly, anyhow.

There's also the dramatizing of the 'genuine mistake.'

In that case, the fumbling and pressing the wrong button might be the workday's first acting performance. Under five seconds, the bit approaches pantomime—the bulging, too urgent eyes seeking the correct button on the panel, the stabbing finger that misses its target, the confounding mistaken choice, the operatic hands communicating fake-regret and pseudo-dismay, the OmigodSoSorryI'mSuchADolt facial tour de force. All that to disguise the fact that (likeliest) you wanted to ride the elevator alone for a blessed half-minute or (less likely but still possible) you couldn't find the heart to make room for an extra body in the car or expose yourself to the infectious germ field of someone else. Despite civility's long reign, such petty, antisocial acts do transpire. For humans, fallibility comes pre-installed.

And besides, you rationalize, how much of a rush could "Hold the doors!" be in that waiting forty extra heartbeats for the next car represented the affront of an unacceptable delay? Christ, there are stairs. There's no IED display speeding to zero on the seventh floor, no bomb to defuse.

If you run into "Hold the doors!" shortly after, there's a chance for another performance: the insincere apology.

For Judaea, altogether a different kettle of trash fish in Marcus' reasoning, the pretence at the panel and the uneasy smile and raised eyebrows of apology did not fit. Instead, tit for tat. Tits for tat, actually. The sound of that, though. No, as she approached the doors bundled for a November downpour, direct evidence—circumstantial would not do—of the deliberate slight needed to be plain, if only to her repugnant eyes. And cinematic too: face cooly impassive, late-'60s Clint Eastwood attitude sliding in her direction and intently holding her gaze, he'd press the >> << button until the doors closed.

From there, repeat, as apropos, until doomsday. Not in my house, woman.

Marcus felt pretty sure she'd tolerate these actions, understand the point of origin and low-road, Law of Nature (*pace* Hobbes) legitimacy. Even so, he ran through a couple of variations. Keeping Judaea off-kilter, he might allow her to embark at arbitrary junctures. Or, if she raised her voice to say "Hold the doors!" (or, worse, "Marcus, really! Hold the doors!") his

Plan B involved reverting to the pantomimed wrong choice of button and the what-a-dolt-am-I facial mask. Picturing that last scenario, the tucked-tail cowardice undermined the entire piquing gesture; and despite not having ridden in that elevator Judaea would still win.

Not much, Marcus concluded after the third or fourth successful if ho-hum episode, but a start holding promise. When *be ye fruitful* surfaced and swam through his consciousness, it loitered with an earworm's doggedness and sounded like permission. Okay, he decided, *multiply* it will be. Pettiness was sorely under-appreciated.

COMPATIBILITY: 1

Wednesday's sole faculty meeting, and what might be the thirtieth he'd sat through during the 2027 school year, awaited Marcus ninety minutes into the afternoon. A guaranteed purgatory of white noise droning to outsiders, in its measured interjections—"Actually, in point of fact . . . ," "Perhaps another productive avenue of approach . . . ," "Yes, possibly, but let's not overlook . . . ," "We might fruitfully consider instead . . . ," "Then again . . . ,"—professorial ears would register skirmishes over power, territory, and the shape of the unit's future.

Attendees frowned on showboating and emotion-tinged voices lifted above the convention-set decibel range. But veterans knew to count on the volleying of courtly insults between heavyweights, dinosaur antagonists keeping ideological strife or personality clashes from the previous century alive. And logical contradictions, when uttered aloud and pounced on, ignited memories of long-ago schoolyard slugfests. Racing blood alongside public humiliation: sated before witnesses, the victor practically swaggered; and that meeting's loser, calm at a glance but outmanoeuvred and tasting bile until the next convening, turned to furious notes and jottings while evading looks—compassionate and not—from supposed allies.

Daggers between colleagues, how long its history?

Granted tenure long before any of his current pupils scampered in preschool, Marcus had patted his own back with an escapade to Italy. Churches and museums and gold-painted aristocratic interiors by the bucketful for three weeks. Wandering stately corridors of the Palazzo Madama in Rome he'd stumbled upon *Council of Elders*, an ironically titled fresco of politicians in togas in a crowded senate chamber. Gesticulating grandly before enthralled peers and would-be opponents, a patrician ham denounced his cowering rival. Craning over the security rope to catch exactly how the painter applied the speaker's blazing eyes and set mouth, Marcus had grinned in recognition. Though painted a continent away and centuries ago, the resemblance to faculty animus couldn't be missed.

He'd wait till noon for sushi. In the meantime, drab busy-work—admin, prep, student work in virtual folders—brought to mind 9-5's addendum to "death and taxes."

Marcus opened the profile instead. Interminable, that work in progress.

A totality of empty boxes accused him obscurely.

To date, he'd struggled to fill out the sections that *enabled*—so he'd read—the company's exclusive proprietary algorithm to accomplish industry-defining feats with a laboratory precision that merited inclusion in ads. That unique algorithm had been formulated for *mature bonds*. Every speck of promotional material stressed the company's unparalleled expertise with maturity, that burgeoning demographic.

Brains still capable of seething with the over-proof ingredients of puppy love evidently required calculations of a different kind.

Happily, Venerati's parent company provided exactly those. And more!

Lifting uncritical information from business magazines and company websites, Syb had described Venerati as a competent unit within the renowned consumer brand holdings of a leading media and internet company. Since launching in Q1 2022 it had met performance targets. With annual revenue in the billions, the online relationship portfolio, one of the company's key verticals, included dating sites for specialized demographics. So Syb established. Apparently, this leading media and internet company operated discrete sites for business executives, Generation Z, Christians, select ethnicities, and the rich, famous, or attractive. Also: old people with enough money to cough up a membership fee.

While wondering about a physical setting where "consumer brand holdings" could be renowned, Marcus' thinking had hovered at the phrase "key verticals." For the one he envisioned a seminar he'd never wish to attend. For its companion, he recalled a meeting with his banker. Apparently vital in ways emails were not, that afternoon's face-to-face "sesh" had featured a neck tie in black and fuchsia, an animated pie chart, the term "key vertical," and the banker's bared teeth accompanied by frenzied if momentary head convulsions—the pantomime designed to relay an aggressively sharkish but still viable investment disposition. Or something. Nodding and saying "Okay, right" while listening, Marcus had felt tricked, sure that a basement division of the bank invented jargon to befuddle clients.

Besides business speak, Venerati's ad agency never failed to place numeric magic front and centre. Over and again, this ostensible fact. Like a blaring SOS. Or propaganda.

For the online dating sector's entrepreneurial romantics, behind-the-scenes equations—a diligent and ceaseless worker nearly everywhere—ushered in True Love. The ads and images said as much. Liberally. The intimacy of a shared meal shot during sunset's golden light, a barefooted stroll with loosely entwined hands, constant bursts of warm toothy laughter, newfound joy, and rediscovered wonderment—all of it securely rested on the bedrock foundation of numeric equations.

Marcus guessed if he clicked often enough he'd find small print. Unequivocal waivers and binding legalese statements about non-liability. Counsel-worded backtracking: *Beware, we promise to deliver exactly nothing, our calculating machines are for show.*

The damned first step, though. The profile, foreboding gateway to a Shangri-la à deux.

Fill boxes with words. Given his job, what could be so difficult about that?

Starting and stopping, typing and deleting, Marcus had already sighed and blown bags of air into his cheeks over the prospect. Agonized, even, if momentarily.

At odd hours he'd logged off exasperated, pictured a ballooning likelihood of failure. An hour or twelve later he'd hear "If at first . . . try try again" in a kindergarten teacher's singsong—damn you, Miss R—and recommit to readying his virtual self for a flesh-and-blood audience.

Stuffing screen boxes with a siren's song of beckoning poetic sentences, fingers tapping on keyboard squares: he'd clicked that—on the Options menu—immediately.

Boss-like dictation to the transcribing machine irked him.

Speaking aloud and addressing a mute glass eye as wires—or photonic beams, who knew—behind that camera lens transmitted the captured visual data for women to later interrogate? That gave him the sense of wrestling with quicksand.

Seated while gawping at the impassive black circle on his home desk computer he'd tried out a few sentences nonetheless: "Hello there, I'm Marcus." He might as well be auditioning for a Director of Funeral Services role.

Smacking his cheeks, adjusting his face and his shoulders, and dipping to bass, he'd leaned in, resting fist to chin to feign a beachcomber's devil-may-care stance. "Yo." Ugh.

Rolling back the chair and crossing one leg over the other while tensing otherwise benched abdominal muscles for an acceptable slimness facsimile, he'd managed to replicate a vintage catalogue model. A stiff.

Nothing worked. The poses lacked conviction. Dignity. In playback his image managed to sidestep charm. That awkwardness—if he could trust his own judgement—would sink him.

Watching the test-runs at night, nose to screen, he measured the results with what objectivity he could muster. Clammy. Jaundiced. A waxen sheen. Shifty-eyed and nervous. Evasive. From a few steps back: reedy, weedy, gone to seed? He came across as tired, worn out, jowly, in dire need of sun, exercise, rejuvenating potions and transplants. Virgins' blood: for centuries that had worked superbly for Countess Karstein.

The sallow tinge, the mottling: business as usual or a warning sign? Perhaps the Department of Vital Statistics had failed to alert him with a CMT news blast: "Attention Client #72——R-3: your liver has begun to fail. Please report to your health care provider."

Varicosing restricted to ankles, there was that, a small mercy.

True, to attain "young for his age" he could resort to image editors and filters. Imported backdrops: hiking a craggy range in New Zealand, boarding a gondola at Alta. Nothing tropical and swimsuited, though.

Or cosmetics. Hair dye. Fruit acid peels. Something dermatological using injections and lasers. A face swept with drug store bronzing powder. *Begummed, besmattered, and beslimed*, he thought, foreseeing the inevitable dressing table with stuffed drawers and jars in stacks that grew higher with each passing year, a rash of withdrawals embarrassing to explain to the tax accountant.

Preservation! He couldn't be bothered.

He'd accept "dignified" and "active," positive terms reserved for his *unique* demographic, so long as they steered clear of any association with *discreet*—a bathroom vanity stacked with Tranquila, special needs underwear with built-in triple protection against leakage, odour, and wetness. Its technology approved by evidently cash-strapped NASA.

Besides, the status quo still managed to give his sex an easy pass.

Patriarchs, heroes, world leaders, and captains of industry needn't bother with mirror time scrutiny when they made the world run. So the story went.

Under the bath of blue-grey light and hazy background, Marcus had sensed a sad air of perversity in the paused images too. *That guy*, one of the spurned figures of the modern age: the sad bachelor-masturbator seated at a desk and reaching out to virtual images while surrounded by take-out containers and plastic utensils, his dingy T-shirt a bib and napkin in one. Marcus there too, an elder statesman.

For all a viewer might tell, this guy devoted every leisure hour to playing ersatz medieval dragon slaying games online. Signing on as Galadriel38DD he'd flirt nonsensically with other gamers. In turn they'd conjure a nerdy wanker's fantasy scenario about unclasping Galadriel38DD's bronze metalwork bra to celebrate victory after an epic pixelated battle. A hands-off romance, chaste yet perhaps worthy of a Public Service Announcement.

Assessing his face's surface area on screen, Marcus had envisioned a stranger in a gallery approaching a black-framed still and making guesses based on skin cast, the message in his eyes: "Hmm, he works as one of those geezer security guards with a walkie-talkie in a bank lobby that spouts 'Good morning' or 'Good afternoon'?" No one's idea of a catch, in other words.

You've got to get back on the horse, he heard from a distant reach in his own head. Heartfelt advice from the chorus of wise receptionists, hopeful moms, and plucky sidekicks in a thousand film scripts. *It's like riding a bicycle. You snooze, you lose. You'll never know if you don't try.* Right.

With warmer light and a background of books, knick-knacks, and antique manuscript pages of flora and fauna behind glass, he'd tried again: "Hello, I'm Marcus." After those words (and their flabby variations: "Hey there," "How do," "Greetings," and "If you're watching this, it means . . ."), only corniness ("I'm a Scorpio . . ."), inane factoids ("I was born in . . ."), rimshot jokiness appended to dull semi-factoids ("When I was in high school, an electric typewriter was vanguard technology"), resigned metaness ("The instructions say 'Tell viewers something about yourself,' and so here I am . . .'"), or dead end improvs that began at the shrill beep prompt chosen from the menu.

He'd consigned each attempt to cybernetic oblivion, praying that no former student and current hacker could fish them out and post the conclusive evidence of desperation: worldwide ridicule in retaliation for a C- five semesters ago.

Typed words, yes. Those he could master.

ACVQ Warm-Up Round

Off the top of your head, what flavour are you?

~~Umami, like any cut of meat on the menu.~~
~~Hearty, salty, bitter, with the astringency (okay, technically that's~~
~~not a flavour) of a Shiraz.~~
~~Not one through and through. People shouldn't aspire to have~~
~~the consistency of a cherry Popsicle.~~
~~A comforting, wintry meal like beef bourguignon~~
~~A Boulevardier: bourbon, Campari, sweet vermouth. Sour,~~
~~earthy, sweet, bitter; an acquired taste but satisfying once you've~~
~~had it in your mouth.~~

A Boulevardier: bourbon, Campari, sweet vermouth. A mélange
of sour, oaky, sweet, tangy, and bitter; it's an acquired taste but
definitely worth trying.

Quick, off the top of your head, list five of your favourite things!

~~A glowing review; Bach's Cello Suite No. 4 in E-Flat Major (Steven Isserlis); Eccles cake; *The White Ribbon*; The Metropolitan Museum of Art.~~

~~*Ali: Fear Eats the Soul*; Cabernet Sauvignon (Napa Valley); a Paris-Brest with a side of espresso; "Immigrant Song"; bread baking.~~

~~A woman dressed to the nines for a special occasion; a dress with exposed shoulders; being met at the airport after a flight; winding through a nighttime streetscape after *un dîner pour deux*; in robes and enjoying a room service breakfast for two.~~

~~*The Road*; *American Pastoral*; *Pale Fire*; *White Noise*; *Bleak House*.~~

~~Vienna; London; Rome; Seattle; Mexico City.~~

~~Cherries; baked potato; Yorkshire pudding; bbq'd ribeye; grilled asparagus.~~

~~The view from the top of a ski hill; northwest coastal waters during a winter storm; fog; thunder and lightning; the desert at sunset and later still.~~

~~Bacon's *Painting*; A.J. Casson's *Algonquin Park 1943*; Munch's *Death in the Sickroom*; Wall's *View From an Apartment (2004-2005)*; Rothko, *No. 7 (1964)*.~~

~~Gardens; ale; chocolate; Ava Gardner; Lucy Liu.~~

~~*Blue Train*; *Safe*; *Bitches Brew*; *Badlands*; *Chinatown*.~~

~~*Vertigo*; *8½*; *Moll Flanders*; *The Beggar's Opera*; "I am the wife of Mao Tse-tung".~~

~~-~~

In no particular order, here are the first five that spring to mind: *Sunday at the Village Vanguard* (Bill Evans Trio); apple strudel with whipped cream; a weekend's driving getaway; the lightning-strike moment that inspires a new project; browsing an independent bookstore.

(I'd argue that you can learn just as much by knowing about someone's unfavourite things.

In the interests of full disclosure, then, here are mine: sports culture; car culture; anyone who talks at length about the minutia of their job; evangelism in most forms; Dulness.)

ACVQ 2

Describe an average day.

~~Quite similar to yours, I'll bet.~~

~~Yesterday, for instance. Wake at dawn, breakfast and coffee, classes taught, etc.; beans on toast for dinner, strong black tea after, some reading.~~

~~Work followed by an evening of inactivity; masturbation (5 decades and counting: you do the math), post-ejaculatory stewing over life's utter strangeness, muddledness, and brevity.~~

~~Typical white collar 9–5, but closer to 9–3. News or reading or pacing the apartment and settling on staring out the kitchen window at the landscape and sidewalk activity below.~~

~~The bread and butter: meetings, classes, admin; at home: the luxury of silence and being left alone . . . .~~

~~Any average, by definition, sweeps away the highs and lows. Days are good and bad, exciting and boring, ordinary and exceptional. An 'average day' only conveys routine.~~

~~A set of goals accomplished during the workday; when the balanced work/life goal is met, evenings are spent in lifestyle pursuits.~~

~~Like everyone else who has gainful employment, my days are consumed with trials and tribulations, accomplishments, setbacks, and procrastination. Evenings aren't that much different.~~

~~The list of averages: 3 meals, several snacks; classes, meetings, committees, transit to and fro; a social event (often work-related), leisure time (at home, career-related)~~

~~"On paper, anyone's average day is a compendium of unremarkable moments. Peer beneath, however, and you'll discover the stuff of Life: triumphs and defeats; discoveries; stretches of tedium punctuated by episodes of pure exhilaration."~~

~~My ball-and-chain, the ol' career, imposes a certain order over my days. My goal, then, is to keep that order fresh and lively. My evenings are my own. I strive to leave them open-ended.~~
~~Descriptions of an average day have a way of making most everyone as exciting as a cog: eat, excrete, work, rest, sleep, repeat.~~
~~Words I keep in mind: "As long as habit and routine dictate the pattern of living, new dimensions of the soul will not emerge."~~

Challenging but rewarding, the varying aspects of my career occupy my full days. For evenings I strive to balance recreation with food for thought (music, reading, current affairs) . . . while fitting in errands and chores too!

PEDAGOGY

Wednesday 1:30-1:45 PM

A ghost town, one third of his weekly office allotments for students wholly disregarded. Rolling tumbleweed the only missing ingredient.

Scrolling through just two of forty-five pages of tumbleweed on a stock images site, Marcus realized that as far as metaphors go there wasn't much there. The sound of crickets chirping, a hooded figure grasping a scythe, an hourglass, a clock face: equally blunt.

On Monday teenage students in a pheromonal semicircle had blurted or nodded promises related to speaking in person at his office on Wednesday. No slacker added "Let's see what the weather's like," "Unless something pressing comes up," or "Okay, maybe, but don't, like, count on it." The electronic communique steeped in the language of melodrama ("Urgent!!!" in the subject line) and sent at midnight on Tuesday? Apparently resolved. Another's 1:03 AM state of alarm, forecasting essayistic disaster and surgical remedies—"necessary to speak," "deeply concerned about," "before it's too late"—cancelled with the light of morning. Each first-year's name in the appointment slot a no-show.

Marcus had learned to temper expectations. Or, at least, not to dwell on follow-through failures and, heaven forbid, take student flakiness personally. Instead, a philosophy of water off a duck's back: "No problemo," "I understand," and "These things happen." The stance —"They know not what they do" supported by neurodevelopmental findings he needed to remind himself about now and then—gilded him with a merciful heart of God patina. Little bloodsuckers, students valued apparent generosity,

responded well to nodded acceptance of the multitudinous mitigating circumstances that resulted in skipped appointments, tardy
assignments, and last-second requests for rescheduled presenta-
tions. For themselves, of course. The lame excuses of other students, rivals all: pedantic rigidity, rules never bent, "deadlines are
deadlines," and "if they can't compete, then maybe they should
consider dropping out."

As for the source materials of Marcus' ostensibly enlightened
philosophy, those didn't matter so much as effect. Unlike
Dorothy, these transit passengers through one semester of his
tutelage would never learn who operated what levers behind the
curtain. Not that it interested them, either. Especially when
screens mesmerized them with unending animation in a virtual
parade.

Besides, orthodoxy dictated that schoolmasterly militance or
"Christ, if you make a fucking appointment then keep it" singed
their delicate new petals. And, deep within the meaning-making
folds of their brains, reaction emerged as "What a dick," "He's so
cruel," "He doesn't even *try* to get me," or "He's terrible at his
job." The reaction-process terminated with indelible harshness
on the various sites where anonymous but evaluative student
voices could be seen and heard until the sun went supernova.

Fingernails tapping the glass desktop, Marcus wondered why
hackers never targeted their exposé attacks on those offensive
web addresses. To broadcast Anonymous (author of the immortal
lines: "BOR-ING. So, I learned he has 3 sweaters, 2 pairs of
shoes, and -100 personality") as Selina G, bubbling over with
hurt feelings and unchecked malice because of a C- average.

Better to work with them, then. This honey over vinegar
tactic was pragmatic as well as serpentine Admin's golden rule.

When he'd finally caved in and ordered an acceptably useful
3.0 version of Syb, one of Marcus' first questions had been instigated by a similar period of no shows, failures to comprehend
basic instructions, and complaints, in spite of irrefutable evidence,
about his F at properly guiding, nurturing, or instructing.

The gist: "What's the fucking deal with teenagers?" Syb had
requested clarification. He'd repeated himself, she'd asked him to

rephrase "fucking deal," and he'd realized that vagueness, a student hallmark, could launch from any tongue. To the desktop machine Marcus queried about late adolescent listening skills, idea retention, and priority ordering. Asked for research summaries regarding the causality of adolescent moodiness, petulance, inconstancy, verbal tics. About age-specific self-infatuation, ire, vengefulness, sanctimoniousness.

With barely a pause, Syb's speaker emitted word after word, enunciated title after title. For the first time, he grasped how much information she could access. In no time Marcus understood that Syb could inundate him with the immense totality of relevant studies as well as the long history of findings that predated current ones—exabytes, zettabytes of information that could not be listened to in a lifetime. She'd therefore need to be halted mid-sentence. Marcus predicted the banks of machines giving sense to Syb's voice would eventually discern the "cut to the chase" embedded in any human query and spare him the effort. He still waited for that intuitive version. Lucky 7.3, maybe.

Per usual he'd taken away a smattering of key words. From a three-minute outflow he'd retained "lagged structural development" and "late development of the prefrontal cortex." Good enough factors to consider for the remainder of a steady career.

As a result, the day's mantra and resolve to Let It Slide. He still got paid, after all. Empty office or not.

And, no use in fighting biological systems as old as . . .

Syb: "While the exact number of early human species is debated, Marcus, Sahelanthropus tchadensis is one of the oldest known branches in the human family tree. This West-Central African species lived between seven and six million years ago, possibly very close to the time of the chimpanzee-human divergence.

"Sahelanthropus tchadensis has two defining human anatomical traits. One is small canine teeth; the other is walking upright on two legs instead of on four legs. It's thought to have eaten a mainly plant-based diet.

"The chimpanzee-human divergence refers to—"

"Thanks for that, Syb."

Right. Since, practically speaking, forever.

At 1:44 a cleaner rapped a knuckle on the glass and asked "Vacuum now?"

The dour visage and haggard, seen-it-all eyes suggested origins in a post-Soviet, post-glasnost, and post-Putin *kommunalka* and total faith in additional portions of the equivalent in a cramped new location until the hour of holy unction.

The thirty-going-on-sixty glumness reminded Marcus of a custodian a decade ago who'd described the colossal, crushing disappointment felt by her family of six. She'd done so with the least encouragement. The occasion of snow, any breakdown of services, between floors in the elevator car.

In the telling, a childhood of constant sacrifices in the name of a promised land across the Atlantic that handed out opportunity like eggs at Easter had become a migratory adventure with a thudding finalé. The photographic still would depict a penniless greatcoated sextet on a gangplank huddling uselessly against a February snowstorm in Halifax. Until she retired the woman had complained out of habit about noise, rain, aching bones, and a thankless employer. "Same shit, different day," she'd answer, unsmiling, to "How are you?" She'd carry on, nonetheless, the cross of futility a reliable sidekick since Khrushchev.

"If you want, sure."

"I don't want, but will do."

"Okay. Yes, yes, do. I go main . . . I'll go to the main office for five minutes."

Positions reversed, Marcus supposed he'd—grow sour and resentful? Make the best of it? Take smoke breaks every possible minute? Put in the requisite hours and clock off the exact second the shift ended? Steal toilet paper and cleaning supplies?

All of the above, probably, depending on the position of the sun.

From the menu Marcus selected a "Back in 5" message for the door panel.

MTL—MoL 2

Nexus Building (Stairwell Negotiation)

In the old building, basically an upright cinder block with windows from the early 1970s and an artifact ruled both démodé and not *historical* enough for heritage preservation by some planning committee or other and so flattened to rebar-ribbed scraps, stairwells hadn't been airy and panoramic. Cramped and functional, their tightness brought to mind submarines, factory warrens, hateful projects housing of the Pruitt-Igoe stripe. Low-ceilinged concrete and budget lit (by fluorescent tubes and, later, LEDs mimicking that sci-fi glare), stairwells operated as building code regulations, the mandated windowless standby emergency exit when elevators couldn't run. In them, two larger men moving in opposite directions would each pivot right to keep the peace. Prepared to mutter a jokey semi-apology that simultaneously pointed the basalt finger of blame at the bygone architect's blinkered worldview, departmental veterans understood accidental shoulder checks and jostling as a matter of course.

The ethos of public buildings had changed and with that evolution formerly obligatory and cut-rate stairways had become handsome, wide thoroughfares or promenades that inspired thoughts of leisurely collegiality or a latte-accessorized stop to admire the widescreen view.

When climbing stairs in the old building, or descending them, Marcus saw, he could have dominated the centre, forcing loathsome Judaea to cower at the hairpin landings or to stop mid-step to let his tank-like width pass (or else suffer the brunt of superior weight).

Wishing for those days was unrelated to nostalgia, he told himself. He had no plans to let that sentiment—a hallmark of the truly aged—settle in his cells and colour his vision. Instead: those bygone stairs represented convenience. Utility. With them he could privilege his claim to space over another's, Judaea's, say. Might is right, and all that. Him a bowling ball hurtling toward the middle pin. Beware!

Being dead centre in the new building's spacious cascade of stairs—beckoning, a standing invitation—and approaching Judaea coming when he was going or vice versa failed to achieve any trophy for retributive justice. While still not much, he gauged the manoeuvre as better than a complete failure: case by case, something usually felt better than nothing. As with a game of chicken, one of the participants would decide to move. His vow: not me, not ever.

If Judaea noticed the defeats, she gave no sign. On and off, he checked her channel for a fresh vlog about gendered microaggression. That'd be about her speed. He'd confirm then whether Marcus-the-Merkava had gotten under her skin.

In the story of vengefulness—his slow-dawning realization—the targeted wrongdoer must not only begin experiencing mounting fear and sense an amorphous but real threat to the order of things. Until the revelations of final act, she must also suspect, intuit, or catch the barest glimpse of the identity of the actor responsible for righting the wrong. The procedure lacked a crucial step or stage without it. So operated the psychology of ego gratification.

MTL—MoL 3

Security-minded and a building code kowtower, the campus was lousy with heavy in-case-of-fire doors.

Marcus had no formal policy about holding doors open, regardless of the user's gender. Sometimes he did, sometimes he didn't. If anybody looked burdened with folders, books, or equipment he'd hurry to or loiter at a door until they passed through. Usually, at least, though only a monster would sweep by a frail golden-ager outclassed by a heavy door. Lapses stemmed from mitigating factors. Such as busyness. Or cumulonimbus moods.

He intersected with Judaea at these thresholds on sporadic instances. He'd catch her trundling reflection in the glass or approach the building as she neared a doorway from the opposite way. The vile woman seemed the very definition of pack-rat tendencies, heading off to a classroom criss-crossed with satchels and pulling a wheeled carry-on suitcase. Textbooks graffitied with colour-coded tags, it goes without saying. She ran errands, undertook coffee or meal runs, or beetled off toward meetings laden with stuff—a messenger bag, a conference tote, a purse, padded envelopes, packages for posting, a tablet or laptop. In another life, she'd have pushed a rickety shopping cart heaped with broken appliances and grimy coats.

Veering left or right and choosing a door adjacent to hers, he'd pass through. As though the woman's self-made plight made no impression on him. Or her person.

He'd keep walking his route, toward the elevator or homeward buses.

Now and then, thoughts about the corporeal purposes or ends of anger would bubble up; he'd tap a query to Syb or address her discreetly.

In the chemical view, with its tale of amygdalic shrieks for molecular goads—"Charge!"—to incite protective actions, all roads led to *On the Origin of Species*. Of course. Whether pinned to increasing social bargaining power or deterring transgression, the foundational explanation for anger could be found in the bland all-purpose phrase "an evolutionary adaptation favoured by natural selection." Exceptions existed, naturally, which Marcus assumed researchers explained away as single generation mutations that natural selection itself would cull. When he learned, thanks to Syb's handiwork, about Reactive-Affective-Defensive-Impulsive Disorder, a rule-breaking impulse common to individuals with antisocial, violent, and psychopathic tendencies that potentially resulted from damage to the neural circuitry that underlies moral decision-making, an on the spot (that being, a seat near the front of the express bus) diagnosis placed him firmly outside the spectrum of antisocial and psychopathic tendencies. Just as well: already iffy, Syb said, treatment often caused hepatotoxicity.

Protection of the self, too, according to Freud, that analyst's touchstone. Anger: one of the psyche's many mechanisms to defend the ego. As vulnerable as an oyster missing a shell, that ego. For it, anxiety—*Die Angst*—meant threat and therefore the precious organism that housed it (the entire universe, as far as *das Ich* could discern) placed in severe jeopardy. And that would not do.

In the long view, then, this conflict and wayward resolution between two consenting adults—she'd started it, after all—landed squarely within evolution's business as usual territory.

MTL—MoL 4

Meeting Room 2B (Mots Trouvés)

A handy borrowing, courtesy of a recollected episode from a flatulent conference.

Windy, a gas-giant of verbiage, the panel speaker had regarded the allotted twenty minutes as a soft figure and a go-ahead to *share*.

He ought to have known better.

Witnessing a patchy audience's resentful silence and low-decibel huffs, clock-watching, and fidgeting ignored or misinterpreted as *Please go on* and sensing the speaker's mistaken confidence that his every word and every extemporizing based on his every word—"That reminds me," "To put it another way," "As an aside, it's important to recall"—ought to become a perpetual motion machine, the moderator cleared his throat with faster and louder cycling. Hints rejected by the self-aggrandizer, a scholar-narcissist caught in a hall of mirrors, the moderator raised his hand, waved it, and then declared, "For future reference, what's typed on that page, if you don't mind. Not the whole megillah. Time's up exactly now, thank you."

Marcus felt gratified by the half-hearted and short-lived clapping.

Another unit meeting, at midpoint. Marcus sat, as one did, listening. He glowered as well from time to time.

With wandering preambles, a parade of illustrative examples, free-form monologuing, and an evidently willful misreading of the room's emotional temperature, Judaea-the-egomaniac repeated that long ago conference speaker's bad habit with a mechanical consistency.

Soapbox grandstanders played as ordinary a part of any meeting as mutterers, whisperers, or those who pointedly disregarded everyone else while waiting for a turn to preside with their two cents' worth of perspective. Simply, they irked. Afterwards, conversations in offices or corridors might take jabs or serve piquant helpings of ridiculing sarcasm.

At meeting No. Severalhundredandchange, and the fortieth or so with Judaea, Marcus aimed for—and, according to his own ears, reached—a tone of voice that registered as perfectly matter-of-fact. The Disinterested Bureaucrat rather than angered, sarcastic, petty, or vindictive Marcus O. He spoke for the good of the gathered unit representatives, clearly, and not for himself alone: "Though we appreciate the effort, perhaps next time present just the salient facts rather than the whole megillah. The surfeit of information doesn't really serve any of our needs. Like you, we're all busy. And like you, we all have points of view we'd like to share. Time permitting, of course. Thank you."

Asking then about the next agenda item, he affected a gotta-be-somewhere-soon posture. As though a misheard coffee order would be equivalent to the contretemps that had passed seconds before. A quickly and painlessly resolved minor incident, all dramatized before a roomful of note-taking observers.

Outwardly, for the room's inhabitants: business as usual. In the sanctity of private consciousness, Marcus felt the glow of a wide toothy smile. Gratification.

Stymied, Marcus began reading. His oldest habit other than breakfast cereal for dinner also doubled as a favoured way to coerce sense from the superabundant world.

Per usual, a Gondwana of points of view.

By the dozen: bullet point advice articlettes of three hundred words cobbled together by been-through-the-wringer authorities formerly sentenced to hard labour and long stretches in the continent-spanning penitentiary called Online Dating.

From them, no shortage of adamant opinion.

He'd paused to read a garish website of flashing banners and testimonials called Been There, Done That run by a woman who wouldn't wish online dating on her last mother-in-law (yuk yuk). For a *Small Fee* BTDT promised to share *Can't Miss Steps* that would lead straight out of *Internet Dating Hell*. Plus, *Hard Won Secrets Learned on the Battlefield* and a *One-Way Ticket to Happiness*. *Rock Solid Game Changers* too. Mixed metaphors proved the least of BTDT's failings.

While this *Registered Relationship Coach* (whose website did not mention where she'd registered) indicated her position as an equal opportunity mercenary, other vets of similarly wizened temperament specialized in and offered *Free* Correctives* to the encyclopedic blunders and habitual fatal errors of the heterosexual male alone. (As for women's many, many red flags and endless public lists of dealbreakers, experts appeared to regard them as eternal givens.) The takeaway: the poor pitiful buggers, as clueless as they are lumbering and so completely illiterate that they needed guidance from knowledgable readers of human nature who could read between the lines as well. Lifting approaches from used car lot operatives, their *Guarantee to Guys* or *My Money-Back Promise to You* reflected legally cautious wording that, to Marcus's eye, proclaimed *I Possess the Secrets to Success* but also *Results Vary*. Their scripts could as easily sell *Next Generation* weight loss pills made from *Recently Discovered* berries from the Amazon that *Doctors Don't Want You to Know About*.

The history of snake oil purveyors, Marcus thought, what lessons would it teach?

Day or night, at differing hours, and during breaks, Marcus noted the dating-advice publisher fashion for insider tips, thou shalt commandments, and numbers—"Top 10 Do Not Do's," "8 Ways to Tickle Her Fancy," "Seven Foolproof . . . ," "The Surefire 5 . . . ."

Seeking a common thread, he grew exasperated by the lunatic diversity of opinion.

The gender in heels since Catherine de Medici possessed staggering biological sophistication, consensus appeared to have decided, and a sensitive internal clockwork thrown off by the least mote of masculinity's toxic dust.

Marcus pored over calamitous musts to sidestep. He learned about criminal descriptors that set off one in a networked system of homogametic alarms. With sage definiteness (of the trial and error, school of hard knocks, and baptism by fire varieties), pros revealed what certain words truly meant and what personal information to carefully sculpt, edit, or reserve for third date revelations, if at all.

Over lunches, Marcus chewed over advice promoted by *Reader's Digest*, which he hadn't known still existed.

Avoid using the phrase "nice guy" as a description: that dodo might as well castrate himself in public. Ditto for "good guy" and "bighearted." Exile "easygoing." These flimsy lies pointed to a man either so out of touch with himself that he believed his own hype or a lug too lazy to bother with actually trying. Nobody was a nice guy. That, or no single lady believed him.

Until he'd grown weary or readied his wings (the picture of himself as a paunchy overgrown nestling had elicited a snort), Marcus vowed to read widely, or said, "Syb, read" as he in opened cans in the kitchen and began his morning shave. With so many search findings available to him and her, Marcus realized he could spend another adulthood preparing; or that, often enough, one expert's bit of advice cancelled out another's. If everyone was entitled to their truth, as a student had once told him, then everyone's belief was true and therefore his truth was the truth he chose. Or, in Marcus's case, what stuck.

Having discarded the video profile option as invasive and a smidge too revelatory, as making him feel stared at or studied like a lab microbe, Marcus opted for text. Easy, a promising start.

And with text in mind—the collective pan-gender wisdom he'd accessed on his computers, in grocery and drugstore check-out lines, in his doctor's reception room, and in throwaway newspaperettes handed out at transit stops—Marcus sorted, paying close attention to repeated assertions from the teeming community of in-the-know authors. Surely, if all these experts and all these veterans publicly sharing their knowledge agreed on a point, it had to possess authentic merit.

He learned—

Don't crow, brag, and overemphasize successes, but have clear ambitions, goals, and accomplishments. No one cares about the breadth or exclusivity of your social circle or what make of vehicle you drive. Don't list expectations; research has proven openheartedness and openmindedness as attractive qualities. Your list of "musts": minimize it and, certainly, don't overshare.

Don't come across as wishy-washy or overly certain. Post no references to sex in any form: a respectful gentleman doesn't ask, doesn't tell, take measurements, or document performances. Don't mention "stamina" or drop hints about "techniques the ladies love." Don't post ideals that are from religious texts, history, literature, films, or cartoons. Don't compare yourself to the same; no woman wants to date Sampson or swallows your strik-ing resemblance to Hemingway, Paul Newman, or George Clooney. Taking a jocular stance and describing yourself as either being a stalker or not being one amounts to a dating taboo; men-tioning 'rapist' is self-sabotage, and air quotes don't help. So too for appearing shirtless in any image. Or holding a weapon. Strike alcohol from the picture. Jokiness, euphemism, innuendo, cloying sentiment: introduce at your own risk. Recreational drug usage too. Don't compare yourself to an animal. Reserve thoughts on the cosmos for (much) later.

Don't be cutesy. Don't rely on clichés: a "real catch" belongs in the sea. Photos of you in Mardi Gras beads, novelty memorabilia related to beer: don't go there. Firmly asserted or held opinions can be alienating. Needless to say, nudity, whether tasteful or crass, tanks a guy's chances. Don't idealize your ex, if applicable, nor vilify her. Don't mention fashion or swimsuit models. "I prefer under 40" is both presumptuous and offensive. A defined age range suggests basal superficiality. Don't objectify. Give no vengeful or accusatory or bitter or longing account of your relationship history; better yet, avoid mention of it altogether if possible. Pining for ideals belongs in bad poetry. Avoid legalese or reference to an easily accessed divorce lawyer. "Simple" is a red flag word. Ditto for "sweetheart," "lovable," "A-list," "discriminating," "misunderstood." Close to your mother and ex or distant from them, they're effectively the vengeful fairy at Sleeping Beauty's christening: keep both out of the picture.

Don't own a snake. Have the decency to wear a shirt that requires buttoning. All caps? A coffin nail. Bad spelling? Another. Clingy, needy: you're an adult, grow up. Angry at the world? Keep it to yourself or see a counsellor.

Don't generalize about the kinds of women who haven't worked out for you. The fact of yellowing teeth signals giving up; women's supercharged reproductive senses automatically zero in on that and retract. Hair past the nape spells vain man-child. Same for pendants on leather string. Smile, but not with the width of a campaigning politician. Punning? A notch above rifle ownership. "Nudge, nudge" belonged with reptile pets, photographed erections, safari poses, and mistaking vanity for self-confidence. "You get what you give" a chief operating principle.

The takeaway: every step forward contains a multiverse of missteps.

Cowed by adamant experts, Marcus relinquished "nice." The word had appeared and disappeared within his boxes before. Typing n i c e, he'd thought *benign, pleasant, thoughtful, reassuring.* And: true, at least sometimes. He tossed the no longer functional word on the populous Use at Your Own Risk pile. Apparently, it belonged with pythons, abundant jewelry, machine-tanned skin, and a subscription to *Recoil.* Mealy-mouthed, evidently, a bland non-word whose very presence tripped feminine alarms.

Synthesized—the praiseworthy reserved and the offensive weeded out—the resulting patchwork figure suggested a pair of ears designed for attentive listening and an equally useful set of arms for hugs, household handiwork, and cleaning up after himself. So far as Marcus could determine from the Alexandria of blog, magazine, and newspaper pieces he scanned, the contemporary answer to Freud's much spat-upon, century old question did not lead toward the long history of warriors, conquerors, or legislators. No, the preferred model descended from the heavens as a safe, nurturing partner with a keen emotional intelligence that intuited a woman's complex and fluctuating psychological states. A neutered pit bull crossed with a golden lab and trained as a guide animal, in short.

The Frankenstein-stitched creature might hump a leg, yes, but only if asked.

Marcus didn't bother with articles offering counsel to female profile-fillers. Not often, anyhow.

Glances at their stunted vocabulary of repeated words transported him to what he'd imagined as an extinct 1950s fantasy—a fever-dream mixture of hausfrau and sexpot with an operating system based on highlighted decrees about wifely obeisance from Corinthians, Ephesians, and Colossians.

ACVQ 3

The best thing you have going is?

The question is asinine.
Just one thing?
Tenure and with it career stability and a good pension; equity.
Normal functionality (according to my CMT)
No sign of male pattern baldness.
The ongoing ability to sire an entire region's population.
Equity via ownership at a respectable address.
A portfolio that's been performing well for years.
A promising familial medical history.
No major vices.
Bridled optimism.
White person problems: that's all I've got.
No signs of forgetfulness or incontinence.
No alimony situation for which I bleed monthly.
Comfort in my own skin.
Substance.

A general certainty of purpose.

ACVQ 4

Describe your perfect first date.

~~Whatever its crass origins (romantic comedies? Those televised dating competitions? the flower, chocolate, or greeting card industries?), the "perfect first date" idea is also an unhelpful myth. It creates unrealistic expectations. And it leads people to believe that there's no reason to continue on if the first date doesn't measure up to the Platonic ideal.~~

~~A meal. A casual dinner, perhaps, so that there's chance enough to learn about the other and get better than a first impression and sense the depth of our compatibility.~~

~~There's no love at first sight or "right away I knew in my heart that we were meant to be." Any first date with eurekas in the "I wanted to see her again" vein or "I couldn't wait to hear more" rates as a better-than-okay dating experience.~~

~~We sense mutual physical attraction. And there's a mutual realization that it's important.~~

~~We've both kept up our end of the bargain.~~

~~We're both curious to know more about the other.~~

~~The bloom is *not* off that rose.~~

~~During conversation we don't sense any overdeveloped neediness in the other. Neither do we hear about lawyerly lists of 'dealbreakers' or see the hardened eyes of someone who's been in 'the dating pool' for too long.~~

~~During a promising first date the moments of mutualism far outweigh points of difference.~~

~~She's kept her figure and thinks I've maintained mine; she comfortably expresses her thoughts about the world and likes when I do the same.~~

~~I discover she's not a prude; she discovers that I'm not a creep.~~
~~We're both satisfied that time hasn't warped our outlooks,~~
~~demolished our physiques, or soured us to the bone.~~
~~A sense of mutual enthusiasm that's not fuelled by vampiric~~
~~desperation.~~
~~Despite our 'advanced' years, we've both formed opinions of~~
~~ourselves, the meaning of life etc without those having turned~~
~~into any kind of fundamentalist dogmatist.~~
~~Whatever skeletons there are, they remain stowed in the closet.~~
~~At least, for a time.~~

Regardless of details—flowers or venue or weather: they're ultimately not that important—or first, second, or third impressions,
or conversational hiccups, when a realistically 'perfect' date ends,
both parties don't hesitate for a moment to express the desire to
set a second date.

ACVQ 5

How much private time do you need?

Plenty. In a crowded world, it's a luxury I value. Even Mother Teresa carved out some down time.

Too much is too much and too little is too little.

If Oscar Wilde didn't have something clever to say about private time, he ought to have.

The answer is challenging to quantify: a little, a lot, a moderate amount, at least an hour each day??

There's a fine line between 'want' and 'need'.

There is "too much of a good thing" and perhaps that's what I possess right now and wish to remedy

Generally, I value the comforts of "private time" over the discordant nattering voices and ceaseless negotiations of "public time."

There's something to be said for socializing; there's more to be said for the value of solitary experiences.

The constant need for an audience, social activity, or conversational noise is a personality flaw.

"When I first read the words 'introvert' and 'extrovert' when I was 10, I thought I was both."

Hmm, somewhere between a Thoreauesque cabin hermit and a regular Joe?

Part of me craves nothing but solitude, another realizes the dangers of that. Those two are in fairly constant dialogue.

"Private time" does not mean solitary confinement. Even when sharing a room with another, I'm able to secure private time.

Frequent public speaking is an occupational hazard. The beneficial counter-balance is solitude.

"One can be instructed in society, one is inspired only in solitude."

~~The older I get the more I enjoy my solitude.~~
~~A pair in a room, friends or lovers. They're seated, occupied with individual projects and yet able to converse: the best of both worlds.~~

Those needs are fluid. On my own, I'm content with the roar of my own mind. While in a relationship, though, I value shared experiences and the influx of perspective from the other person.

Pedagogy

Friday 1:30–1:45 PM

Glossy hair a protective baffle against Marcus' dour visage and tested patience, the girl paper-shuffled and expelled her signature nasal huffs. Even with the fantasy name signifying European glamour and its attendant riches, L'Oréal was finding neither the strategy nor the courage to first address and, tougher still, dispute the 58 or its implied—and, to her mind, consequential—verdict.

It's your dime, Marcus thought while also pondering a wired pay-per-use communication system that had once, for ten cents, allowed users to speak for a set period, contingent on geographic distance. Outmoded technology. Might as well try explaining *carbon copy. Papyrograph.*

Better nothing.

You're polluting the office air with anxiety, Marcus fumed behind a facial posture the years had perfected as *encouraging.* He imagined transmission—L'Oréal a Typhoid Mary figure unleashing molecules that would waft into his lungs; they'd fasten themselves, multiply without hesitation. Smiley face first responder cells would fight uselessly against the onslaught of distress.

Conjuring a scenario—himself molecular, a two-dimensional cartoon, paddling through the tepid waters of her neural pathways in a nano-canoe—Marcus wondered about the girl's agenda. His adult change of heart instigated by her sad plight? Hope for the best? Negotiation girded by spymaster stratagems? Tears, crocodile or otherwise? Gaping silence, intuiting that both nature and professors abhor a vacuum? To reveal the 58 to her frowning screen-parents only after the last chance meeting's

failure, or to pray that constant career demands kept the entrepreneurial dynamos too frantic to inquire? For all he knew, the
student could have displayed the damning number and its messy,
handwritten rationale already and currently acted on her mother's
tigerish advice.

A wallflower, Marcus thought, changing tracks.

When boredom intermingled with impatience, he could
depend on the frivolity generated by his own mind. Less a habit
than a point on a newly identified disorder spectrum, no doubt,
something for which a costly pill regime equally surely existed.

Wondering about etymology Marcus guessed at a Victorian
coinage for wallflower. Austen maybe. "Mr. Darcy fixed on a
bank of wallflowers, perched far from the elegant females intend-
ing to plague him," etc. As for L'Oréal, Ms. 58, he'd forecast the
freshman's party trajectory to a lone corner. Shrinking Violet.
More Victoriana.

Put off by the bank of hair and the juvenile—or allo-
genic?—sniffling from behind it, Marcus speculated about the
student making that apt selection from a retro game's avatar
menu. Phantom Girl. Charma. Infectious Lass. Enchantress.
The Wasp. Miss Fury. Hellcat. Invisible Girl. Such ludicrous
feminine options: shrink, disappear, use gendered wiles, pass on
disease, be clawed and vindictive, a secretary in a cape pining
for matrimony.

As a boy he'd adored Saturn Girl—haughty, canary haired,
bullet-breasted—and gently rubbed comic book panels that
showed her belly button's home planet medallion. He'd feared
the Legionnaire too. The mind-reading had stopped him cold. If
raw and rank thought were meant to be known, he decided, the
species would have given birth to the requisite organ, just as we'd
sprouted eyes and a voice box. Give or take, Marcus had stayed
adamant about that.

In semester two as a Master's student he'd earned and been
stoked, as he'd then said, by a nod from a professor famed for Ivy
League connections and a distempered tomcat manner. In view
of Saturn Girl's first appearance in 1958—just five years before
Valium's release to the market to help "reduce psychic tension"

in women especially—did it not make sense, he'd asked, to draw a correlation between fear of 'women's intuition,' 'masculine anxiety,' and the 'regulatory apparatus' introduced to suppress one and ease the other?

Replaying the memory, Marcus cringed at his toadying, Marxist posturing, and grotesque appetite for finger quotes. Postsecondary education: forever trying on masks to impress evaluative audiences. Young Marcus and L'Oréal would probably overlap considerably on a Venn.

Eulerian Circles? Marcus would swear John Venn had used that name for his idea. Syb could tell him after the girl's departure.

About to reach for the dermal monitor glued—"secured," the doctor's assistant had corrected him—to his right trapezius, Marcus stopped his hand. A bad habit, that reflex. He preferred not to draw attention to infirmity, whether actual or perceived. For the same reason, he kept pharmaceuticals safely at home. Cleaning staff got curious, after all, and gossip thrived on every human tongue.

He smoothed a hank of grey along his nape instead.

Announcing its own foresight at a hospital-set news conference, the regional government had initially recommended Compact Medical Technology for anyone belonging to a risk group—those with family histories marred by breast cancer, heart disease, diabetes, and so on.

Scandalized activist groups reacted predictably. Their media-blitzing hurled panic-button words like "stigmatize" and "pariah," before finding precedents in yellow stars, scarlet letters, and the inevitable Big Brother. Protestors with home-drawn placards—"100% silicon-free zone," "Keep your tech off my body," and so on—blared from headlines and transit screens until coverage about foreign IED devastation and momentous political scandals resumed.

Later, pundits questioned the timing. A "proactive embracing of the future" on an election year of the anyone's guess variety, how typical, what jaded bread and circuses realpolitik.

A public relations rebranding effort soon swept the inflammatory duo "high risk" out of public sight.

Converting the prohibitive cost into "MediTech LTE" and offering tax incentives to *individual clients benefitting from the health augmentation associated with regularized CMT usage*, the follow-up cross-platform campaign achieved a market saturation to crow about. Shortly after: full success and heightened poll numbers. Newly viewed as benevolent, as visionary in partial thanks to "Yesterday. Tomorrow. Today." With that inspired if empty-headed tie-in campaign motto, the government gained seats and kept its passable majority.

Since prostate cancer typically attacked men over fifty, Marcus had contacted the physician before well-intentioned support staff came e-knocking.

State of the art, he heard from front staff and technicians. LTE. Cutting edge. Long-term cost-effectiveness. As though they'd been coached by the same press release.

The molecular bonding agent and mimic-polymer—terms the MD had insisted on—promised to adhere perfectly with a seamlessness that didn't tug or resist. That *breathed*, the thin waterproof interface practically a second skin. So much for claims: Marcus sensed the CMT's blanketing shape. It looked identical to bandage plastic, a quit-smoking patch. Promoted as a gateway to a dazzling future, the CMT met with skepticism. Locals made cracks about placeholders, Edsels, and Clippy. That landslide of buzzy and "revolutionary" billion-dollar product launches that arrived DOA.

Offered a choice of what his MD's tablet displayed as Ethnicity Spectrum Tones, Marcus had perversely and regrettably opted for Natural. The non-colour recalled beached jellyfish.

Embedded in a translucent rectangular derma, the silvery labyrinth of sensor circuits kept track of organic and reliable but sporadically failure-prone bio-machinery. These circuits transmitted messages to analytic processors warehoused somewhere else. Or something: uncurious about the device's fine points,

Marcus had deferred to the MD's familiarity with jargon, with its faith audibly reliant on the all-purpose prefix "nano."

Elsewhere still hummed dense magical boxes of networked supercomputational brawn dedicated to the constant medical assessment of human bodies by the million.

For a monthly fee, pet owners could sign up: Obesity Spectrum Disorders and cancers afflicted Tiger and Rex too.

As an entertaining, gee-whiz afterthought, the MD had let Marcus know that he could watch vitals transmitted by the eavesdropping patch all day on a screen if he wished. Should the mood strike, Marcus could sit at a desk, ride transit, run errands, or sip tea at a café while gawking at the pulsing of his own heart, or track the regular chemical processes called Normal Range Functionality. With a stargazer's awe, the MD rhapsodized, Marcus might observe the release and catch of hormones, or the steady reproduction of healthy cells. Or, waiting for the traffic light to change at the intersection of X and Y he could witness the first anomaly, which might spell doom (or excess salt at lunch) and certainly worry until authorities diagnosed the mystery.

Not quite Narcissus entranced by his reflection and soon to be drowned, Marcus believed, but close. To the MD, he'd offered enthused nods that implied *I cannot wait to watch that screen.*

Should CCAP or K-levels sink, LDL or WBC numbers grow, GABA production rates subside, or any cellular abnormality emerge and persist, the instructional lecture continued, a signal would fire from the synthetic derma appended to his lumpen body. It'd pass through a gallery of patent-protected scientific ingenuity developed, named, brought to market, and shipped to a global network of addresses.

Eventually, the MD gushed, the network would synch to other lifestyle segments, monitoring client food purchases, recreational choices, and workplace seatedness rates, for example. Individualized recommendations for healthier alternatives would ensue. "C'mon, why eat cheesecake if red algae chips are just as available," proclaimed the wiry man with the prop stethoscope who organized his vacation schedule around metabolic rate training retreats. The man publicized every accomplishment in a black frame.

The specifics of the pan-continental system eluded Marcus. Along with the rest of the population, he accepted these gaps as both characteristic of the times and, should he choose, a fix as easy as asking any nearby product laden with silicon wafers. An office coffee maker, perhaps. Marcus only half-doubted that the Kaffeematic's array of tiny interfaces, coloured diodes, and transmitters could usher in an international conflict. That spy-novel incident with the hacked garage door opener and the pulverized Honduran diplomat still drew sweat from the worry-prone. Vacuums could be made to snap, security systems and ovens turned traitorous.

He'd never found cause to address a terminal with any query.

Marcus supposed that at other addresses—identical grey-toned cubicle farms in tax haven industrial parks built atop the bulldozed shantytowns ringing Mexican, Indian, and Malaysian cities a solid bet—monitoring faces employed by External Service Providers would scan data for oddball indicators and dispatch a non-external maintenance crew.

Back when he drove, an opportunist had smashed Marcus' passenger-wide window and snatched his wallet. He'd grumpily ordered replacement identification from the Department of Vital Statistics. Marcus imagined the building's basement retrofitted now with metallic ventilation and stacked black machines. Some statistics had greater vitality than others.

The MD: within a few human exhalations the electronic alert arrives at the medical facility and undergoes instantaneous analysis. If alarm-worthy, the client—"That's you, Marcus"—will get an auto-communication with instructions of where to go and with what urgency. All colour-coded for his convenience: act immediately if red; book a convenient appointment in the case of amber. Green, of course, promised "proceed as usual." A false red or false green? Don't sweat it; system redundancies weeded those out.

To Marcus, the derma's presence felt potent and dual: a constant yet cheerfully-hued reminder of mechanical failure and death but also a forestalling, a sidestepping and technologically-aided running from both. A prosthetic augmentation.

His doctor had acted nonchalant, a parent reassuring a child with a bandage and "There, there, now you're all better." Marcus had remembered the boxes of nicotine patches he'd slapped on his shoulder in his twenties and how futuristic they'd seemed then. Little had he known.

To Marcus' joke about the DEW Line and all the good it would have done—words intended to take a whack at the man's hard facade of medical confidence—the MD replied with professional vagueness that early detection could open the way for intervention. "It's all about timing. Or maintenance," he chuckled, which summoned images of older model vehicles with overworked belts about to fly apart, plugs whose corrosion thickened until they no longer sparked.

The MD recommended placement near the carotid. For "optimized efficiency," and so on.

Marcus refused. Even with hair he kept unfashionably long for the 55-Plus demographic, the high-tech identifier of his susceptibility would show.

Oh yes, her. There—still, again—the overdressed adolescent who'd christened herself after a leading tissue engineering research company, nanotechnology patent-holder, and hair dye titan.

The girl steeled herself to speak and expose the maelstrom that must feel unique to her but, to Marcus, more or less typical of a student visit.

Her glance crawled across folders, factory-made surfaces, glass panels, and a sampling of old books. Before addressing the grandfatherly man that circumstance—Fate, the indifferent universe, pure chance, bad luck—had dictated she challenge, L'Oréal's face reflected youthful perplexity: brow and forehead in the shallowest of furrows, half-pursed lips strangers to weathered striations. Quizzical about the bingo ball cage, her head tilted a few degrees. Turning further, her eyes met the vitreous vista of Marcus' desk.

"Professor Marcus . . . how do I do better?" The voice soft-spoken, a notch above a whisper.

Phew, Marcus thought. So preferable to a solitary midday plunge off a bridge, storming into a classroom with a cocked rifle, or a locked door meltdown in residence chased by junk food, bubble tea, and an overnight marathon of anime.

Could he help her? Of course. Marcus felt certain the girl's question would be better formulated as "Will you show me how to achieve complete mastery over language, research, and course-work, preferably now, in the slim handful of minutes until my next class, and if not, then before the next assignment's due date?"

Testing out fresh wording for the day's third "Alas, there's no easy answer" answer, Marcus bowed his spine. He aimed to establish eye contact.

Within reason, of course. Too much impedes reasoning, Syb had informed him, but too little broadcasts a deadly waning of interest.

The sclera flashed, he saw. The left eye actually flashed. How . . . distracting.

Marcus squinted, leaned toward the girl, careful to appear attentive to her scholastic needs rather than physical person. He discerned a metallic disk affixed to the surface of the white. Between the iris and tear duct, a heart shape about the size of a pin head. Of a thickness measured in micrometres, a decoration apparently updated from a few years back when girls wore heart-shaped metallic—platinum, titanium?—disks that reflected but did not emit flashes of light.

Another in a snaking line of technological achievements with zero value. Marcus thought of cyclically popular Tamagotchis, plastic eggs manufactured and thrown away by the hundreds of millions. By now, how many landfills had they conquered?

Immediately reminded of girls in high school who outsmart-ed iron-fisted parents with firm rules about eyeliner and revealing blouses, Marcus wondered if the decoration—marketed as Scleradots?—counted as rebellious.

And, perhaps the flashing meant a capacity to record and transmit.

He checked her hand, noticed a ring design he recognized as functional—connecting to machines for sound capture, transcription, and storage. His voice and its endless assertions and questions, maybe his face too and all its oldness: files stored within assorted drives and clouds for a time and then deleted or forgotten. In classes he politely asked that students submit permission forms if recording. He told potential rule breakers where to find the download link on the university website. Nobody ever did.

Personal space, copyright, intellectual property: inside classrooms owned by a public university the territorial borders grew murky.

Apparently—and in spite of lawyerly efforts—students could upload clips to risible channels that specialized in much-viewed scenes of spectacularly droning or questionably attired professors. Meltdowns, specious claims, and wardrobe malfunctions captured for the sake of smug, derisive laughter. Worldwide.

Though tempted Marcus hadn't followed through in search of his own name. Who needed the bruising?

"Yours is a complicated question, L'Oréal. Addressing the matter in the final"—he gestured toward the screen—"ninety seconds of your appointment will accomplish nothing very much. Next time, all right. We can proceed from there. Yes?"

"Yes, I see. Yes, I will come here tomorrow."

"I won't be here then. Office hours are listed on your syllabus and—" Marcus cleared his throat. *And I might have mentioned that fact, oh, about a million separate times in class.* "Sign up on—you know where." The so-called learning technology's current name had slipped his mind. Relay™? Relate™? Entwine™? Convey™? Compass™? Compress™? Over the semesters there'd been so many. "And we'll work out a strategy then. See you then. Oh, and before that, please, consult—." Consult™, yes, that was it. "Please consult the syllabus about recording devices."

"Yes." L'Oréal shot out of the chair. When she chose to, the girl could move so swiftly.

Condition-of-employment obligation served, Marcus checked the corridor for stragglers. He offered one a quick cordial nod and temperate smile. The hooded boy—whoever he was—returned his eyes to the screen on his lap.

Once, Marcus had meant the practiced facial arrangement as "Within the terms of my contract, I care" with an articulated suffix of "There are reasonable limits. Now go." Fully cultivated, the habit gradually became automatic, a personal trait bolstered by muscle memory and neural patterning. He'd observed the same in politicians and sales clerks. And mothers with children at the look-at-me stage.

Any professor's early semesters taught the necessity of setting terms, pointing to boundaries to student voracity, and defining the amount of give available. Instantly a part time parental figure, Marcus had immediately picked up on the septic teenage brew of self-absorption, neediness, insolence, and contempt. And the tricks for keeping it at bay.

Tears followed by hormonal rage followed by a peculiar vindictive silence that nevertheless communicated the snarling contents of a scalding review: he felt only puzzlement and small grudging admiration—ordinarily given to endurance sport participants—for those plunging headlong into the full time parenting gig. He kept stony about that viewpoint, though. Alongside the billions with faith in divine creation or hands-off governance, true believer Moms and Dads displayed little and no tolerance when challenged with any critique of their investment.

With that circumspect muteness, Marcus had realized, he joined the majority staggered by the appalling opinions and ridiculous convictions of others and saying not a syllable about them so as to keep the peace.

If faced with an exam question—"What is civilization's greatest accomplishment?"—he'd have a ready thesis. Not the wheel, not tools, not the microscope. Knowing when to shut up.

Marcus nudged the door, catching the peripheral movement of the hydraulic arm that guaranteed its steady, gentle closure. Click.

In a minute or so he'd resume work on Interstitial Knowledge Relatedness Unit 3: Economics, Energy,

Environment, Essaying. One of the unit's Humanities Renewed™ courses meant to illustrate the benefits of cross-disciplinarity study and highlight the Interconnectedness of All Things™ to would-be pharmacists and adolescent gunners for C-Suite bonuses who loudly protested "boring and irrelevant" but mandatory courses. His last year's Taylor (Frederick Winslow) + Eliot (Thomas Stearns) + Einstein (Albert) + Eisenstein (Sergei) had been a real barnburner.

A mechanical peacekeeper, the door's standard device barred the human instinct for communication via slamming. Also, being hurt, angered, or offended by a door shut with passionate intent.

One microaggression triggered another. Better to nip escalation in the bud administratively via engineering consultants before another shocked news cycle of headline exclamations and pundit handwringing led to widespread murmurs of "hell in a handbasket" and network-variant calls for *more*—policing, weaponry, monitoring devices, psych evals, pills, leadership, faith-based instruction, or quality family time away from animated screens whose animation purportedly championed bloodshed and anti-social *Weltanschauungen*.

With doors that gently clicked an institution's global reputation could be maintained; unsightly litigation would be lessened as well.

Marcus hadn't heard a slam in years. Likewise, the raised voice had been effectively banished: monkishness, he believed, nestled deeply in scholarly DNA.

The familiar environment of his former office—an uninhibited door and laden shelves of various woods, walls in a bygone institutional parchment tint—had comforted him. The shoe fit, Marcus felt.

Even the wood grain melamine of the old four-drawer desk now sorted into parts and recycled, he supposed, or else degrading in a landfill at a geologic rate, had come with a ready-made idea of being a definite link in a long chain of men who struggled and pushed on to create work reliant on flat surfaces made from hewn and reformulated tree trunks. A Romantic delusion, perhaps. He could live with the mirage.

No such tradition could be extracted from the cool industrial products currently within view.

Angular brushed aluminum forms, inquisitorial white walls, pulsar-like LEDs housed within chromed plastic, and green-tinged glass panels by the truck load, the ingredients of wood's forward-looking replacement, continued to strike him as alien, as a set for a film in which he'd been miscast. As though without a second's hesitation he ought to embrace self-regulating fabrics developed by lab PhDs and donate today's soft baggy corduroy trousers—teddy bear brown cotton purchased within sight of Bond Street—to *Professorial Aesthetics*, a smirking sartorial exhibit at one of the campus exhibition spaces. For display next to horn rims, elbow patches, and footwear apparently ignorant of fashion's breakneck pace. Community-building through snideness.

Instead, conforming to the glass-residing new order, he might develop bio-weapons or perfect age-reversing injectables. Edit chromosomes. Develop avant-garde performances for world premieres in Graz. Conjure forty-word nano-articles predicting key trends—body jewelry, the pierced brow revival, blocky heels whose screens looped footage of Laika locked inside the *Sputnik* 2 or a clip from *Eraserhead*—sure to trigger consumer frenzies next season.

Installed at regular intervals along corridor ceilings, opaque blister-form security lenses added to the sensation of being monitor-able for crimes that might range from theft of institutional property to the apparent non-productivity of staring out a window. A persistent reminder too, if subliminal, of a possible need for police scrutiny, *post factum*. Cue silent lo-res footage of a cracked student, professor, or custodian and the collective finger-pointing of pundits, relatives, and passersby.

Just below Home Health Aide, Syb had informed him, Security Technology was a rapid growth field. In the name of reassurance, campus policies ferociously embraced the latter.

Marcus peered through the polished surface of the desk—the committee had ordered the least stark from the three ultra-minimalist models on offer. What sadist built desks without sets of drawers?

His gaze settled on fabric-swathed thighs and sturdy brogues resting on one of his former committees' accomplishments: commercial-grade carpet with high molecular weight.

With low molecular weight, whatever that might be, trouble would surely follow.

About the distinction, he'd queried the sales rep, curious rather than zealous.

Scanning the doomsday article "Life Span of Litter" in anticipation of the rep's presentation, he'd zeroed in on a prediction that future soil would be categorically perverse: with a microscope, an eye would stumble upon crumbs of organic matter interspersed with the sediment of diaper linings, baloney packages, doll parts, flea collars, and devilled ham cans thrown out in the 1970s and earlier. Bits of toy microscopes too. Enough bag plastic to displace an ocean. Practically everything had formerly been unholy nylon, polyester, or vinyl. Wigs, leisure suits, sofa upholstery, sedan bench seats, house siding, office chairs, all discarded and buried in incalculably huge pits. Ads for once not lying by boasting *Lasts forever!*

If the carpet is nylon, he'd asked in the aquarium-like meeting space, what is Renu-Ably Sourced™—he'd said "tee em"— if not placating doublespeak?

An old hand, the company agent trotted out an on-book answer for the committee: the fabrication utilizes rapidly renewable building materials and products (made from plants that are typically harvested within a ten-year cycle or shorter) for 5% of total value of all building materials and products used in the project.

"5% of the total value . . . ?"

"Yes, that's correct," ignoring 95%, the figure's looming evil twin. "Our Green Matters™"—she added "tee em"—"microsite can answer further questions relating to this crucial issue."

Once her professional, smile-set face left the room, the Design Committee quartet made Orwell-referencing quips and joked about grape Flavor Aid.

Marcus had lost count of the committees he'd joined. As a faithful apparatchik, he joked to himself, he really ought to track down a copy of Lenin's official portrait for his office.

Problem was, there'd be no space for it.

Amid sleek technological spareness, Marcus missed the shadowy and arguably musty cavern where book spines pleased him and glass was reserved for window panes. Soon he'd become further out of step. Rumour persisted that planned summer upgrades—smarter doors, faster communication, sharper screens—would extend into the autumn.

Years earlier, when incandescent bulbs had suddenly become as iffy a proposition as race-, religion-, gender-, size-, ethnicity-, disability-, or sexuality-based zingers at the office, he'd adjusted to the change automatically, even while disdaining the blue-tinged surgical light that represented an environmental good.

The air plant in a spherical mini-terrarium distributed to every office as regulation greenery, he'd accepted too.

Acceptance. He'd instantly pictured an Edwardian curmudgeon railing against light bulb filaments and mourning candlelight's passing in rhyming couplets. No one hangs out with that guy, he understood. Out with the old, etc., etc.

Before the big move, he'd been informed he must requisition shelving. Via a discouraging bureaucratic portal, of course. The administrative and architectural attitude implied judgement: since whole epochs of texts—all the works that anyone could ever hope to read—could be accessed electronically, nostalgia for books that consumed so much space visually as well as physically signified a retrograde practice. He may as well have cut, hauled, and burned peat season after season when installing a thin silent bank of solar cells could easily do the trick. Or, long for the days when servants washed bedding and combed their superiors' hair.

In keeping with "Innovatory Mindfulness™," the trademarked mouthful phrase evangelical teams of recruiters hawked while pinning on lapels at fairs, drives, and forums in core territories and emergent markets—Singapore, Mysuru, Shenzhen, Santiago—the scale on campus had changed alongside its materials.

Visually, impact-wise, that meant upcycling. Like straw beds and outhouses, chalkboards and bolted desks made sense only as items in a museum display.

Aside from new wine in old bottles: growth. The Office of the President—if asked, Marcus could not point out its location or define the extent of its reach but conjured something tentacled and Vatican-like and atmospheric with rituals, mysteries, motives, and the continuous production of agendas—had begun, decades ago, with a Strategic Campus Plan it publicly defined as visionary.

A formerly modest habitat of buildings dwarfed by stands of trees on three sides and a flat Pacific expanse to the west had steadily added functional structures. Groves are fine, but they hardly announce the arrival of a new destination on the global map of postsecondary institutions with brand visibility. In the next phase, serviceability gave way to the visually arresting and ethically sound, to architecture worthy of media releases. The term "starchitect" had cameoed for a semester or two before disappearing as an embarrassment.

On the cover of a pamphlet or as part of a promotional clip, a row of stodgy, backwards-glancing rectangular structures made an impact of the wrong sort for prospective students and the parent-benefactors capable of subsequent endowment bequests. Penitentiary-mirroring buildings with warren-like rooms cause shudders to potential clients, bring to mind words with dystopian connotations: regime, dictatorship, indoctrination, totalitarianism. Institutional, the opposite of innovatory. Nobody ever pined for a no-frills classroom that could double as a military boot camp.

Innovatory could not happily co-exist with the passable or boxy nearby. Facades, though, retained their value. Stone-face bits that pointed to an Ivy League lineage or family resemblance to one of two UK campuses gave the campus a historical gravity that dropped hints about the august spirit of inquiry therein. With visible—if sporadic—signs of those heavyweight materials, the institution had nevertheless begun a process that wound up at here and now. With close by soaring glass of irregular shapes. With angular spaces dedicated to alchemical purposes—theorizing quantum scale particles, training brilliant young minds to use gene editing tools. All lit by automated bulbs that lasted several lifetimes and consumed kilowatts with the appetite of cacti.

Pluralistic utopian crystalline forms, exotic geometry that evoked the promise of unfettered potential, fantastical elements of engineering whimsy along with the earthen and subterranean that promoted a perennial reverent organic oneness with the biosphere. A mindful city of mind at the edge of a coastal city of spired glass. What magnificence. Luminous with plenitude and potential, secular cathedrals where nearly every last mystery had been explained.

Marcus thought of telling Syb to open the door. While no heresy, any shut door sent a troubling message of unavailability. It implied "I'm not here for you, I don't care."

He felt confident Quality Assurance had sent faculty a bulletin about the psychological impact of appearing uncaring. Deleterious, no doubt.

For the time being, he'd risk leaving the barrier intact. Any drop-by would survive the disappointment.

MTL—MoL 5

Meeting Room 2A (Ice Cream Social)

He'd done scant research. Sometimes, just like that, the bare minimum serves well enough.

Still, the stakes looked higher. The new escalation involved greater publicity and hence demanded greater caution. Backfiring: not an option. Witnesses witness, after all. And, heartbeats later, they gab. For true victory, he'd shape that story too.

The unit's latest panic belonged to the first of two perennial crises. On the current cycle, instead of a blindsiding budget cut, enrolment fall-off had triggered wringing hands and the squawking about doomsday's imminence. And with the unaccountable dwindling numbers: dire visions of cobwebbed hallways, collective dodoesque extinction (non-survival of the least fit), and a budding existence where employment placement officer bots knocked with virtual briefcases bulging with samples of thousands of degrading jobs. Behind the bread-and-butter worries, existential ones: how could critical thought have become irrelevant, uninteresting? Also: what's this idiotic world coming to? The unit's faculty, critical thinkers all, articulated stupefaction at the emergent way of things. O, the Humanities!

Troubling for all too: one crisis related to the other. Fewer students meant cancelled sections, which encouraged the perception of plummeting departmental needs for funding (that in turn produced an announcement from tightwad HQ about a dreaded budgetary contraction).

Triggering questions microscopically coated with norepinephrine and cortisol wafted along airwaves—"*What* can be done?", "What *can* be done?", "What can be *done?*"

Plus: "How can we rebrand ourselves, revive our image?" and "How can we get *them* [students, those ungrateful, no, *tyrannical*, heirs apparent] to pay attention to us and clamour for our invaluable course offerings, those first class tickets to becoming good, culturally literate citizens and exemplary models of a livable future?"

Answers could be—and often were—circuitous and ponderous, relating to late-stage capitalism, gigabytes of metadata indicating a lost cause due to a decades-old drift of the university away from an airy-fairy Liberal Arts education toward a prestige career to make parents beam (doctor, lawyer), or at least to come to think of their offspring as acceptably practically-minded (B.Comm, B.Pharm). If these graduates couldn't explain "glasnost," place "It is impossible to suffer without making someone pay for it; every complaint already contains revenge," or situate the Spanish Civil War in the correct century, they shopped and played electronic games like champs and settled into their eventual office pens as readily as Huxley's clones.

Jaded faculty muttered "C'est la vie." Or "Que sera sera," its resigned double. Hopeful pockets of faculty espoused adding relevance by speaking to the kids on their own terms and shifting toward the popular. Becoming "cool," in other words, like a stodgy department store throwing money at a design and marketing agency and waiting for news of the exciting new look dictated by polling agency findings.

Or, more laughably, taking a stab at "sexy." The very thought!

Others still: the unit's a leaking and eventually sinking ship, such is history, no use in Luddite protesting when you're a lost cause.

Boom year through bust, in Marcus' experience all these stances resulted in nothing except worry wrinkles, frown lines, and circular meetings in an exhausting series. One response: hopeless, like David and Goliath minus God. The other, a low-key celebration of the thick insulation offered by tenure: "Historically speaking, career categories do change and dry up, oh well, and am I ever happy that I'm near the end of mine and can retire with a comfy pension as our world burns."

Between cynicism and despair: the proactive, practical, and doable. Put up better and brighter and bigger posters that spelled out the real-life advantages of studying Feminist, Gender, and Sexuality Studies, Art History, English, or Philosophy! Become a Philosopher-King! Help Change the World Through Articulation! Spread Knowledge to the Globe's Underprivileged! Curate an Important Exhibition! Work at the U.N.! Rehearse for Courtroom Rhetoric! Write a Screenplay! Save the Planet One Cogent Idea at a Time!

Alternatively: punchy, trend-aware course titles that suggested the relevant, fun, and adventuresome (yay!) rather than the paper dry and exacting (boo!). From high up: faculty, please aim for course conceptualization that speaks to student interests—Post-Literacy (and the Second Coming of Visual Culture); Diasporic *Kawaii*; World History in Memes; Ethics Case Study: Superheroes; Inside/Outside: Genitalia in the Pre-Modern World; Psychopathology + Leadership; Humanness After Biotech; The Invention of Street Culture; Gamers, A Brief History; Heavy: Electric Guitars From Hendrix to The Ruins of Beverast; The Semiotics of Virtual Anonymity; From *Kar-kid* to Sex Worker: The Global Politics of Prostitution. Also, keep in mind students' magpie-like affinity for shiny bits: tinfoil over toil.

And, please, either sneak in for cameos the non-photogenic Miltons, Wollstonecrafts, Aquinases, and Kants—so serious, so powdered and Eurocentric, so many paragraphs and so few pictures—or ditch them altogether. Who needed word-choked treatises when the Web could spit out inspiring quotations from those éminences blanc in two-, three-, and four-line threads?

Of all things, Judaea chose a tone-deaf and fatuous revival for her gesture of innovative proactivity. Like a cotillion or a formal afternoon tea, the relic she opted to dust off—an Ice Cream Social—conjured a fantastic spectre of the Good Old Days, that Currier and Ives panorama of community through rose lenses, when congenial politeness ruled with a velvet fist and godly, goodhearted folk took a breath to appreciate life. The warped view, the treacly nostalgia, the fetishizing of quaintness, the falsity: in the years before the Social's abandonment, Marcus had skipped every scoop. The ritual had been an entrenched (and, word was, beloved) tradition when Marcus started. Decline started at the advent of lactose intolerance. By the era of phablets, the tradition—a simulacrum that made as much sense as a barbershop quartet, a Sadie Hawkins Day Dance, or a Homecoming Queen—had withered, become a penny-like semi-curiosity. A sliver minority of undergraduates embraced the playacting. Of course, those same students would do so for an ink-making exhibit or quadrille lesson. An impromptu scene from *Measure for Measure*. The rest: "OMG. That. Is. So. Lame."

With the latest crisis: central office discussions, closed-door discussions, corridor and elevator discussions, glacial meetings starring theme-of-the-semester discussions. How bad and how-to-respond the marrow of them all. Then Marcus heard that Judaea planned to revive the Ice Cream Social. "It'll be a hoot," reports had her enthusing, and he'd thought of word sent by Mary Shelley about reanimating the dead.

At the meeting Judaea didn't utter the word "hoot" but that was the gist. Her unending preamble trotted out "conducive," "opportunity," "acculturation," and "communalism." She even managed to fit in "interpellation," a term that hadn't been fashionable since the 1980s, her Marxism a plastic star worn by a child sheriff.

The meeting's Chair had invited suggestions and thanked everyone with a diplomatic blandness that implied the equal value of all suggestions. She opened the floor for comments.

Marcus waited for a few and then spoke to the air once the Chair offered him an auctioneer's nod.

"I have to wonder . . . ," he began. "While we might appreciate the sentiment, we have to consider the appropriateness of this Ice Cream Social. Is it an outmoded social practice we should condone by reviving? Do its values adequately represent our mission statement and pedagogical outlook? In short, is it a cultural form that warrants resuscitation?"

In case anyone missed the questions' rhetorical usage, he continued.

"Way back, when the dominant culture instituted the first Ice Cream Social, women were chattel, still decades from voting, slavery a rampant insult, and class divisions were naturalized. Entrenched. Needless to say, Aboriginal peoples were feeling the brunt of colonial expansion and minoritized social groupings of all kinds experienced daily and systemic criminalization or repression. These facts represent the foundation upon which this so-called 'Social' is built. Aside from being an uncritical exercise in deeply problematic nostalgia, it strikes me that the whole enterprise reflects a hankering for the good ol' days that for many were anything but." (Unstated but implied: how any politically-conscious woman could undo generations of progressive effort for the sake of a measly career perk is beyond my comprehension.)

And: "Other than the scion of an American founding family, what student today could respond positively to this? What would her perception be? We might as well host a minstrel show, burlesque dancers, or an 'Indian'-themed 'pow wow.' Perhaps there's a vitality to the thing, a utility, but I can't see its heart as anything but, well, fossilized."

Sensitive to the least oversight, the smallest hurt feeling caused by any mote of impropriety, or any environmental change resulting in a cooling social climate and the development of a deeply if vaguely sensed lack of safety, security, or comfort, faculty condemnations, quibbles, and alarmed calls for reevaluations bleated around 360 degrees. Not for the first time Marcus recalled that tight circle forming around schoolyard fights.

Marcus had speculated about whether Judaea would defend her proposal. The fool might say that its retrieval stood for a political act of recasting meaning, just as, he'd heard from Benjamin during a vociferous radical phase, using "queer" signalled a way for an oppressed minority to redistribute power. As though anything ever worked out to be that simple. Alternately, she might opt for a critique of his critique, essentially saying that sometimes a cigar is just a cigar and that circa 2025 an ice cream social had no meaningful relationship and certainly no political continuity with whatever had happened way back in the United

States before the Civil War. Untethered from human history, it meant what it seemed: ice cream served in a quaint setting to foster communalism. Bottom line: what's the harm?

He'd decided she wouldn't dare. Ahistoricality? Tantamount to heresy. When the Chair permitted discussion, Judaea (was that tension in her jaw?) offered, "Let's put it to a vote." Certified as unviable, as folly *avant le fait*, the Ice Cream Social revival plan expired in plain sight.

"Resolved: for the time being, the proposed Social does not speak to the unit's immediate needs."

"You can't win 'em *all*!" Banal even in defeat.

Marcus stared through the window, letting the room understand his readiness to address the meeting's final item. With the Ice Cream Social debate so completely dead and buried, wouldn't they all benefit by moving along?

Home Office (Isthmus of Brunswick)

S ervice. In appearance, a nothing word.
In one context, a simple choice: "Full or self-service, mister?"

During the interim he'd driven his mother's pristine red Miata, transport for short-legged free spirits, Marcus brought the car in for service when some panel's warning light activated or steering pulled right. He'd stuffed the records in a sealable bag, an act the woman he'd sold it to appreciated.

Handing him a business card, she'd smiled and said he'd be shocked about how many people neglected to keep receipts. Marcus swallowed any rejoinder.

An accountant with a business plan based on house calls that she characterized as "really exciting," the go-getter divided the world neatly: the respectably organized and those sad cases, strangers to ledgers and Excel who couldn't bother with a budget, never mind reserve file folders for tax purposes.

Itching to unload the car, he'd commiserated. Tsk, tsk, small wonder the personal debt ceiling had managed to climb so high.

As the CPA photographed the car panel by panel ("for my records," she mouthed), the outpouring of her personality—Mother Superior set of mouth, puritanism, no evident capacity for humour, a real pill—struck him as oppressive, if remarkably free of doubt. After further small talk at the insurance office and the ritual relinquishing of license plates, he felt nothing but relief watching her adjust the mirror, sanitize the steering wheel, and exit the parking lot after a cautious three-point turn. A taxi would be no problem, he'd insisted.

Beyond cars, service's nuances grew complicated. An existence of cleaning up after your social superiors, for instance. Syb had told Marcus that according to the latest data, India maintained the world's largest servant class.

Or else locker room talk and its corollaries. He'd tried out that with a freewheeling half-semester girlfriend in graduate school—"Service me . . . ," the jocular tone intended to disguise urgent desire. (Wisely, he'd trailed off before vocalizing "bitch," the very word on his tongue.) Single and nursing the sting a week later, freshly jilted Marcus replayed the fallout, which included Astrid's lecture—a slow-building but definitely outraged diatribe all the more impressive for being off-the-cuff while she sat on the futon dressed in nothing more than a black AC/DC T-shirt—about objectification and the mistake guys habitually made in thinking that they could learn anything from pornography, especially that being treated as a prostitute and servicing Marcus Jr. turned on Astrid, Woman herself at that instant, in any way. *In what universe*, her refrain.

That hurt. He'd never so much as implied that he'd assigned his penis a pet name.

Marcus had kept the episode to himself. Why kvetch out loud?

He didn't wonder if she'd done the same. Men and their ridiculous, endless presumptions and lessons never learned, Example #794: graduate school sisterhood was cemented on such offences.

Not for the first or last instance, he wondered then if he should buy a dog and be done with it. True, the man and best friend arrangement lacked a few significant perks.

In a postcard—West Coast totem poles in a tourist-friendly cluster—a few years earlier, ever-theatrical Benjamin had printed "I feel more helpless with you than without you" sitting atop the unneeded request for "some space." Before checking, Marcus read the words and guessed song lyrics from Joni Mitchell or Janis Ian. In an earlier missive, Benj had sent Madonna lines—a different diva for a different phase. That heart of his. Always on his sleeve and never where it belonged.

Marcus had pondered that statement of helplessness after the 'service me' incident, tentative in his conviction that some men were fated, as though punished by a god of antiquity, to yearn for something only to fumble once it reached their grasp.

Bouturodactylos, Tantalus' unsung cousin.

Innocuous-seeming on the unit's list of primary hurdles before tenure and promotion, service followed teaching and research. He'd once pictured it as incidental: a committee here, a meeting there—an obligation no more momentous than washing the dishes, a task to sneak in between class lectures and no big, time-sucking deal.

In the first tenure-stream semester he'd joined the Safety Committee. It met once a year and peaked with the distribution of an updated sheet about earthquake readiness and the posting of 11x17 signs in neon informing rule-breakers to keep fire doors shut. A canary-like elderly woman ran the operation with gargoyle watchfulness. Nostalgic for Cold War fervour, the Senior Clerical Administrator's chirpy militance melded unsmiling North Korean officiousness with Nancy Reagan's coiffed inquisitorial fervour. Her zeal in turn summoned wartime words: coup d'etat, putsch, mutiny, revolt.

He'd stuck with the colossal tedium of the *Robert's Rules*-led discussions as well as the Madame Nhu delusions of grandeur, muttering "Do it until you've framed your Tenure Granted form."

For institutional service, he came to learn, the trick involved strict boundary maintenance.

Word got out about an unguarded willingness to fill a chair on a committee.

And that willingness implied broad transferability.

Service begat service.

If you agreed to join committee A, then why wouldn't you also join hiring committee B, chair committee C, consider offering input for departmental website D, gather news and articles for newsletter E, take on unpaid editorial work at journal F, peer review a submitted article for journal G, write a letter of reference for student H, send a letter of introduction about student I to an in-demand colleague at the university in Nottingham, read and remark on the undergraduate Honour essay of student J, the Master's thesis of student K (also: student L's dissertation), join a graduate student committee in department M, moderate that panel for conference N, help organize and advise for undergraduate conference O and graduate conference P, vet papers for session 8c at conference Q, review a publication for journal R, pore over the manuscript of colleague S (directly beneath it: colleague T's vexing article), write an assessing report about a bulky manuscript for university press U, advise informally on a federal funding grant for colleague V (and student W), ditto for the funding committee selecting unit picks for university grants X, Y, Z? And repeat, with variations, each effort recorded in a CV file that expanded constantly, a microcosm of the cosmos.

All that goodwill, a finite substance, and all those stolen minutes. Exhausting. From what enviable well had Mother Teresa sipped?

With the exception of clerical masochists who took jolts of pleasure from giving, giving, giving to an ultimately thankless and perpetually voracious dictatorial system, faculty found their collective backbone and quickly outlined exactly how often they'd give. And how much. In defining strategic priorities, they accepted plum roles while letting the boundless, tenure-securing need of junior faculty, cannon fodder, pick up the slack. Deep within, *paid my dues* and *the-way-of-things* bounced around as molecular chains in the brain segment where rationalization takes place.

Service: a polite request with pleading undertones from the editor of *Isthmus*, a mid-rung journal based in an American east coast college, came with an attached file. *Offer advice, please, and one page of critical commentary, Yours respectfully*.

Marcus parsed the article, waited a few weeks, and advised strongly against publication for a short list of certain reasons.

Though the author's name had been stricken from the document, he'd recognize Judaea's underwhelming work anywhere.

Ethico-precarity, Post-Wattsian Spectacle, Interface Studies, Eco-Judico Feminism: on the unit website, she'd opted to list those as the Primaries of her specialization portfolio. Morettian Novel Analytics. Postures, postures, postures. Marcus doubted Judaea changed her own car's fuses, the hypocrite.

Of course one of the journal's interns would transmit the usual rejection template—so many submissions, such exceptional quality among them, so little actual space per issue.

In a lapse of decorum, the dolorous email might also sprinkle in some of the terms from Marcus' evaluation. He hoped for *dim* and *reiterative*. He'd typed *banal* and *derivative* too, but doubted they would make the cut.

The effort to shoehorn a word, any word, with "fossil" as the root, threatened to turn into wearisome farce. Marcus opted for "irrelevant," the first runner-up, instead. In a perfect world the editor would let it slip in and his disappointed reader would put two and two together.

Homeward's bus ride: in the ballpark of twenty minutes when workdays coincided with regular traffic and repair crew-free roads. Marcus' stop concluded with an unavoidable minor decision.

One option meant backtracking and twelve extra minutes of walking.

Vigilant about tracking and assessing, Marcus's CMT relayed Healthful Tips, perky automated notifications that outlined the proven benefits of daily exercise. Or *lifestyle*, a word he imagined as invented by ad men.

The "Did You Know" PSAs brought clients up to date with wellbeing. Studies, research, findings, constant beneficial news beaming in. Science, to be applied. Make friends! (Close social ties protect individuals from life's discontents, assist in delaying mental and physical decline, and are better predictors of long and happy lives than social class, IQ, or even genes.) Move! (Leisure-time physical activity is associated with longer life expectancy, even at relatively low levels of activity and regardless of body weight.) Get laid! (As an individual's sexual frequency increases, so does their risk of death decrease.) Pour a modest glass! (Consensus indicates that red wine can boost a range of health factors.) Smile! (Results lend strong support to the prediction that a smiling person is better liked and evaluated more positively than a non-smiling person).

Eat sea vegetables, purple berries, black seeds. Additional lines on the do-to list.

Then again, pshaw. By the metrics that counted, he was doing just fine.

For the school year's two hundred or so trips, the messages added up. Marcus would delete the alerts and wonder about how and when unsolicited helpfulness—Limit sitting, Eat red grapes,

Fear saturated fats, Consider a grilled tomato instead of bacon, Embrace mindfulness and steer clear of toxic emotions—had become such a loudly nagging industry. Suddenly craving a plate of rice crackers, sliced dill pickles, kielbasa, and cheddar, he'd remind himself to ask Syb about permanently shutting up the silicon chip Samaritan and promptly neglect to follow through. The next day: information bundles in chipper tones highlighting a new study's revelations about the essential good of lowering this or increasing that, or an exclaimed motto—Make the Extra Step! Take Another Minute to Stride! Try a New Route!

Following them he'd presumably mobilize himself into immortality while doing his part to help the state trim annual healthcare costs.

Grumpily, he'd silently argue that such coddling led directly to reactive evenings of TV (gunfire and car screeching, the occasional laugh track interlude) with nothing but a bag of tortilla chips and cubed Swiss for dinner. Or that the upshot of intermittent Every Choice Matters segments—"Did you know that the increasing obesity rate hinders efforts at healthcare expenditure containment?"—was everyone collectively feeling worse about their fellow citizens. And, in the majority of cases, themselves.

The closer-by stop represented hassle in olfactory form. Perhaps created without malice by an egalitarian computer or transit planner in a far-off office, it forced riders to wait and disembark near a crosshatch intersection of vehicles across fourteen irritable lanes.

That locality featured a T-shaped fetid nanoclimate absent from any tourist map. Its accidental offspring—a swampy miasma of airborne beef patty and deep fryer fat from a 24-hour exhaust port venting into a brick alleyway that functioned as a *pissoir* and smoke-stop for vagrants and drunk restaurant-goers—gave off an excretive reek fluctuating with the seasons. August—the cruelest month, no contest—claimed the prize for unbearable, nearly assaultive pungency. Not even the hardiest pamphleteer of God's word, wrath, plan, and wisdom could bear to distribute the latest prediction there.

For today: twenty accelerated paces of mouth-breathing. A former habit of holding his breath for the same now struck him as juvenile. Not to mention harder to sustain.

Two blocks up and one over, the Warfield presented a home absent of worries in late afternoon's benevolent light. No evident leaks, no broken windows or fallen bits of facade, no smoke or fire, not even a dandelion or discarded dog bag on the two squares of front lawn. An empty lobby auspicious too.

On days with loud or noteworthy tenant complaints (or calls already made or needing to be), blue-aproned Mrs. C swept the walkway or hummingbirded in the lobby attending to Christmas cactus leaves and buffing the mirrors. Covering for her husband's questionable grasp of or level of comfort with English, she'd become his proxy and familiarized herself with the basics of Marcus' schedule. She'd hover until Marcus checked the mail.

Better her than a tenant, Marcus thought. By hiring Mr. and Mrs. C he'd taken pains to distance himself from both ownership of the building and responsibility for its burgeoning ailments.

Turns out, aging wasn't just an affliction for creatures, and carpenters had hammered the Warfield's last oak lobby panel just after the Battle of Inchon.

A teacher even in retirement, Marcus' father had had photographs enlarged that showed the construction crew toasting completion with beer steins on the front stairs and again, legs dangling, atop the roof.

He'd dug up other photos at the library's main branch: local war victory celebrations in taverns, carnage framed by tropical palms stored on microfiche, MacArthur in khaki and aviator glasses wading through the Yellow Sea toward a beachhead. All caught in black and white. Smudgy photographs reproduced by the thousand on newsprint that he'd photographed and then ordered as enlargements: Marcus' mother had declared it—"Hen's art project"— worthy of exhibition. Marcus still wasn't sure if she'd meant praise; over years his parents had developed mutual ribbing as a relational hallmark. In any case, she'd had the images framed and insisted on hanging them for the rotating audience of tenants—a pair in the lobby and two sets in each hallway of the first floor.

As proprietor Marcus kept them there. They'd grown on him.

Despite his striving to create the impression that he was just one of the Warfield's tenants, the renters knew better. Tenants preferred a face-to-face with the man in charge and not paid lackeys—his smokescreen, his peacemakers. They understood that seeing a rat in the alleyway, hearing scavengers in the garbage bins, or having a radiator make strange, worrisome sounds—"as though there's something trapped inside," Mrs. C had recently passed on, her tone perplexed and accusing—required an authority whose very physicality assured resolution. Otherwise, well, who knew. Perhaps Mrs. C would tell her husband. He might do the bare minimum or nothing at all. Or, Mrs. C could affect a smile and enthused appearance but say nothing whatsoever to anyone. Whereas, tenant thinking went, the boss's evolved sense of duty, his personal responsibility, or his ethical obligation would guarantee satisfactory results. He resided directly above them, after all; thanks to a common skeleton of planks and wires, their business became his too.

"I'd like to speak to your supervisor." From campus IT to ISPs over the years, Marcus understood the impulse.

His old-fashioned short stack. Well, his and Benjamin's. Just two storeys over storage, laundry, and a quartet of basement suites, the building's quaint size and details—from popular (stucco pebbled with glass, diamond-shaped bevelled glass panels) to complaint magnets (swelling-prone wooden window frames fitted with single pane glass)—marked the building as historical.

Marcus had resided in its penthouse for decades.

Growing up without a pot to piss in taught a man the value of a dollar, his father had enthused at opportune moments, such as Benjamin angling for department store clothing. Marcus later learned that all dads seemed to warehouse the same philosophy.

A vacation request denied, the necessity of a paper route, a reluctance to spend good money on brand-name sneakers the boys would outgrow in six months: each incident resurrected chapters of the rags-to-Buick Riviera story. With an inexhaustible supply of parables about hardship, sacrifice, and self-denial, the man cracked open the pages of his youth like a TV minister at the pulpit.

Before growing suspicious of the stories' claims as unsullied truth, the boys made fun of the supposed hardships—they peed anywhere, so who needed a pot.

In the late '70s their dad started with "putting our money to work for us," speaking the phrase with zeal, as a man swayed by new found scripture. He eventually confided that his lifelong banker had retired. The replacement, "the reckless type," had set up an appointment to describe the retiree as a dinosaur, a dodo, long out of step with the times. Mattresses stuffed with bills belonged to the past. Conservative rates of return meant a nose thumbed at opportunity. Speculation had grown safety nets since Black Tuesday. Yuk yuk. Warming to the man and forgiving the callousness toward his predecessor, Henry admitted "what he's telling me makes perfect sense."

The young banker goaded him to "get real," and he promised to give the modern approach a shot.

Previous to the meetings: a household budget and an accounts ledger kept in a kitchen drawer, dinnertime sermons about expenditures. Also, gifts that doubled as lessons—coins in sealed sets, pink ceramic sows wearing a sash painted with "A Penny Saved is a Penny Earned" (kitchen, bedroom) along with piglet banks for the boys. At irregular intervals Henry played a game called "Now or Later?" with silver dollars. He claimed to have invented it. When a professor referred to the Stanford marshmallow experiment two decades later, Marcus had guffawed at recalling his father's reapplication of it. Once Henry explained the rules both sons had invariably chosen "Later."

Under the banker's spell former advice and practice—cautiousness, scrimping, foolproof government bonds—gave way to Henry's readiness to "play the market." And to his apparent comfort with "educated guesses."

"Hen, my educated guess is telling me to point to the elephant in the room. Maybe a man having a middle-age crisis? Should I be worried?" Agatha cracked.

For months Henry took solitary drives in up-and-coming or down-and-out neighbourhoods, returning home with news about a "considerable investment opportunity" or a surefire business that was—somehow—a bargain too. Nodding to his banker's urging for a leap of faith, the follow-up investigations nevertheless revealed underlying reasons for bargain prices and the fine print of can't-miss schemes. Muttering about shysters and rackets run by chiselers, Henry gave residential real estate a go. The city's market growth—then on the slightest of inclines— matched a need for caution he couldn't easily shake.

On the May long weekend in 1978 Henry returned home to the family's aging suburban neighbourhood but kept the car idling while he made a call. With an invitation for a family ride across town to a property their eventual dinner guest realtor swore to be a diamond in the rough and a real gem, they piled in.

Along the way, their mother agreed to the purchase—"in principle"—with one condition. As his pet project, the Warfield belonged to him; he'd be its beast of burden. Everything: property tax, lawn maintenance, bleeding the radiators, midnight-run vacancies. In case of divorce, though, she joked, they'd split it right down the middle. And in case of going belly up they'd get a divorce. In the boys' ears the second quip sounded less funny.

"A deal," Henry replied, "she's money in the bank." At traffic lights he described the building's good bones. Abandoning his teacherly decorum, he conjured a vision of the first step in a real estate empire. Strapped in the back seat, the boys waited for the ritual of their mother's rejoinder. Agatha looked dreamily out the window instead.

Drawing nearer their father told his passengers they could "kick the tires, but at a distance." That afternoon the real estate agent had other commitments.

During the first pass-by, Marcus's mother acquiesced: "Money in the bank takes all kinds of shapes, I suppose." On the tour around the block, Henry came to a rolling stop in the alleyway to point out the fortress-like solidity of the carport; he stopped altogether to savour the barely discernible hum of nearby traffic. Even the secure latch on the back gate held promise.

The shack on top drew the boys' eyes. A boxy add-on apparently slapped together far after the original structure, its cladding of faded shiplap suggested a child's fort or treehouse. Marcus' mother wondered about the legality of pigeon coops.

"Already on it." Henry tapped the spiral notebook, ever-handy in his jacket's breast pocket.

Over dinners Henry described the months of negotiations—meetings, phone calls, paperwork—as closing the deal.

He'd characterize a lawyer as either sharp as a tack or a slippery as an eel. The offices of city hall: a nest of vipers, a bed of sloths. Inspectors: licensed thieves. Notaries public he deemed as useful as tits on a bull. The menagerie, he swore, could be out-smarted.

Henry never met the man selling the Warfield, learned only he was an only child unloading his father's estate, and physically unavailable for any meetings. Dinner table speculation included a jailbird, a gambler on a losing streak, and a hermit.

Henry's enthusiasm for closing waned only once: the lawyer's adamance about the rickety penthouse tenant. The lawyer passed along one of the will's numerous stipulations: the decedent's brother would reside there until he decided to vacate. He'd pay no rent. "In no uncertain terms": Henry saw the point as an obstacle intended to challenge him only. The tenant himself didn't bother him so much as the inability to make the obstacle budge.

A mid-morning eureka resulted in Henry successfully proposing a separate contract with the tenant that could be rene-gotiated every second year. "'In perpetuity,' my ass": he declared the negotiation a victory.

For years the property had been an income source for Marcus. First with lawn care and vacuuming carpets on week-ends. He and Benjamin regarded it with ambivalence when they assumed ownership. One any given day the Warfield could be a nuisance, the cause for a throb of nostalgia or regret, or a pay cheque whose regularity felt as good as a blessing.

As resident and daily manager, Marcus grumbled about the grind, soon realizing the heart of a customer service representative didn't beat within him. Once Mrs. and Mr. C took over workaday managerial tasks (and Mrs. C revealed a gift for prospective tenant interviews and choosing the quiet and respectful), only the shared title of ownership irked the reluctant partners.

A holdover, it sat in a neigbourhood that, like all of the city, illustrated the startling process of time-lapsed redefinition. The houses dating from the 1930s and converted into rooming houses had been sold and demolished first, followed shortly after by the two-storey places erected during the Depression and after the war. Stucco-faced constructions from The Waltons through to the Miami Vice eras had succumbed last. Their concrete replacements, always described by marketers as exclusive and distinctive, dwarfed the Warfield.

For reasons no one could trace, the previous owner's father had added a penthouse for his brother. The lawyer had offered "troubled" and "anti-social." That guess gradually hardened into fact: the tenant's case requiring special handling.

Poking around the unit—permanently vacated, it turned out, after Agatha spotted the tenant climbing into a taxi clutching a small brown suitcase—Henry concluded they were lucky the Warfield hadn't burned to cinders, so plentiful the newspaper towers. Meaning to ready the unit for tenancy himself, he put the work off for a month, then six. He told Marcus he needed to find a guy to do the heavy lifting. Marcus figured Henry lost the taste for the steady demands that came with ownership. After the Warfield's first year, he certainly never brought up an empire of holdings again.

Accessed by an exterior staircase at the building's first floor fire exit, the penthouse perched on the roof and looked little different than a river shore shack from which Huck Finn might have fished.

Preparing to move in, Marcus hired student painters and a flooring guy. Before his fall and decision to return to Montreal and a nursing facility close to a sister, the tenant had evidently smoked in spite of rules. He'd also fed himself with tea, soup, Spam, and tinned chicken spread. A two burner hotplate sat atop a hulking stove that would have been old-fashioned in the 1970s. Between it and the kitchen window, the tenant stored garbage bags stuffed with cleaned and crushed cans (and two more for their folded labels). He'd slid them under the the dining table and pushed the rest into entryway and bedroom closets.

In a closet jammed with woollen coats and bread bag-stuffed garbage bags Marcus had found a hand-cranked iron cage tumbler for wooden bingo balls. He placed the device on an office shelf visible to students for subliminal messaging. Yes, my dears, fate did come in many guises.

Except for the aluminum wiring—"heresy" that caused the contractor to rail against boneheaded amateur renovators and shake an appalled head at the number of death traps throughout the city, the Warfield included—the shack passed inspection. Weatherbeaten and decrepit at a glance, the cladding housed a spacious and airy residence. If tenants and passersby assumed the worst about its inhabitant, Marcus could accept the false judgement. In reversed circumstances he might do the same.

The best way for someone to notice you is:

~~That depends on who the "someone" is. Who edits these vaguely worded questions??~~

~~In the case of a desirable professional contact there's ____. In the case of a social contact, there's ____. With a perfect stranger, it's . . .~~

~~Hmm, this question makes us all look like mutts performing tricks for edible treats.~~

~~Play to my strengths, keep my weaknesses out of sight.~~

~~Lacking a peacock's feathers, I capitalize on my best colours: ____, ____, ____.~~

~~If an eligible woman grabs my attention and I hope to capture hers, 'reading' her personality and matching it to parts of my own is a good bet.~~

~~I am myself. If that captures someone's notice, then great. If not, pretending to be someone else isn't going to help matters. Eventually, I'll have to resume being myself. Even Tom Ripley had to accept that.~~

~~Purchase costly doodads and be shameless about showing them off. Generally, I don't calculate about strategies. Life isn't delivering winning pick-up lines in a singles bar.~~

~~I know, I know, competition and survival of the fittest, and so on. It's depressing. As a clothed male ape within a larger community that's basically striving to win the attention of an available-and-sought-after female ape, I can attract notice by beating my chest (publications, status, bank account figures) or highlighting my utility. I haven't quite figured out which one works best.~~

~~While not becoming 'that guy' (the supposed life of the party, the fatuous spouter of opinion, the predatory, muscle-bound alpha), asserting the unique value of my person and utility.~~

~~Present the most outgoing and engaged version of myself (without turning into an insincere glad-handing politician).~~
~~Keep the snark, the complaints, the cynicism at bay.~~
~~There's something to be said for the parental advice: "Just be yourself." Desiring and obtaining a crowd of people to notice you through conscious efforts strikes me as the problem neurology of a teenager seeking constant validation from the outside world.~~
~~-~~

It's my hope that I don't need a "best way" to become noticeable. If in a room of strangers (or a virtual room, as the case may be) and tasked with the ambition or goal of attracting notice, I have no doubt that there are those who would view the circumstance as a competitive sport along the lines of "He who has the most toys wins." Instead of accepting that Midas-like greed for attention, I prefer to think that mingling in that room and presenting myself 'as is'—face, body, demeanour, voice, opinion, social skills—will charm, impress, or attract a person or two. Likewise, others will step away or judge me as a waste of time. C'est la vie. In the former case, the initial point of mutual interest might lead to friendship, romance, or a collegial relationship. That will grow of its own accord. Or not.

ACVQ 7

What journey do you envision for your next five years?

~~"Envision"? I leave that to psychics, astrologists, interpreters of tarot cards.~~

~~I rarely assign myself five-year plans. Those are for dictators, bureaucrats, and CFOs.~~

~~1,824 lunches, that's almost certain.~~

~~Give or take, more of the same.~~

~~Safe to say, nothing radically different.~~

~~Give or take, more of the same. As far as a 'journey' goes, that's not a bad thing.~~

~~Journeys. Well, there's actual travel in the works.~~

~~To and from work, basically.~~

~~Carrying on. It's gotten me this far.~~

~~The question has teleological presumptions . . .~~

~~This question is designed for individuals who also pin up colourful vision boards in their offices and send positive energy out into the universe with the odious belief that because of natural cosmic law they receive it in return and their dreams will come true. A reasonable person cannot swallow that tripe.~~

~~Five prostate exams and, possibly, hip replacement surgery. One change of lens prescription.~~

~~I'm possessed of one of those minds that peers only a few months—at best—into the future.~~

~~Hazarding a guess strikes me as foolish.~~

~~I'm at the top of my game . . . As the saying goes, there's nowhere to go but down.~~

~~Realistically, I picture and am planning for the gradual reduction of my salaried profession.~~

~~Securing a replacement as the current one ends? Hopefully I'll find it soon . . . .~~

I'll confide that long-range planning has never been a strong personality trait of mine. Looking ahead, however, I foresee accomplishments (work-related project completion) and change (a steady march toward semi-retirement). As a result of those, I expect free time to unfurl. With that: travel, new hobbies, leisure activities.

ACVQ 8

What is the core code of conduct you live your life by?

No carbs after 7 PM.
Wash, rinse, repeat.
"Neurosis is the inability to tolerate ambiguity."
The Code of Hammurabi (+ Don't sweat the small stuff)
"The right of nature . . . is the liberty each man hath to use his
own power, as he will himself, for the preservation of his own
nature; that is to say, of his own life."
"Do unto others as you would have them do unto you."
Since ancient times, philosophers have maintained that to strive
too hard for one's own happiness is self-defeating. Take it when
it's there, but don't expect it as a constant state.
"Every day we act in ways that reflect our ethical judgements."
Do no harm, do what you can.
Do no harm, relatively.
Do no relative harm and help when possible
"Each of you should use whatever gift you have received to . . ."
Put in the effort, or don't bother. Help deserving others.
Situational kindness, generosity, and when necessary asser-
tions of what's right and wrong
Remember: between shit and piss, we are born.
"Life is a lottery a lot of people lose." Don't forget your wins.
"L'enfer, c'est les autres" (the popular understanding).
"I should premise that I use the term Struggle for Existence in
a large and metaphorical sense, including dependence of one
being on another, and including (which is more important) not
only the life of the individual, but success in leaving progeny"
                                                    —Charles Darwin

~~At base we're all equal, from bowel movements and mortality to capacity for insight. The accident of birth (affluent, destitute, devout, atheist) and the fact of societal conditioning changes and upends all that. It's important to keep that in mind.~~
~~Clean up your own mess.~~
~~Learn to play well with others, or at least learn to fake it well enough.~~
~~"The ways by which you may get money almost without exception lead downward."~~
~~Nice guys do finish last; women fare better with the same.~~
~~"To burn always with this hard, gem-like flame, to maintain this ecstasy, is success in life."~~

Find satisfaction and, better yet, a contented happiness. When possible, aid others in finding it too. Also: look before you leap.

PEDAGOGY

Friday 8:25 AM

Wedged in the rubbery seal of his office door, a card. Translucent plastic, parchment-hued: Lanyard Holdings. Web address, contact information beneath.

Despite the year and technology, sales reps and used textbook buyers—who lugged sample cases and proffered ready hands and wary eyes and stood on visibly worn shoes as though auditioning for Willy Loman—showed up at the beginning and endings of semesters.

"Yeah, living the dream," one guy liked to crack, the sarcasm discomfiting and revelatory at once.

Literally door to door salespeople knocking on empty offices and peering through the glass with cupped hands, they left cards on which, like this Lanyard outfit, entrepreneurial types added Holdings or Group to the small business name—a species of misdirection, Marcus thought, peacocking to obscure the fact of meagre holdings or in-name-only conglomerates.

Making the plastic rectangle bow, Marcus thought to ask Syb about recycling options. He tilted the card to catch the light. Type 3, Type 4, Type 5? He added it to others already marooned on a shelf. Walking down the corridor to the proper receptacle could wait.

PEDAGOGY

Friday 2:44 PM

Personal email:

"Dear Mr. O—
You may be aware that the real estate divisions of Lanyard Holdings have been doing their part to enhance cities worldwide for over a decade.
Recently, one of our residential property development analysts identified 1186 West 11th Avenue ("The Warfield") as an eminent prospect for consideration. . . ."

Pedagogy

Monday 4:05 PM

Mrs. C removed flyers and business cards taped to the Warfield's intercom or wedged in the front door. Though Marcus had given her the go ahead to recycle any and all, his building manager slid the material under the door of the penthouse. Executive decisions belonged to the owner, apparently.

In the half minute between picking up the sheafs and throwing them in a bin, he'd wonder vaguely about their effectiveness at drumming up business.

After reminding Mrs. C on a few occasions—and resisting the vestigial urge to simplify with "No keepee" and deploy the hapless tourist sign language of forearms in an X that meant "Don't"—he gave in to the process. Some past mishap, a disastrous clerical error or such, had locked the woman into the routine of archiving negligible, ephemeral scraps of paper.

Working with C's system? Easier than not.

The same business card clipped to a standard business envelope waited for him with pizza, souvlaki, moving services, and gutter cleaning flyers. Inside, a brochure for Lanyard Holdings that showed a globe red- and green-dotted with projects in varying stages of completion, with concentrations in Malaysia, Thailand, and the North American west coast from San Diego to Oakland.

Office 205 (The Court of Duty)

Although the House of Duty contained many rooms, Marcus preferred to picture a Court. With its bows, curtseys, and intricate rituals, the latter demanded schooling in diplomacy applied to the usual spread of pupils and grades, favours and factions, codes and inferences. Despite the absence of wigs, outré shoes, and silk, Sun King ghosts roamed faculty hubs and perfumed the atmosphere with the musty notes of their manners and underhanded methods.

Marcus had expected the Head or a rep from the unit's Committee Formation Committee to drop by. A light knuckle rap on the door frame and jokey "I happened to be in the neighbourhood" before disclosure of the ulterior motive.

New hire funding meant striking a Hiring Committee. Its work: informal polling of salient faculty, a defensible, non-litigious, and nominally inclusive profile for the prospective candidate, a job posting with every other word choice representing seeming hours of talk, CVs by the crate to evaluate, and a shortlist to settle on—all before visits from the quaking, overly eager candidates, a day for each of glad-handing, queries, unofficial assessment, further temperature-taking from faculty (aka, "What's your impression?"), and an arduous weekend of meetings to finalize a choice and a spare just in case, to be presented to the relevant Office of the necessary Dean before the actual call.

Guileful Judaea, baldly pledged to reshaping the unit in her image, kept watch on budget windfalls, sudden transfers to better positions, and yearly retirement announcements. When tenure-stream positions opened as a result, the dear made sure to get word out that although barely hanging on with a hectic schedule she'd squeeze in committee work. To Marcus, the transparency was remarkable. Machiavellian would not be one of the charges ever levied against her.

What might have been tolerable prior to the Incident—important committee work in one institutional room with a single conference table while facing a semi- or unappealing colleague or two—now struck Marcus as a no-way-in-hell affront. He'd glower and seethe and become accusatory or erratic, each member interpreting the behaviour differently and, perhaps, deciding on a collective prognosis once he'd left for home. Sulking, acting out: the mystifying performance annoying to the other committee members (though not Judaea, he imagined, wonderstruck by her own ability to cause harm) not least because of its near resemblance to a tantrum, a behaviour acceptable in senior faculty only when whispers identified its root cause as medical—so sad, such a loss, but hardly a surprise. Either way, word would get out about early onset senility, or else ridiculous, unprofessional, questionable, and inappropriate showboating. From there, social exclusion—from lesser exile to pariahdom—unspooled in many forms.

Marcus knew he could have pleaded with the usual humblebragging—presidential busyness, a calendar graffitied with prior commitments, "too much on my plate"—like anybody else.

Instead. Insinuation, the inferential. Gossip for gossip. Speculation, word of mouth, the cruel lessons of the Russian scandal game. Disinformation. They would reliably carry on their eternal work.

"Thank you, but that's impossible, I'm afraid. Without casting aspersions, and"—leaning in, to convey the lie of the secret's exclusivity—"between the two of us, the provisional committee make-up strikes me as untenable. To assert their worth, some younger faculty make the mistake of adopting an almost feline imperiousness and manifest a reluctance about the collaborative process that's unequivocally careerist, distasteful, and ultimately counter-productive for both committee and unit. If a revised list materializes, however, consider me a candidate."

The only other woman on the list, practically sainted for dependability and self-sacrifice—"No, Really, I Don't Mind At All" to be lasered on her eventual gravestone—couldn't ever be associated with the feline. At a pending meeting, the members of the CFC would hone in on the slight's target. None of them would dare spout any corporate-speak weekend retreat truism related to "Team" and "There's no I," but the gist of their conclusion would reflect much the same.

With luck, an informant for one of the discreet Risk Management task forces operating from Quality Assurance would hear whisperings about a conviviality downtick and pass it along.

Possibly symptomatic, this failure to get along prompted ameliorative response. Any potential or actual prelude to perceived reputation in freefall could spell trouble for the overall institutional brand and make student recruitment work in emergent markets a potential red flag for quotas.

Unleashed: Furies in the guise of soft-spoken and quick-smiling Kathys, Karens, Darryls, and Daniels attired in comfy office casual of oatmeal shades. One would materialize from an elevator car, lob mild questions, show instructional videos, and allude to a return if further troubling news reached their spooky building. After, the unit would seek to identify the species of thought criminality that, like black mould, could replicate steadily and perniciously. Faculty loathed academia's New Corporatism, but played along for fear of a QA officer requesting a randomized 'Let's touch base' about performance metrics, at both unit and individual levels. For Judaea, analysis of apprehended value quantification and core competencies would establish on what side of the 80/20 Rule the newly buttonholed employee had landed.

Marcus pictured Judaea squirming as a QA officer droned about synergy and the unique opportunities afforded by and responsibilities attendant to world-class employment. Because suboptimal morale negatively affected unit functionality it must not take hold, never mind persist. Following the remediation request, another—Judaea's prescription for a single-use occupational benzo—was sure to follow. Ask for extras, though, and Vital Statistics initialized a diagnostic outreach. While an automated routine, the nature of the process—a questionnaire and evaluative meetings, to start—worked either to discourage excess or encourage loophole discovery within the system. For the DVS, pharmacological tolerance represented an anomalous reading. Once an alert within the system, any irregularity pinged as a matter for addressing, classifying, and processing. Dealt with, as students said.

MTL—MoL 7.5

Meeting Room 2A (Talking / Not Talking)

The anticipation of reasoning lapses and scoring of debate points animated unit meetings. With the exception of Judaea, Marcus partook in the ritual.

During her turns, though, he ordinarily checked his nails, stared out windows in sequence, took a break to pour a glass of water, wrote notes, adjusted his socks, checked a screen for mail, doodled, and tipped his chair back 45 degrees. He fidgeted and sighed, puffed his cheeks and blew out volumes of breath. The woman's unimpressive chest belied an evangelist's long-windedness.

Judaea's action mirrored his, he noticed. Or vice versa. Only scrutiny of a near eternity of security footage would solve that chicken-or-egg riddle. And who had the inclination?

His performance read as petulant, no doubt, a child exasperated and bored with whatever activity kept adults in thrall. Just as, he gathered, walking up to her and saying "How dare you" would come across as theatrical and overwrought. As risible, despite the earnestness.

As soon as Judaea finished, Marcus resumed with attentiveness, questions, and contributions. He met eyes, acknowledged the comments of others. He'd ask for an example, refer back to a similar proposal that had been defeated or else briefly implemented and then retired, or say "How would that play out?" Stretching his gaze around the table, he'd slide over or under the place where his nemesis sat.

If asked, he felt prepared to explain, "I just zone out when she speaks."

No one brought it up.

Worksites A-Z (The Rumour Mill)

Unleashing wispy-but-insidious rumours, poisoning the well. Ordinary, petty, misguided, and habitual. Further child's play.

Older than Egypt as well. Syb had informed Marcus about an inscription on tortoise shell excavated in the Indus Valley: "Jushur of Kish smells of donkey."

Beginning in 2023—nothing written, nothing traceable, but as primitive as a string of words launched into the proper ear canal in unit offices, corridors, or elevator cars. Ethical lapses, behavioural offences. "Her vlog has non-permitted branded content," for instance. "This remains in the room, but I was told she's become a shill for Pearson's North American markets division."

Heretical acts, pocket-sized.

"I heard . . ."

"This might comes as a surprise, but . . ."

"According to the grapevine . . ."

"There's a rumour that . . ."

"My understanding is . . ."

"It's just speculation, but . . ."

"Between you and me . . ."

Marcus read theorists: gossip as workplace violence, as an act of social control, as empowering/disempowering, as coercion, as an aid for large group bond maintenance, as having different signification contingent on what gender spoke or was targeted. He came across no one claiming the practice could function as a crude but effective form of retributory justice.

At arbitrary instances Marcus dropped his voice or trailed off when malignant Judaea rounded a corner or appeared in the main office on an errand. He might be speaking about IT staff, student work, or budgetary news. The weather. The subject was immaterial. To the interloper the abrupt change of environment would look rife with implication. Though she'd jump to wrong conclusions—*I am being spoken about* or *They are excluding me from that conversation*—the net effect of hurt feelings struck him as apropos.

COMPATIBILITY: 4

With amorphous evening voids at the Warfield to inhabit, Marcus sped on—fascinated, appalled, and confounded.

First astonished at the drastic transformation of the dating ethos, he later concluded that the commandments—a voluminous bounty of contradictory certainties—could answer the hoary human question posed since the dawn of Neolithic farming: "Why can't we all just get along?"

Sarcastic or hostile (gauging the tone proved a challenge) but professing to save steps, other sub-literary pieces, glossaries of a kind, mined common and outwardly harmless dating stock phrases for their supposed actual content—"emotionally secure" = on mood-stabilizing medication; "feminist" = fat, hates men, castrating; "free spirit" = junkie; and so on. Every possible term turned chameleonic, a species of misdirection, a lie, a disguise, a distant early warning transmission. Nothing safe, honest, or unvarnished truth: a self-defined "voluptuous free spirit" suddenly a ravenous, putrid glutton from Dante's third circle. A guy with "a couple of setbacks" probably filled police, social worker, and bankruptcy lawyer files. His "back on track now" underscored any woman's need for kid gloves, saintly patience, and makeup talents to mask the occasional bruise.

The problem with words and their pliancy wasn't exactly news, though the severity caught Marcus unprepared. In the near future when he'd read hand-picked selections of words in profiles and decide how unstable they might be, or else scratch through the gleaming surface in order to reveal the toxins beneath—"I'm a cat person" = flee from me, as I'm stagnant, a mazy swamp of neurotic compulsions—his own would be likewise read by others. Of course: give and get, fracture for fracture, lie for lie. Blonde, brunette, or raven-haired, their souring direct experiences or baptismal education via advice gurus could only push them toward hardened, unkind translation. He might type "well-educated." Between retinal input and nanoseconds of meaning-construction in her brain, she'd generate "pompous." A second viewer, a third, and so on, might settle on "boring," "uptight," or "snob." His profile abandoned, blocked, swiped away, or annotated with a black heart icon that defined him as a candidate for Hazard Zone or Do Not Revive.

"Bookish," "comfortable," "mature," "companionship": despite the forthrightness, these nouns and adjectives turned into traitors.

Instead of "nice," then what?

The literal millions of pages tabulated by search engines felt equal to a suspect but unthreatening stranger's invitation, as though a hoarder had exclaimed "C'mon in!" After a moue of distaste and an instinct to retreat, practically anyone would step over the threshold. If only to see what's what. Cats can't claim the monopoly on curiosity.

Marcus also puzzled and frowned over documents by women and men (possibly: who could ascertain where these word strings in fact originated?) that seethed with vitriol. Unlike plucky dating advice entrepreneurs, these indictments from the walking wounded rebuffed a lemons → lemonade philosophy.

One page stated that women were proof that Satan existed, another that God must be evil since his "Let us make mankind in our image" created an eternal situation in which two sexes that cannot stand each other for long nevertheless needed to play house for species survival. These incensed and fixated authors revived "thee" and "sayest" eagerly but failed altogether to learn succinctness and so fell in line with the world's writers of demented manifestos.

In turn their commenters, most locking the cap key and claiming to be red-blooded males—who implied that other alleged brothers agreeing with the status quo must possess the cut-rate, anemic stuff of a wether—railed against women with a half-handful of anatomical expletives, gruesome calls for rape and dismemberment, or brothel-camps and non-metaphorical chain-ings to the kitchen sink. For these part-time traditionalists, Stepford embodied the pinnacle of futuristic civilization.

Marcus hoped the furious outbursts represented fringe ele-ments, reflected deformed thoughts caused by parenting disasters, neurological disorders, serial hurt feelings, broken hearts, or per-ceived loss of privilege decreed by their gods way back when. Or, the usual healthy-if-ugly sublimation, giving off steam rather than acting out and realizing horrific psychotic actions and fulfill-ing visions of sexual torture.

Within minutes, he clicked them off his screen. Such acidic ugliness and contempt had to be corrosive.

Other hours of night, other facets of the same. Dating sites accessible without memberships, helpful articles geared to new-bies that reprinted typical questions and how to tackle them so that answers possessed the widest appeal. SAT-prep for singles, essentially.

He'd think *This could be useful* or *I can master these*. In a few instances, *There's something here*, while conscious of the long odds of follow-through of an ensuing project or article.

"Quick, off the top of your head, what do your favourite shoes say about you?" Marcus muttered "Fuck off" and left that one blank.

"What's your favourite age and why?" Ditto. The meaning-lessness, the ambiguity. Both "The Age of Reason" and "32" could be equally valid and neither revealed much.

"What journey do you envision for your next five years?" Fatuous. Questions on par with those lobbed by corporate job interviewers. "I dunno" and "Well, I haven't given it much thought" not acceptable; "Alive and employed" a glib warning sign; and "Part of a viable team!" pro forma and scarcely a pass. Every winner expected to be a self-actualizing mini-Stalin with five year plans, firm quotas—with the famine, death, pollution, and prison labourers raked out of the picture, of course.

The idiocy, Marcus huffed: keeping a chock-a-block career vision board at home (and its image stored on phones for emergency check-ins upon setbacks) and wearing an aspirational gold chain—with a two-tiered pendant spelling *Maximized Potential*—at the just-for-now lower floor office job. Dream catchers, a positive attitude begetting riches, daily wishes upon a star, time lines to actualize what the new you will become in three, six and twelve-month intervals. How had these farfetched idea gained such traction? The fantasy of the eternally plastic self and willed success exactly that.

What would a woman who might capture his interest hope to discover within those boxes? How would answers about favourites—"apple strudel *mit schlag*," "Howard Hawks comedies and Michael Haneke dramas," "fog," and "mid-twentieth century Americana" come across? Would calculated untruthful responses—manliness conveyed via "a Porterhouse, baked potato, and Cabernet Sauvignon combo," "the feel of a stick shift," and whatever *Cigar Aficionado* awarded Cigar of the Year—be preferable, strategically-speaking, or would information pandering to the continent-wide audience reading about him on screens assure better results? A beach-view vacation? Quiet moments communing over honey-dabbed chamomile tea, heartfelt murmurs about nothing in particular? As for the question about the half-decade journey, the dead and buried drudge's remark about same shit, different day sounded entirely apt. But how well would that test in the target demographic? He hadn't come across "Don't sound cynical" in the articlettes, true, but that, it would seem, indicated how obvious advice didn't warrant publication.

Here and there he'd consider the ingredients of a profile, mull over answers and effects. Further questions mushroomed. How could he begin without grasping precisely what he wanted? Marcus thought of lures and prey and discarded the metaphor.

At his age, when he'd known himself for some half million hours, how was it even possible to lack self-understanding for something so basic as desire? What does a *woman* want? Ha.

And he couldn't just brush off the renewed impulse for companionship as a psychological hiccough, pre-senile romantic longing. Judging by the adolescent geyser of vivid tableaus—sexually orgiastic—his mind had lately conjured in dreams, he was evidently missing *something* in his waking hours.

If asked, he'd have said he expected age-appropriate dream images: ravens, skulls, tombstones. Worried forecasting, anxious wintry episodes drained of colour. Tick, tick, tick.

ACVQ 9

How often in the last month have you felt misunderstood?

~~I'd expect to find a question of this sort on a psych eval given to military and police recruits.~~
~~Anything above an acceptably low number is an instant red flag meaning Should Not Have Access to Firearms.~~
~~I've *been* misunderstood several times. As for "felt misunderstood," that belongs to the script of an adolescent, along with "It's so unfair" and "No one even tries to get me," and that hormonal sense of being a square peg in a world overrun with round holes. After that, feeling misunderstood belongs to narcissists, the woefully immature, the clinically paranoid, and that population segment for whom life plateaued too soon and at too low a level; they're resentful of that fact and need some external force on which to pin the blame.~~

In my field, being misunderstood is inevitable, an ordinary part of the job description. As for feeling misunderstood, that's not at all common for me on any month.

ACVQ 10

Describe your physical self in a few words:

~~Taller than average by two inches. Proportionate . . .~~
~~Fit~~
~~Virile~~
~~Well-preserved~~
~~Good bones~~
~~In a police lineup: taller than Pierre Trudeau and with more hair;~~
~~shorter than John Updike but with longer hair; at a distance sim-~~
~~ilar to Paul Newman yielding where there'd been resisting, con-~~
~~vex supplanting flat, drooping rather than taut~~
~~Trim physique (bulges here and there)~~
~~'Gently used' but no work done.~~
~~Grizzled (front only, the god of genetics has spared me a hirsute~~
~~back).~~
~~Could be better, could be worse~~
~~Hazel-flecked green eyes. Moss green eyes. Green eyes.~~
~~Nothing that a few months and a gym membership couldn't fix.~~
~~6' 1", 34" waist, clean shaven~~
~~"It surprises me to discover, when I remove my shoes and socks,~~
~~the same paper-white, hairless ankles that struck me as pathetic~~
~~when I observed them on my father."~~
~~Worn but not worn out.~~
~~Standing at an impassive mirror my roving gaze records the~~
~~accretion of consequences caused by time and experience. Erect,~~
~~capable, steady, and purposeful: my mind's eye discerns these. As~~
~~a third party, then, the evaluation is yours to make.~~
~~Robust~~

Walking toward me on a busy city street, your eye might be drawn to my above-average height and stride. Closing in, you might notice: proportionate build, slightly shaggy grey hair, erect posture. Closer still: bright green eyes, expressive brow, pleasing smile.

What do you look for first in others?

~~It depends. This goes without saying.~~
~~"Brain trust"-sanctioned vagueness again . . .~~
~~Probably, like most, I look for compatible qualities. In short: someone like myself.~~
~~Well, when I'm looking for an accountant, I'm interested in cost and credentials. In a repair-person, much the same. At a conference, though, a different set of guiding principles comes into play. Back during the 'speed-dating' craze, I'd have sought . . .~~
~~As with everyone, it varies. Friends, colleagues, tradespeople, etc etc. Each one has its own set of preferred characteristics.~~
~~I don't really spend much effort collecting a retinue or entourage. Courtly and celebrity cultures are not promising role models.~~
~~Generally, intelligence, thoughtfulness, egos under control, generosity, a settledness that hasn't turned stagnant or moribund.~~
~~By "in others," it's safe to assume the vague question means "in a woman I might want to date"; if it does not, then, I look to see if "others" are packing a weapon or appear weeks into medication-free binging.~~
~~A sapiosexual.~~
~~As Aristophanes was reported to have said: "And the reason is that human nature was originally one and we were a whole, and the desire and pursuit of the whole is called love." When we find it, we know it.~~
~~To return to the (virtual) room filled with a variety of wome . . . unmarried; not younger than forty; not in any clerical, commerce, real estate, or custodial field; not pointedly athletic; not notably talkative; not matronly, virginal, or a 'project manager' when it comes to men (I can dress myself as I see fit, thank you); agnostic~~

~~perhaps, but not devout; of average height or taller; a B-cup or larger; experienced in life but still curious and relatively free of battle-scars, wounds, and deep-set damage.~~

I respond rather positively to brunette hair falling past the shoulders, a trim physique, a quiet confidence, a knowledgeable way in the world, a glint in the eye that's mysterious but suggests a certain comfort with irony.

PEDAGOGY

Monday 8:46–8:50 AM

Work email:

"Dear Dr. O—

You may be aware that the real estate divisions of Lanyard Holdings have been doing their part to enhance cities worldwide for over a decade.

Recently, one of our residential property development analysts identified 1186 West 11th Avenue ("The Warfield") as an eminent prospect for consideration. . . ."

Before deleting the sales pitch, Marcus scanned paragraphs that transformed the simple business of mutual profit into a radiant instance of moral good.

He'd sell, the company would build, and the world would become more beautiful, one address closer to utopia.

Accepting the rhetoric of this strange literary form—which packaged thick concrete mega-coops as Exclusive Residential Opportunities and cuboid habitats with bucolic names like Avalon on the Park and Boxwood Mews as concierge-equipped pinnacles of the architectural arts—required that Victorian beast *a willing suspension of disbelief* to work around the clock.

Even vultures wait until the body is dead, Marcus thought.

Approached by wide-lapelled real estate scouts and, later, dark-suited and open collared acquisition agents, his father had called the men's work both a necessary evil and philistine. Sharks, whited sepulchres, and sow's ear purses too. Agatha said that "snakes in the grass" fit the species to a T.

Marcus shared the ambivalence. The last associate to contact him, who'd actually pressed the penthouse buzzer and requested "a moment of your time, Sir," had read Marcus con artist-style and assumed—correctly—that Sir's reluctance (for who wouldn't sell and walk away with millions if he could?) stemmed from foreseen loss: that once bulldozed into scrap, any trace of the Warfield would remain lodged in memory alone or be converted into electronic archive digits in some library's catalogue of rarely accessed storage.

Mouth close to the Warfield's intercom, the junior associate made a vow he couldn't hope to fulfil. The development's residential exterior design managers would keep the gist of the building, "probably, anyways."

The gist, Marcus had replied.

"That's right, Sir, the basic idea. The general impression a place makes."

Standing on the entrance's top stair, the associate evidently interpreted Marcus' "Hmm" as "Do explain yourself further, please."

"For instance—but I'm no expert, okay?—those diamond-pattern windows might wind up in the development's facade. Or else, I don't know, I'm not all that creative, the stucco here with the bits of glass in it could get turned into a kind of textured concrete. In a nutshell, though, I'm pretty sure the essence of the Warfield would be preserved and live on inside the new development. Or, I guess, you could think of it as a facelift."

Immortality, oh goodie: Marcus had thought of donated organs. "Thank you for the offer. I'll consider it and get back to you." One boilerplate falsehood deserved another.

A few years before that another flurry of rezoning had erased blocks of middle-aged apartment buildings and mom-and-pop shops in low-density strips. Immense billboards announced new mountain view districts and sold bohemian live-work hubs built over bulldozed warehouse blocks.

In turn, successions of pitched, angry, regretful, celebratory, and acquiescent conversations had pondered the evolving identity of the place. The city's apparent future as clean but soulless and as hermetically-sealed as a moon base drew applause here, sneers and calls to action there. Elsewhere, no doubt, dinner party quarrels broke out about the importance of maintaining an architectural time-line in the form of preserved buildings. Equally, grudges were nursed about high-density residences supplanting lawns and post-war suburban sprawl. Also: tut-tutting over the stratospheric prices paid for property A or B. Miscellaneous blame and scapegoats assigned.

Outrage and aghast sentiments, Marcus had thought, the great unifiers.

Within this network of accusations, elegies, and debates, one addition story—reported as a "human interest story" by media announcers who did not seem to realize that only humans watched TV—had gained traction.

The objective facts soon blended with the rumoured, the half-remembered, the wishful, and the embroidered. Mythification, in short.

A popular recounting, a folk hero narrative, starred an elderly white woman who owned a basic wood-sided tract house that a child might draw: a blue square with a blue triangle sitting on it; three shuttered windows supplied the details. The home was the remnant of a row of mill worker habitats erected some eighty years previous—this span an impossibly distant past within a city renowned for building cranes, line after straight line of reflective condo towers, a powdery concrete-scented air of newness, and quizzical visitors who asked "Didn't this address used to be . . . ?"

The wizened owner resided on a block that caught the attention of a foreign-owned development corporation.

The story's paths fragmented from there.

One version, widespread and yet ridiculous, depicted the elderly holdout as somehow gingham-attired and vigilant on a porch rocking chair, cocked rifle across her lap. Pie-baking Ma Dignity, guarding her stake. Fending off invaders. This icon of folklore embodied snowy goodness while the corporation, along with its implied avaricious VPs, legal teams, and BoD members, contributed to and reflected television plotting: good versus evil,

David versus Goliath, heartland values versus Wall Street, the little guy versus the faceless monolith, and wholesome local versus barbarians at the gate; all in one.

In another that circulated, the woman no longer lived and breathed at all. External parties utilized her image as ploy, a negotiating tactic. In fact, a variant story went, the owner had died years before but her savvy children capitalized on the grandmotherly signification in order to obtain a substantially higher price for the address. Before the cycle ended altogether Marcus had heard a forking of that story involving two businesses. One owned the house and created leverage via the plucky old lady character. Business A took its rival, the eventual developer, to the cleaners.

The virtuous elder woman embodying plucky but cantankerous goodness who turned her back to filthy lucre and dared to shout NO to The Man had been embraced as a rousing tale of grassroots political action by residents of downtown concrete towers that overlooked that now legendary tarpaper roof. A line drawn in the sand, the conflict warmed citizens' hearts.

If choosing between walk-to-the-office centrality and a three-hour daily commute from that eight-lane desert of big boxes, burger franchises, gas stations, and cineplexes, though, they'd have signed an expropriation motion—as necessary to civic wellbeing—in an instant.

People love an underdog story, Marcus had thought, so long as its plot doesn't undermine their own property values and right to profit. Or comfort and convenience.

Conference Space 1 (Job Talk: Children's Media)

A gathering of the tribe—a marvel of pecking order complexity, a study in the nuances of collegial interrelations—the job talk for a tenure-stream position also ushered in a festive, if Flavian, atmosphere. Marcus imagined Romans had experienced similar adrenal moods on *munera* days with gladiatorial contests on the bill.

What good, evolutionarily-speaking, did witnessing a gutting serve? Did bloodlust somehow trigger an instructive memory about fundamental human animality? Marcus made a note to ask Syb about findings.

Shuffling toward the podium, the applicant looked out of her element as well as plucked from the era when Henry Ford's Model T grabbed headlines. Even without the carpetbag and umbrella, she brought to mind a composite of Mary Poppins and Bertha Mason. Glancing downward, Marcus supposed her shoes might be a find at an estate sale held by the relatives of a deceased Old World governess.

In light of the desirable Children's Media position, Marcus considered the applicant had brought in irony as an integral aspect of a projected stand-out performance—anything to induce the committee to overlook shortlist applicants two and three. The intent, if that, had wound up closer to a severe B-movie women's prison warden or a fervent member of the latest antichip cults that wove its own cloth than to any London nanny with magical capabilities.

The applicant looked sallow, but not far outside the regulation hue. Having drawn the short straw and been assigned the inaugural visit and presentation, she had to be preoccupied with making the winning impression. A showcase, for display: capable and perhaps tilting toward significant research, topic in an emergent-but-fecund area, reputable academic chops. Ideally, a correct profile for the unofficially unmentionable expectation that she fit in while doing her part, of course, to keep the institution's global ranking on the profitable ascent.

In head, heart, and gut the candidate would intuit that the material and her selling of its merit needed enough staying power to endure until the Hiring Committee reconvened three or so weeks later. Marcus had sat in enough of those post-mortems to know the easily forgotten nature of applicant talks. During the final meeting committee members would scramble, referring to notes in the manner of map-reading tourists in a hectic foreign city.

Despite the absence of any glaring floodlight, the applicant shielded her eyes as she first addressed eight rows of audience. She clasped the top edges of the dark woodgrain podium, leaned into the mic, and said "MUCH." Along with the startled audience she turned to the IT clerk at the corner console. Already tapping a screen in response, he raised a hand in apology.

Volume adjusted, the applicant proceeded with a cliché: "Much academic ink has been spilled . . ."

She halted, surveyed the audience, and pondered her clutch of cue cards before laying the lot down. A sermon commenced instead.

"There is a certain dubiousness—an obscenity, in a way—of resource usage . . . jet and ground transport fuels for global conference attendees, non-renewable resources for print journal production, and even trees . . . when it comes to contexualizing the *pornography of suffering* in Hans Christian Anderson. So much waste for so little substance. Early, in fact, as early as the juvenilia of 'The Tallow Candle'. . . ."

Oh boy, Marcus thought, extempore with antagonistic provocation toward anyone in the room who'd flown to a conference. That meant everybody. That degree of recklessness had to be unprecedented. At the podium, *go big* and *blaze of glory* must

have crackled along neural pathways the instant before the applicant set aside the notes.

The moderator signalled the hopeless speaker at the twenty-
minute mark. The subtlest of tugs at a sleeve to reveal a
wristwatch, the gesture nonetheless relayed the Grim Reaper's
finality: YOUR TIME IS UP.

With a meek "Okay, I see, thank you," the applicant
stopped mid-sentence.

Her face reflected the understanding that she'd thrown losing
dice. Worse, already digesting her new status as the unchosen
candidate—third in a field of three—and a kind of cause célèbre
whose name would be circled as soon as another Hiring
Committee began sorting through its stacks of application
envelopes, she'd recognized as well the painful course of the next
stage: fifteen minutes of questions from an offended and punitive
home-team audience. The temptation to abandon the cards,
snatch her briefcase, and leave the audience with only a vivid
impression of a hasty adieu must have been overwhelming.

Waiting for the moderator, the candidate readied herself at
the podium.

From the rearmost aisle seat Marcus watched hands shoot up,
Judaea's among the first.

Permitted to choose her tormentors, the candidate began
with a graduate student. A wise move: generally, that demographic could be counted on for a meandering, name-dropping
question. With a sheer enormity meant to convey intellectual
complexity, the question instead grew both serpentine and
entangled. Ultimately, there was no there there.

With her next choice, the candidate opted for an elder in her
field. The woman's emeritus position excluded her from Hiring
Committee duties and, it was accepted by everyone present, true
relevance. The woman's question could have been lobbed from
the graveyard of exhausted critical approaches, and the applicant
indulged it—"A good point . . ."—with a performance of defer-
ence the audience saw as I'll Let the Deluded Old Dear Cling to
Belief in the Validity of Her Outmoded Stance.

Her third, seemingly arbitrary, snagged Marcus' full attention: Judaea.

Already rehearsing an acceptable exiting excuse to whisper left and right, Marcus stifled the effort.

He'd heard people speak of their experience of a migraine's appearance. One moment it's business as usual, then next there's a sense of a hard concentration of discomfort, like a stone expanding right in the nucleus of the skull. Although Marcus didn't see red or feel a fist in his brain, when he heard Judaea he could suddenly comprehend both.

Judaea's mustard-gassing preamble—"my research," "I've found," "I'd argue," "it seems to to me," "what I've discovered," "it's become apparent to me": as though her singular devotion had produced a limitless clean energy device—coalesced as the emblem of everything wrong in the human world.

For the moment, Judaea held the room hostage. Marcus imagined variants of his thought—"Oh, for the love of God, will you please shut the fuck up for a blessed minute"—seething inside every head filling every row in the room. The candidate. The IT guy. The Committee. Faculty. Graduate students. The woman from Food Services counting down to tea and coffee pouring.

The grip of manners was such that despite the near-perfect majority (36:1, in fact, he counted), the mic on the recorder would replay only a shuffling or cough or chair squeak besides Judaea's voice touching on, meandering through, and publicly documenting intellectual feats and nonpareil insights. He heard the vain malice of the witch in "Sleeping Beauty": it's your hour, yes, but let me make this all about my needs.

Judaea capitalized on an inexplicable social phenomenon: if someone interrupted her mid-question, the episode would be perceived—and recollected later—as an act of rudeness visited upon victimized her. Onlookers would regard Marcus with disdain ("How uncouth!") or derision ("So typical!").

Nevertheless. He'd risk Hydra-headed censure. He'd deviate from the group mind.

Marcus stood. He raised his hand and showed the Head the face of his watch. Her attention triggered other heads to turn; for a moment Judaea's voice faltered as she too craned to witness the usurper daring to steal her thunder. Making for the glass door, he wondered if the candidate felt envy.

As he descended the stairway, Marcus realized he couldn't trace his display back to the Incident, not entirely.

With nearly anyone holding an audience hostage with their untended self-absorption, he'd do the same. In every demographic, people confused a right with a privilege too readily.

Meeting Room 1A (Bare Knuckles)

The revival of body language as grounds for a tut-tutted conversation had begun a season of costly rural wildfires or so after microaggression and manspreading as the topic on everyone's tongues. (*Everyone*, of course, means that largish segment of the global population exposed to the episodes of North American TV/radio/podcast/YouTube/news media content that outlined, reacted to, and expressed both feelings about and scalding experiences of—firsthand, secondhand—body language, and thereby in fact excludes several billion individuals.)

About body language's folded arms, tilted heads, akimbo legs, or assertive shoulders, fractiousness and outrage erupted in select circles. Derisive snorts and that singular facial arrangement broadcasting *I can't believe this is a* thing *again, get a life already* to the world weren't uncommon either. Places where pickup trucks revved and Old Gringo boots were worn at New Year's parties never breathed in the least waft of this campus-wide tempest.

Marcus remembered the trend vaguely, along with Teflon Age, a flimsy tag invented and briefly circulated by whoever or whatever generated media headlines and content, to describe a social historical blip when, apparently, no one trend dominated or persisted. Or stuck, get it? Wocka Wocka Wocka!

From the vantage point of 2020 something, the upheavals and ideas struck him as baffling, as deeply and widely felt episodes that in retrospect flattened into vapid trivia and fleeting moments of "Remember when?" that made little or no sense and could never be explained adequately.

To students born in the homely, unloveable new century he'd opted for the convenience of dismissive shorthand: "Oh, it was the _____ [Seventies, Eighties, Nineties, Aughts]" followed by a shrug, the universal one implying that accounting for the mystifying fixations of past decades or generations amounted to a lost cause. Neck tattoos, Y2K, performance art, flash mobs, grunge, food sensitivities, booze cans, bomb shelters, the Fourteen Words, lifelogging, braided headbands, Tea Partiers, the simple living movement, Disco Demolition Night, the Low Information Diet, Bronies, "Talk to the hand," Transcendental Meditation, Promise Keeper stadium rallies, bling, panic rooms, Chronic Fatigue Syndrome, cosplay, psychic hotlines, nouvelle cuisine, "We are the 99%," Iron John retreats, post-irony, the futuristic illustrations circulated with Ronald Reagan's Strategic Defense Initiative, and on and on.

"Do you have a spare hour?" he might retort jokingly to a class of confounded faces.

Gendered microaggression, Teflon Age, body language. Per usual, digits of blame got pointed.

One group took the brunt, another assumed the position of outspoken victim. Generalities were aired, contested, adjusted, recanted. Quarrel outflows like flu vectors, or patterned—crest, trough, repeat—in echo of a sinusoidal wave.

On news channels, progressives blamed conservatives. Their rivals broadcasted counterpoint.

Weekly, on *Circle of Love*, Pastor Maggie 'Sister' Graham chose unholy targets, agents of the Beasts of Revelation—the godless, philistines, feminists, radicals—whose shamelessness foretold the End Times.

Across dinner tables, one generation talked smack or threw shade at another.

And so forth.

Coinciding trends motivated fierce conversations while also redirecting the focus. A self-published diet book by a former doomsday prepper (and ex-day trader, media sources revealed) gained widespread visibility; its popularity reignited or intensified longstanding talk about the great divide between men and women.

Not only resulting in a fresh round of celebrity revelation ("I tried it for just a week, Terry, and already I'm an entirely new person" and the like) and expert riposte ("Besides lacking scientific rigour its social implications are toxic"), the diet craze caught the eye of television programming reliant on conflict. Also: morning radio hosts specializing in smart aleck zingers for an audience wedged in the first and last of the day's heaviest traffic.

Between invisible wave emitters and invisible wave receivers, the air swarmed with words from one nutritionist cadre aghast about the dubious premise of foodstuffs that allow men and women to embrace their essential selves (red animal protein for men, naturally, and estrogenic bird food—seeds, dried fruit— for women) and another that foresaw only civilization-improving brilliance.

Further tie-ins: media content nuggets of trend-following, or smirking newsfeed lifestyle reporters at timely previews of restaurants in Toronto, Portland, and Austin that specialized in sex-specific menus and featured private rooms that could be booked for all-meat or all-seed chef's menus. Timely as well, transgender, androgyne, gender variant, and drag activists holding placards for a silent vigil in San Francisco on the day cis-ladies-only aviary-themed bistro Gynocene opened her filigreed doors. Either naked or in expressive attire, the group vented outrage while simultaneously drawing it, and gave audiences further cause for the mouthing of opinion.

Elsewhere, speculating about the coast-to-coast disorderliness, the mystifying lack of consensus at every level and in each habitat, media commentators, young people, old people, standup comics, and anonymous comments section finger-typists zeroed in on the continuous incursions of social media, screens, and AI gadgetry, which incited panic here, reaction there, and— always—experts from think tanks, university offices, and a stunningly varied assortment of citizens' groups identifying what it all meant while pausing to predict the gasp-worthy implications for the future—visions already popularized as bleak cautionary tales during the golden age of pulp science fiction.

Bus stop cranks, postal branch queue philosophers, and coffee shop wags didn't hesitate to crowd the air with decibels and wrap up with "Well, that's my two cents anyways."

Spoiling for fights, myriad demographic swathes blamed the vexing planetary alignment or Year of the Water Tiger energies. Further demographic pie pieces spat their assertions into the air: multiculturalism, El Niño, La Niña, sunspots, climate change anxiety, the new rudderlessness, the new permissiveness, the loss of Traditional Values, the loss of standards, the new normal, capitalism, the System, the Man, late-capitalism upheavals, the rich, the poor, the middle class, the erratic boom-bust-boom cycling of the Pax Americana, the tectonic uncertainties caused by the Pax Mongolica 2.0, weak fathers, deadbeat dads, pushy mothers, single moms, lax parenting, the monkey brain, the reptile brain, the fissuring related to emergent Resource Scarcity Anxiety Syndrome, Shifting Baseline Awareness Syndrome, and Trophic Cascade Syndrome, neo-conservatism, or neo-liberalism, the Welfare State (or lack thereof), the Nanny State (or lack thereof), the younger generation, the older generation, cutbacks, handouts, rightward and leftward trends in world leadership, pervasive toxicities (gendered, environmental, ideological, systemic), back-to-basics pronouncements from Houston, Mecca, and Rome, the liberal media, Fox News blowhards, shock jocks, feminists, the international old boys club, God's mysterious ways, feminized children, the absence of master narratives, the educational system, secularism, food additives, celebrity shills hired by energy drink conglomerates, an adulterated water supply, globalization, isolationist reactionaries, off-gassing petrochemical home products, radioactive space junk, and Nietzsche.

A prominent Sensitive (who, despite her protests, people called a psychic) proclaimed on any daytime talk program offering a flight and a four-minute spot that the human race had evolved right into the throes of either birthing or growing pains—she used the two interchangeably, as if they could be. Attuned to the Beyond, she envisioned an imminent New Age that would unfold as categorically distinct from the earlier New Age with its charivari of gongs, crystals, Tibetan singing bowls, whale songs, and essential oil diffusers. Full of godly certitude and wrath, meanwhile, telegenic megachurch evangelists (broadcasting globally via satellite from the Ivory Coast, United States, Nigeria, and Lagos) witnessed in her a minion of Satan and with select quotations proved how the indispensable Apocalypse of John had predicted all this Babelian chaos as a sign that soon enough the wicked and the righteous would be assigned their respective destinations in Eternity.

Having come of age with a 6 PM news-fostered awareness of the Energy Crisis and Nuclear Arms Race, Marcus viewed the upset and outrage and bother caused by body language and related topics as small potatoes. If anything, the skirmishing registered as something passé that had been mistakenly disinterred. Fondue, or shrimp cocktail. A top hat, a seedy bar with a Ladies' Entrance.

The divisive controversy, so labelled by pundits, reminded him of subliminal messages, sexual liberation, feminist separatism, and astrological birth charts—ideas suddenly and utterly and briefly relevant and meaningful beginning lifetimes ago in the turmoil of the late 1960s.

As a subject for media columnists and students, body language had appeared close to but after the Cultural Appropriation Wars as the tag-happy media branded these skirmishes when they resurfaced as topic of debate and a means to carve out audience share. Way back, Marcus' own undergraduate professors had dedicated whole classes to appropriation of voice. Or else, they'd delivered a two-minute verbal footnote meant to shut down current and future discussion while dissuading ardent (if censorial) students from handing in seething judgmental essays. "Burnt books are nothing but moral cowardice," one had proclaimed.

To Marcus, this "ethically problematic" (or "allegedly ethically problematic, but in fact a tempest in a teapot" from a Hemingway scholar who also regarded discussion of canonicity and the phrase Dead White Males with the impatient swat of a regent hearing complaints from a chambermaid) social norm merely evolved into "inappropriate," a festering old idea with new wide-reaching applications beginning at the start of the new century. No doubt, in the Seventies and Sixties other terms for the same basic concept had come, gone, and reemerged as something else. Old wine, new bottle.

Another 2026 unit meeting, another unit agenda that only an expert could distinguish from the previous seventy-five. Marcus entered the room, mouthed orthodox hellos and "busy, busy" along with everyone else, sent nods to those further along the table.

Judaea, flustered, as burdened as Atlas with a bookstore tote, phone, tablet, and file folders, arrived late and, per tradition, sucked up the energy in the room with the effort of getting seated—an action that for any other body involved pulling out a chair, sitting on it, and sliding forward to the table's edge.

Marcus, on cue, felt irked by the woman's very existence and by her perpetual and evidently unconscious need to dramatize her *process*, her busyness, her ceaseless, never-plateauing popularity that made her—*forced* her, when she paused to think about it—to run late and hold up proceedings: "How could a professor with a gram of humanity say 'No' to those needing guidance?" She'd nominate herself for sainthood should a position open.

And like any trained pop star Judaea managed to convey her gratitude (without you, my legion of fans, and a Greater Power, I'd be nothing) while hinting how burdensome, how wearying that very popularity could become. Really, though: for colleagues the performance did not appear to differ meaningfully from an infant wailing only when an adult stood within eyeshot.

Once settled, the Chair began to strike off the points of discussion.

Marcus caught Judaea's glances toward him. Noticing induced her to face away. He registered that, strictly speaking, she hadn't been gawking at him, not the entirety of him but the vicinity where his wrists met the table's corner angle. Half-listening to the Chair's expert balancing of the meeting's steady forward momentum with the catalogue of sounds and movements that meant *I'm listening to each and every one of your points*, he measured the line of sight.

Fists, at rest.

Suggestive, in one view.

Practically meaningless in another since just one of a set number of options for human hands: flat, splayed, steepled, folded, curved into soft hooks, relegated to a lap, clasped prayer-style like olden days students televised as rural calico-clad innocents, hunched into a half walnut shell shape to allow for fingers to sequentially tap their owner's impatience.

Fists. Atavistic, evoking harmful intent and a primal striking force: pain driven into an opponent's body. Or: fist clasped around a makeshift weapon. Kubrick's apes weaponizing bones, Cain clutching a deadly stone. Scenes so often screened that they'd taken on the sobering grandeur of archetype: a woman appears in an ER with a flimsy excuse for her injury, wears telltale black-lensed sunglasses for coffee with a friend; a guy bashfully smiling about the shiner he brings to work.

These referenced reality, of course, factual and ongoing everywhere for all time. But they had nothing to do with him, either in the conference room or ever. No, in those closed hands—an argument could be made that they were not fists at all; the correspondence only a visual accident, just like those Messiah-shaped food items reported as newsworthy since the Age of Idiocy began—no hint, no whisper, no promise, no threat, no essence of violence. Any correlation to actual violence? Case by case only.

He'd hurt a fly, of course, and would again. Office spiders and home silverfish too.

After that, though, he could claim innocence, at least where people were concerned.

In Marcus' history, no playground scuffle, no hormonal territorial dispute at any prom, no feud turned physical thanks to pub night pitchers. He'd explain away the battles with his brother—with their jabs, kicks, charlie horses, and headlocks—as pranks, as masculine socializing.

In classrooms students had accused him of indirect violence ("You probably buy clothes made in Myanmar!!"), or indifference to it and collusion with the evil of its systemic ordinariness

("You eat steak!!!"), or harm via sound wave ("By stating that, you're causing actual damage to me."). Adopting some species of radical feminism for an instant, his brother had accused Marcus of embodying violence simply through the curse of being heterosexual and male.

To his brother: "Fuck off. You're a tool and have always been."

For students: placating staged thoughtfulness accompanied by slow nodding, to imply both "Fascinating, this is news to me" and "Bless you and thanks, your unique young person's ideas are worthy of deep and enduring consideration."

Nonetheless. If Judaea's overheated subjectivity conjured a fantasy—a pugilistic narrative that transformed his benign hands and their faintly calloused, tablet-tapping fingertips into merciless agents of violence, pain, and crude masculine agency, while she shrank into a cowering victim, merely one example of a fairer sex incapable by constitution to defend her frail virtue from manly *force majeure*, what did he owe her? Was the situation parallel to keeping company with an acknowledged alcoholic and pushing away the wine list in a show of respectful solidarity? Even if he didn't loathe her, if she merely represented a colleague belonging to a different gender category than his own and therefore carrying out a historical dynamic so old it might as well be immortal, did he have any responsibility, any ethical obligation to un-fist, to telegraph messages of peaceful intent (I Mean No Harm) via Jesus-y or yogic positioning? By being an ally and painting his nails a rosy pink? Should he also soften and diminish the stentorian voice, cut himself off at the knees? Booming and towering: were those not also forms of aggression, of dominance, of commandeering space?

These questions, as the Head liked to say, "could be revisited." Being infinite, the future offered abundant real estate for mulling over intellectual knots.

For Judaea, let her squirm.

The two pale fistiform hands opposite her? A monster of the woman's own making.

In the penthouse one midweek night and reluctant to pick up a book or face the camera and mic, Marcus had tapped a few words and soon begun swatting away endless pages of pornography, that vortex.

An off-putting virtual reality where sexual appetite was the sole emotional state and physically synonymous with breathing, and strait-laced abstinence the only pathology, its characteristics—and, in truth, very existence—confounded him. A kind of Pop Art, its metrics eluded his analysis.

Via lingering glimpses he learned that contemporary porn—an enormous counter-reality, a constant global filmic subculture of twos, threes, and fours fucking that took up more cultural space than the combined images of people eating, praying, and sleeping—still promoted young performers (animated ones of an astonishing variety as well as the standard flesh, blood, and silicone couplings) with pendulous oversized attributes or acrobatic talents and a convincing ability to simulate perpetual sexual voracity.

Surprising him, silver foxes (typically cast as executives, politicians, wardens, and professors) showed up in dribs and drabs.

A few of their ample-cleavaged counterparts, foxes who were anything but grey, also worked as CEOs and professors and demanded favours from careerist underlings. The majority, though, bore a familial relationship to antique farmer's daughter jokes, Russ Meyer plots, and femme fatales smouldering but stuck in one stoplight towns. Dressed now as then in stilettos and satiny robes, these imitation bored housewives invented alternatives to sedative addiction: the serial monogamists seduced counterfeit mailmen, landscapers, and neighbouring freshman quarterback sons before taking drives and continuing on with willing fake gas station attendants, traffic cops, and hitchhikers.

The older, the more specialized their roles and the more literally open they were shown to be. Hardcore grannies took on football teams, chain gangs, hobo camps, farmyard beasts. Harrowing and grim, Marcus concluded, both the fantasy scenarios and the true-life stories behind them, where dignity was sacrificed for a pay cheque and dubious fame. He spotted nothing equivalent for toupeed geezers with dyed moustaches. Pornographers forced these guys—no longer money makers or even second stringers—to degrade off-camera, a small dignity.

Peeking at the ricketiest clips—archetypal bland interstate motel rooms and the like in powdery aqua and peach, or their set replicas—Marcus had guffawed even as nitric oxide worked its evolutionary magic and his penis swelled against the underwear's soft cotton.

Pornography—the bankrupt lines of script, the wooden delivery of them, the baseline of chasing crumbs. The hoary implicit narrative stretching from dreams kindled by a high school run of *Oklahoma!* and parental applause to a punishing stretch without casting callbacks along with an Inland Empire joe job in the meantime. The would-be member of the Academy of Motion Picture Arts and Sciences winds up chatting with a producer. Naturally, this networked individual knows a guy who knows a producer needing fresh talent. That real-life origin story as threadbare as "I'm afraid I don't have enough left over for a tip," still spoken by slinkily-wrapped Mrs. Jones to comically wide-eyed Pizza Delivery Guy. In the same scene moments before she'd uttered mock-naïve dialogue with misplaced inflections: "I just *had* a han-*ker*ing for *sal*ami." Garlicky cured meat? Marcus would maybe buy the bit if she wore a babushka and rode a *mitteleuropäisch* train in the grey days of deprivation after WWII. The pastel-tinted foyer of a southern California rancher demolished credibility. Not that it mattered to the crew, which captured shots at air-conditioned noon and uploaded them before midnight.

Would subtitles help, Marcus wondered? What about muting and closed captions? He wondered too if Syb could suss out the year of the first appearance of the delivery guy, that porn staple.

Marcus imagined pornographic clips as everywhere, any spot a man with a recording device had stepped, as in a virus outbreak script where a room of frantic scientists on Day 6 project the rate of transmission. On Day 1: the virulence contained within a manageable cul-de-sac-sized area. By Day 14 it—represented as a red stain spreading at end-of-days velocity—will paint the entire globe. In the case of commercialized pornography, planet Earth was at Day 25,550, give or take. The planet as coated with it as with fecal particles.

Curious but questing too, Marcus had swiped through the pages, typed in new combinations of words. So much specialization, such variation. Alaskan Dominatrixes for Submissive Bitch Men, Wet Nurses for Executive Adult Babies. He felt no need for Syb's assistance, her retention.

Marcus learned that globalization applied to prostitution disguised as cross-border friendship services: for a processing fee, a plane ticket (Economy class), and a detailed (binding, penalty-slathered) contract he could order an extraordinarily chipper Asian, Latin, or Balkan lady.

The computer spat out other sites with profiles in grids of presentable—neither modelesque nor ill-favoured—youthful women dressed in what struck him as clerical-grade garb: pantsuits, electric blue blazers with ivory blouses, uniforms for a recent but bygone office or politician. Or overstock from Luhansk Airlines.

The obese, if permitted a spot, had been corralled far from the leading pages.

The rest—a keen tribe of Eligible Single Ladies named Mei and Svetlana with unnatural frequency—claimed to reside in D-list regions with flatlining opportunities for worthwhile careers, not to mention marriage. For the interested gentleman, Marcus read, the ESLs would happily relocate.

The sites highlighted the good values, solid work ethics, and general willingness of these self-starters in unassertive packages. The promotional material also implied that a sexually-compliant housekeeper was available to any male (women shopping for exotic brides apparently too minor a market to address) whose e-transaction got approved. For competitive prices the sites pitched the sheer adventure—a "journey to foreign dating" and "eventually a foreign marriage"—in a way that suggested the singular pleasures of a hike up Kilimanjaro. *No way in hell* had been Marcus' only reaction. He'd prefer the relative simplicity of domestic dating.

Stalwarts with a few nips and tucks, the matchmakers just drew his titters.

Outfitted for the Silicon Valley age, Marcus saw they'd given up the tradecraft of hands-on divination. Evidently outmoded, the Romani palmist routine wouldn't get a bite from anyone tablet-savvy.

Self-defining as a "rare and special breed," these workers in the *intimate knowledge economy* did retain circus gypsy terms— "intuitive" and "foresight"—but threw in databases, trademarked products named EliteXMatch and CompatAssure, and a rhetoric that wedded the barest whiff of Old World mysticism (astrological truths, guiding spirits with spare time on their ectoplasmic hands) to chip-based calculations, accuracy, and secure, encrypted, and industry-leading discretion. Marcus saw that gypsy costuming had been discarded; sartorially, the matchmaking women aimed for a sitcom real estate agent's pantsuited and go-getting professionalism. The vibe, though, felt the same.

Hundreds of taps and prompts later, he sought the fine print in Venerati, which offered "Exclusive Romantic Matches for Discerning Professionals in the Mature Demographic." "Discerning": a flattering euphemism for "last kick at the can." One could, Marcus believed, reach a ripe old age and be far less discerning than he'd been at 50 or 30. Or at 15. Whoever had first preached the line equating old age with automatic wisdom, perception, or insight ought to be congratulated for selling an idea so completely that was also so often demonstrably untrue.

For this class of websites, he read, the golden age lifestyle began at fifty-five.

Unlike the one with a personality test with three hundred imbecilic questions—eg, Q5) "Are you a (1) happy or (2) sad person?"—that assured matches with another industry-leading success rate, this one limited itself to twenty for its AccuCoreValu Questionnaire.

Marcus had sighed, skeptical of an industry with such a large cohort of industry leaders. He puzzled over how to read between line after line of bumf and promises no televangelist would dare make. He'd signed up, which cost him only the price of supplying an email address to a probable info-selling or scam front operating out of a shack in a breakaway republic or favela that simultaneously packaged cocaine and acted as a way station for human trafficking.

A credit card came into play only after clients submitted the ACVQ to Venerati's exclusive population of crème de la crème golden-agers. A place where Quality was everyone's middle name, Marcus read.

The world reminded Marcus—and had striven to for some time, happily it seemed, tapping his shoulder with more force than strictly necessary—of limits, of the need to face facts, to accept the allotted territory that eroded in gradual but steady increments.

The expectation for less, he understood, was his to claim.

At the height of his prowess—though he'd quibble over both *height* and *prowess*, the connotations misleading, an overstatement—he'd only staked a modest claim. No Red Sea parting when he entered the room, no "Eye Love You" from adoring front row undergraduates in tight cardigans that Professor Jones had had to ignore.

When he'd once read the epochal definition—"A man and his body are like a boy and the buddy who has a driver's license and the use of his father's car for the evening; one goes along, gratefully, for the ride"—Marcus had immediately quibbled a "Well, yes, but," to elaborate, to identify the metaphor's flaw: there were virtually as many makes and models of cars as there were types of fathers. And if a Rolls Royce, a sports car, or a Ford truck with a lifted suspension represented a social cachet that drew in grateful women for the ride, then there were others, clogged roadways of Tercels, K-Cars, Pacers, and Aztecs that even when right off the lot possessed a milk carton's magnetic draw. And don't forget the ones at the mechanic's, or on blocks in the front yard.

And between the extremes, well, everything else. Broken driver's side mirrors, duct-taped windows, corroded mufflers, nicks and dents, detestable or laughworthy design.

He'd once been serviceable, an economical model running well enough that didn't draw jeers. Or instantaneous caressing glances of appreciation. Though a solid frame and adequately cared for, that same model approaching the end of its run couldn't count on much positive response.

His willingness to pursue, to grab the bull by the horns, to command a place at the table, not a dynamo in the first place, had waned in concert with social cues shepherding him to the fewer and fewer locales welcoming his demographic. Where to *cruise*, the premise lifted from Benjamin? A non-believer attending church services to chat up widows and never-married types warped by solitary years? Faculty events with tedious crowing, funding complaint marathons, and the overall watchfulness of a spy movie that made any carpe diem gesture—"We really ought to try ____, I hear the pasta's incredible"—a matter of public record? Lingering and friendly questions to clerical staff, graduate students? Tutoring offers to custodians, with just one ulterior motive? No, he'd read those novels, the prof a preening egotist, fool, or jackass at best. An embodiment of straight WASP privi-lege, that figure persisted as a cautionary tale about white collar men whose intelligence lacked the scope for honest self-regard.

He'd weighed other options. He hadn't stepped into a singles bar for years. He was fairly certain no one had called them that since the 1970s and pretty sure that walking up to a group of women would be regarded as some incarnation of the inappropriate—damn that word!—or a prelude to sexual assault, perhaps a currency exchange. Maybe too, a younger woman—45, 50—would size up his potential and opt for the hope of a better incoming offer or suddenly remember gourmet ice cream and TV at home. Happenstance, a conversation about purchases in common in a grocery store lineup, a door held open and a welcoming comment about old-school chivalry? Like the Big One, it could happen. Chances were he'd be incontinent or addled by then.

No one wanted awkward pauses and stilted small talk. And who'd choose the expense of a dinner when both parties had realized incompatibility well before being seated?

Anything younger? Simply trouble with unresolved parent issues. Or else a mercenary.

The latter, his once ever mistake in a hotel lounge, hadn't turned into a transaction. Sad-smiling but kind, she'd said, "Sweetie, there are no freebies." Embarrassed and angry for being tricked, at accidentally playing a starring role in a movie moment, he'd paid for their drinks. All the while he'd been assuming they were clicking and the conversation's liveliness resulting from authentic chemistry, she'd been sizing him up, pandering to his ego. He'd been a conference mark, help for her to meet a quota.

Dating. Its failures had supplied stand-up comics and sitcom writers with gags since the Depression. "Men, amiright ladies?" "Women . . . Guys, can you believe those crazy bitches?" Cat ladies, slobs with delusions, etc., etc. Everyone tittering at the gaping chasm between the heartbreakingly earnest goals (enduring companionship, a family, sunsets viewed from rocking chairs) and both the span of minefield before them and, once attained, the mirage the whole premise turned out to be. O, the eternal pleasure and pain of being human.

When the stand-ups quipped about the peculiar idiocies of men and women, the ridicule encompassed a demographic that was single but vital (20-35) or recently divorced (30-45), or jaded but rusty and warily trepidatious about the quest's second leg (with a cut off at about 50). Neither in their audience or a part of their purview, oldsters—defined by insurance providers and retirement planners as 55+—and the dating pitfalls they faced had zero cultural traction. A revulsion, at a low level like queasiness, was reserved for the subject. A "Gross," "La, la, la, I don't want to know," or "Behind closed doors, I'm begging you."

The truth was sadder yet, Marcus imagined. No punchline, no incredulous rehashing of idiosyncratic habits and beliefs. Instead: an anxious business-minded meeting set in a restaurant or café with a set conclusion. If asked: "Oh, that didn't work out." Possibly a few such meetings before the details added up to a vote of non-confidence. A polite "good luck to you" and a hope, fervent, to never cross paths with the person again.

Or, likelier still, no meeting at all: a face on a screen whose details—hooded eyes, a frail or provisional smile—failed to spark interest. Or: an appealing face at the centre of the image, with side details (the image originally captured at Disney World, a bowling alley, Caesar's Palace, in a pew, or while holding a bridal bouquet) that the analytic brain behind the watchful primitive eye instantly categorized as "Danger, danger, not in this life-time." Somewhere else, of course, women read about age and profession, wondering about the impact of over four decades of adulthood or financial wellbeing. Same (give or take) eye-cortex combo evaluating, computing, conjecturing. What image to post? Teeth bared or not? Listed as optional, the recording camera. Should he resume addressing and describing himself for ninety seconds? No. She might detect a slight tremor, determine that it foretold hardships to come.

Dating. The hopeful recklessness of carpe diem or the wis-dom of treading carefully?

A profile? A start. Maybe a finish, ha ha. Well, an eleventh-hour reboot, marshalled forces. Last-gasp, last-chance, last-resort. Something.

ACVQ 12

What do you consider your five best qualities?

~~Honesty, scruples, saint-like patience with asinine questionnaires.~~
~~An artistic eye and ear (though average artistic capability)~~
~~Doggedness. Punctuality. Articulateness, the reliability of a Honda.~~
~~Joie de vivre, easygoing, outgoing.~~
~~Emotional Intelligence. Empathy. Compassion. Consideration.~~
~~Fortitude, steadiness, intellectual acuity.~~
~~Selflessness, analytic competence, surety, balance,~~
~~Follow-through, self-aware . . .~~
~~Stick-with-it-ness, steadfast . . .~~
~~Generosity, kindness, sincerity, acute perception, advanced education.~~

After some thought, these are the frontrunners:
1. Self-reliance
2. Ambition (minus the Icarus association)
3. Intelligence
4. Generalized competence
5. Sturdiness
As for my five worst qualities, I'd start with . . . well, if you're curious, please ask.

ACVQ 13

Do you realize there is a difference between intimacy and sex?

~~Of course.~~
~~In both cases one is possible without the other.~~
~~Although there's some overlap, they're distinct ideas.~~
~~Jeez, can anyone reach their 'golden years' and not know this?~~
~~Yes.~~

I do, yes, and value both.

ACVQ 14

What dreams do you have around achievement?

~~*Did* I have, well, there's a story.~~
~~At the beginning of my career, like many young men, I allowed~~
~~myself empire-sized dreams. In the case of academia, that meant~~
~~invitations to be a conference plenary speaker, a name that was~~
~~celebrated and equivalent to "respected authority," and intellec-~~
~~tual renown. Now, though . . .~~
~~"Old age is far more than white hair, wrinkles, the feeling that it~~
~~is too late and the game finished, that the stage belongs to the ris-~~
~~ing generations. The true evil is not the weakening of the body,~~
~~but the indifference of the soul." André Maurois~~
~~Arguably, I've passed the age of conjuring outsized dreams of~~
~~achievement. Been there, done that.~~
~~"Resting on laurels" has negative connotations. There's some-~~
~~thing to be said, though, for being satisfied with the notches~~
~~you've already got on your belt.~~
~~Prospering. Contentment.~~
~~Now: ongoing soundness of mind and body. That sounds defeat-~~
~~ed or pedestrian, but it's not. Trust me.~~
~~Measured by popular standards the American Dream of residen-~~
~~tial real estate, a fleet of cars, and constant exotic vacations I lack~~
~~in dreams of material achievement.~~
~~"Achievement of your happiness is the only moral purpose of~~
~~your life, and that happiness, not pain or mindless self-indul-~~
~~gence, is the proof of your moral integrity, since it is the proof~~
~~and the result of your loyalty to the achievement of your values."~~
~~Yes, that's Ayn Rand.~~

I do not hanker after larger piles of possessions. And in most ways, I believe that I've said whatever I had to say. There is such a thing as repeating yourself (or staying on the stage too long). Offering what assistance I can to help others attain their goals: this remains for me.

Comforts, challenges, exposure to new ideas and perspectives: as before, but different.

Things do not appeal to me as much as they once did. Experiences large, medium, or small do.

When a man's physical strength and sense of virility begin to flag, it's thought that he either slides into dentures and doddering senescence or consolidates what power he has and grips it tightly, presidentially, because it's the only proof that he still matters. The third option (and mine) is to continue on as before while permitting yourself the luxury of taking moments—hours, days—off instead of burdening yourself with expectations of constant productivity. You've laboured for decades, so why not 'stop to smell the roses'?

PEDAGOGY

Wednesday 1:00-1:15 PM

Eyes once again sequestered behind a thick hedge of bangs, the girl shuffled in looking prepped for Mars after sunset. As she settled, Marcus listened to the squeaked complaint of synthetics forcefully moulded around the chair. Beneath a raincoat fashioned from transparent vinyl printed with 'It's Slo-Baked Wonder Bread' and balloon circles in yellow, red, and blue, the student had swaddled herself in a dress—tunic, caftan?—of metallic bronze fabric quilted in diamond shapes that brought to mind Mylar survival blankets. She kept the coat's ribbon of Velcro fastened from mid-calf to *qipao* neck. The blunt toes of heeled rubber boots printed with English roses and circled letters (MK) in swirling chains pointed in Marcus' direction from the chair.

Slumped again—defeat? exhaustion? adolescent solitude?—L'Oréal directed all of her attention to the carpeting between two outstretched feet.

Years ago the girl's costuming statement, a case of semiotic chaos, might have stimulated Marcus to analysis, queries. Allusions, irony, appropriation, subversion, pastiche, *détournement*: all caught his attention. No longer. He'd be astounded to learn that she'd actually selected the items to convey any message or stance. Chances were, she'd felt cold ·that morning and thought clouds might bring rain and so reached into her closet, itself the product of compulsive recreational shopping. End of story. In twelve hours another hodgepodge of items with equal meaninglessness.

Over an interval of four minutes—experienced by Marcus as that eternity Huxley had chased so avidly with mescaline tea—he extracted what he'd expected. Decades of meetings with panicked students flailing in their first semester had taught him they could break from patterns but usually did not. This latest one, L'Oréal Zhang by preferred name but in fact the third meeting on a Wednesday morning of a career spanning some thousand Wednesdays, regarded the course as "so difficult." In spite of the will and the hard work and the hours of dedication and the years of preparation before she'd ever taken her first step on the west coast, clarity of expression and essayistic insights eluded her. Style too. Idioms. Reading entire pages of text.

More to the point, she sought but had not found an acceptably high grade.

A small mercy: L'Oréal did not attempt to complain or establish any line of reasoning based on *unfairness*, that adolescent bestie. Marcus leaned in to catch the words: she wanted to do better. Oh, yes, she'd expressed that sentiment in the terminal minute of another meeting the past week.

So. To read broadly, become culturally informed, or conversant in philosophical topoi? No, no, and not a chance. The matter was not nebulous; L'Oréal did not suffer from a vague but nagging sense that she could refashion herself into a salon wag, a wit of the Dorothy Parker kind, or a salaried motivational speaker. If known to her at all, these traits would not energize her mind.

He'd characterize L'Oréal's interest—and the sole reason for the office conversations with the ancient professor currently fidgeting three steps away from her supplicating form—as pragmatic, numeric, and dictated by an external source with absolutist tendencies: "Minimum grade of 60% or 'C' required."

Worse, for applicants, campus watering holes and the very air carried news: increasingly stiff program competition had long ago altered the apparent simplicity of the statement. Minimum meant that if you obtain a 60% grade when everybody else has achieved much better than you, expect to prepare a Plan B because you will not enter the program and will then accept whatever flimsy comfort Plan B brings to you and your watchful family. Likewise, 60% meant consider 65% the true minimum, and don't trick yourself into believing that's good enough either. Aim for a 75% if you've centred your ambition on a BA from our esteemed

School of Business. Okay, it's not Wharton, Rotman, Georgia Tech or even Nanyang, but it's better than New Brunswick and Cleveland State. Pay heed.

With her very future at stake, L'Oréal and her familial backers must obtain a better grade. Without it, the Dystopia of Mediocrity sent out a cubicle-beige summons.

Perhaps, Marcus supposed, in anticipation of a high-stakes adult career founded on entrepreneurial bibles—*Influence*, *Getting to Yes*, *The Art of War*, and the rest—the girl offered him a selection of questions that also contained her solutions.

This once, would he make an exception and allow her to re-write the essay? And then mark the newly improved piece?

No. Afraid not.

Perhaps he'd recalculate, taking into account how much she'd tried, the blood from a stone effort?

Quantifying *trying* represented pedagogical folly; he graded written work alone. Virtually everyone tried.

Could he reduce the value of this essay and give the next assignment greater weight?

No.

Could he bell curve it?

Never.

Could he factor in her status as an international student for whom written assignments in a second language presented peculiar hardships?

That would be unfair to other international students, wouldn't it?

Would he consider re-reading the essay to see if he missed its worthiness on the initial pass through?

Sorry, no.

Reconsidering, Marcus offered an apparent concession: "I do re-read essays upon student request. Be aware, though, the grade can go down as well as up."

The student's next strategy, familiar too, appealed to his professionalism and do-gooder's faculty of duty: "How can I improve?" (Magically, right now, without more effort).

The basic answer, essentially unchanged since Marcus' inaugural semester: there's no miracle cure; the fast-acting panacea you're hoping against hope exists has no material form because if it did everyone would activate the requisite switches, jump back in time, and tell their younger selves to do this, don't do that, and—please!—be wholly aware that five, ten, fifteen or forty years from that moment the person you become will appreciate every syllable of warning.

Faculty Lounge (Whirlpool®)

Over a few semesters of a first-year composition course years back, Marcus had assigned excerpts from a memoir about, its publisher advertised, an "Average Joe who fell through the cracks. Hard."

During his thirties said Joe had battled depression with steady, copious amounts of alcohol. That ushered in erratic 9-5 performances and job termination. In free-fall, he severed family ties, flushed medications with their symptoms of cloudy-mindedness, and burned through credit cards. The former white collar management type's rock bottom, he recalled, took the form of "a September brunch for one" scavenged from a Baltimore alleyway dumpster and swallowed while seated with his back pressed against hard warm metal florid with rust. Famished and desperate but not yet educated about the ins and outs of consuming discards heated by 79 degree weather, he'd suppressed the urge to gag and fed on tossed chowder simmering in a take-out container. Cold sweats, diarrhea in waves, and an ER's bureaucratic disdain assailed him over the next eighteen hours.

The man's account of visceral shame and humiliation had been matched by the description of the queasy disgust he felt while picking through putrefying garbage. As for the author's passage about flipping open a Styrofoam lid and reluctantly pouring the glutinous—and, he discovered, septic—mixture down his throat, Marcus broke down its techniques for classes as model forms for their own essays.

The kids' schooling had favoured standardized exam prep or effusive diaristic indulgence over literary writing, and Marcus enjoyed watching a handful of them successfully grapple with newer forms of expression. Far better, he spared himself the weighty disappointment of poring over thousands and thousands of uniformly lifeless sentences. Labouring in a morgue for that long could, he imagined, cause permanent damage to anyone.

Marcus' own response to the man's plummet—a kind of sympathetic revulsion—had led him to think the chapter would serve well in class. It had. The essayist's treatment of his subject never failed to polarize students. A few blithely judged the man for allowing himself to get into the situation at all. Others wondered why he hadn't gotten counselling. A few seemed matter-of-fact about scrounging. One: "I'd rather rob a convenience store and risk getting caught than eat garbage. At least you get free meals in jail." At an adjacent desk: "Yeah, totally. That's totally gross."

Marcus recognized that food could and frequently did trigger infantile yet fundamental emotional reactions about possessions, territory, and power. "That's MINE," in essence. "Take it and you've defiled me and my home. If you do so, you're a dead man."

A meal denied, access to it thwarted? Please stretch out on the couch for a few sessions, dear analysand.

Pondering a new poke-the-bear episode midday one grey Monday Marcus ran into unexpected internal balking in the vein of—"Now you're going too far"—at the faculty lounge.

He'd switched on the kettle for tea and grabbed the Whirlpool's door handle for milk. Spotting a plastic food container with a lid marked by "JUDAEA R." along a band of masking tape, he bristled with annoyance at the obnoxious "R." As if a whole alphabet of Judaeas roamed the corridors—that, a shuddersome vision of Hell. Why not "Dr." and "Ph.D" too?

The crass woman's daily choices seemed designed to antagonize him, a perpetual sliver of wood wedged under a fingernail.

Ignoring any better angel with its "enough's enough, old man" Marcus weighed the happenstance of "dish served cold," a refrigerated meal, an empty room void of security cameras, and an opportunity presenting itself upon the literal opening of a door. If the universe had nodded a "Go ahead" in its special way, who was he to demur?

Besides, he reminded himself that, in all likelihood, Judaea hadn't limited her smear campaign to just one listener or one instance. Why would she, when doing so would run counter to her nature? After all, any *campaign* necessarily involves steps, movement, zigs and zags, feints, its fullness revealed over a longer span. The blistering conversations that must have featured him and his irrelevance in the privacy of the woman's office, for instance. Or, during mealtimes and breaks between lectures. Phone calls. As for actual proof, he'd caught the baleful sideways glances, the constipated moues, the finger taps when he spoke. At a certain point, he thought, circumstantial bits and pieces solidified into a preponderance of evidence, and those materials added up as sufficient for a conviction.

Marcus sipped sweet milky tea, glad for the quiet lounge but irked as well by the ample uninterrupted period that had turned him into some creaky old play's scheming villain soliloquizing at length on centre stage. Would his dastardliness reverberate with the audience, or merely produce derisive laughter? Would a critic dismiss the performance as paint-by-numbers? Scene-chewing?

"JUDAEA R.," he'd read moments earlier. In black permanent marker printing with a firm hand that spelled assertive confidence. The inclination to fill as much surface area as possible reflected superabundant self-regard if not an autocrat's textbook hubris.

Marcus opened the fridge door and leaned his forehead on the cool stainless steel. What action for optimal results?

Moving the container to another shelf? Too subtle.

Peeling off and discarding the tape strip? Ambiguous as intent.

Taking out the container and leaving it on the counter? Invasive, perhaps, or weird. Or just someone's thoughtlessness, an accident.

Chucking it out? A distinct possibility, if one-noted.

Spitting? Unsatisfying, as knowable only to the spitter. (A typed note—"I spat on your lunch"—altogether perverse.)

Flooding it with piss? From what rank swampy pocket had that thought sprung?

Inspired at last, he settled on eating half. A salad of some kind with dried fruit, nuts, and rice.

Marcus apprehended that to achieve the same effect he could shovel out half and drop the mass into the compost unit. But he felt compelled to consume the food, shovelling down a meal created by Judaea and packed into a container marked as belonging to her alone. Somehow—he didn't care to analyze the desire with much force—the act of consumption heightened the insult's grievousness, the trespass. Marcus thought he'd savour the disgust the act would induce.

With an eye to the room's only door, Marcus dug a forkful, then another, the plastic receptacle close to his mouth. Whatever he'd expected to feel—a criminal glee or, likelier still, a rush of vindication—coursed through him in no way whatsoever. Instead, he thought of the dropped-tail look that had raced across Haystack's face when Agatha chastised him—"No, bad dog!"— for begging as she prepared dinner. That picture gave way to febrile Aschenbach, dyed and powdered in Italy, a delusional grotesque, all the more pathetic for knowing the rules of the game.

Swiping away these silly phantoms, Marcus reminded himself of the icy set of Judaea's eyes on that afternoon years ago. The bone-deep malice.

Corruption begets corruption, perhaps.

He finished the half he'd assigned for himself. She'd seasoned it surprisingly well. In another world he'd compliment her, ask for the recipe.

Ridiculously, Marcus grabbed a sheet of paper tower and wiped the container's surface for prints. Just in case.

To ensure that Judaea comprehended that no mistake had been made, he repeated the gesture on Friday.

Thereafter, he found no container besmirched by her name.

Penthouse (Hypnos' Children)

After a few steps into his quest for tenure the plots of Marcus' dreams underwent a sudden and permanent change. A new class of them developed overnight.

Decades into his career, long after the first cohort of hundreds of students had been forgotten, he still awoke to quicksilver memories of everyday anxiety dreams. He felt miffed by their obviousness—labyrinths of endless corridors, locked classrooms requiring keys he'd managed to misplace, doomed flights from authority hobbled by midget shoes—and perplexed by the dreams' persistence when he stood such a distance from the early handful of semesters when he'd actually fretted, anticipating next day's dead air, flubbed quotations, and visibly resented classroom exercises.

Adolescent dreams of a different nature—psychedelic or whimsical or fantastic—seemed overtaken and extinguished by this invasive species.

Then from nowhere: dreams with static figures out of an allegorical play. Their appearance perturbed Marcus in part because they seemed poorly designed—evidently generated to relay significant information (he was cognizant of that as the dreams unspooled) but without any ability to pass on their messages.

A convincing explanation for this latest development—assuming one existed—eluded him. These figures recurred. In whatever scenario they materialized, the handful of them stood for the same idea; the symbolic property never changed.

In any sampling of dreams—crawling in an underground passage or transferring to wrong buses and winding up further and further from the correct destination—his brother or father or his first girlfriend from grad school manifested dressed as themselves. As though they'd turned a wrong corner and stepped into the spotlight. In the dream, though, their appearance triggered fear and panicky emotions. The figures stood in the distance, uninvolved but wafting ghost-like and attention-grabbing. Whether showing up in a tedious dream set in a meeting room with locked doors that he conjured after nodding off in front of the TV or in what could pass as a fragment of actual memory, Marcus' sleep-state mind immediately associated his brother with abjection and despair. In appearance he was Benjamin, with a trend-conscious hair colour or cut and clothing that proclaimed one of his fits of passion. Despite that, within the dream world Marcus understood that his brother represented a weighty and doomed state. Though wholly himself, he may as well have possessed the empty, pained eyes lifted from Edvard Munch canvases about melancholy or anxiety.

Likewise, Janine, as gushing and upbeat in dream form as her real life counterpart in grad school, registered emotionally as worn out and defeated by the constant assaults of poverty.

Oddly, his parents turned up as comic and elderly, cracking wise and complaining amiably. If he woke up right after, Marcus would be smiling, feeling happy to have passed a moment with this squabbling duo that lost glasses and misplaced car keys and then pelted each other with ginkgo biloba capsules. The dream mechanism flattened them, though, simplifying their complexity and sanding off the real-life abrasiveness and intermittent waspish criticisms. As for any residue of ambivalence stuck in his head, the dream blocked it. Unlike his brother, the dream transformed Agatha and Henry into walk-on figures from a sitcom. Their casting call: Comical Married Couple, Geriatric Age.

Within a month of the Incident, another dream citizen surfaced. Judaea. As the latest resident, though, she defined her own category. She entered any scene as an urban wildwoman—wobbly shopping cart filled with books and computer equipment, frizzy hair knotted and unkempt, jackets, cardigans, and coats over a ragged kimono and rectangular wooden *geta* that scraped the ground as she trod. During the dreams Marcus accepted her at face value. Rather than a violent monster posing a threat, the creature was Judaea, the familiar treacherous colleague from work. For her brief pass-throughs, she approached, but in such a dilatory manner that she never reached him. The fear she induced came from the association. In the dream world Judaea embodied authority and the sheer capacity authority possessed to assign blame and apportion punishment. Somehow, this stricken creature stood for a boss from HQ visiting a branch plant. Or, a black-clad officer from the Ministry of Love.

He'd always done something wrong in these dreams (forgotten to wear shoes, neglected to answer an imploring student email) and her appearance signified the institutional response. Judaea: Quality Assurance personified.

Marcus resented the woman—a one-person plague—in any guise, of course. Now he resented himself, or, at least, that part of himself that spun dream images, for granting her a star-turn role as an imposing figure, as a villain who had advantage over him and the ability (in his psyche, at least) to damage his reputation, career, and physical body.

Syb:

"Radically altering dreams through conscious effort in order to undermine their power is largely a fiction of screenplays, Marcus.

"The term 'lucid dream' was coined by Dutch author and psychiatrist Frederik van Eedan in a 1913 article titled A Study of Dreams.

"Studies have shown that by inducing a lucid dream recurrent nightmares can be alleviated. Lucid Dreaming Treatment, abbreviated as LDT, has been used therapeutically for chronic nightmare sufferers. It's composed of exposure, mastery, and lucidity exercises. The essence of lucidity is increasing dream recall and acknowledging that it is possible to realize when you're dreaming. Most techniques begin with dream journals."

Marcus bought a journal.

COMPATIBILITY: 6

That's awfully *personal*, Marcus thought.

Absentmindedly he reached for the self-prescribed candy dish of tortilla chips, touched oily crumbs. Waist-watching: he resented the very fact. Still, he acquiesced, substance abuse assumed many guises. Life's little serpents; one must be vigilant.

He'd been on a spree all evening. Hopscotching through scads of trivia. The history of hair dye. Fitness and diet guru pep talks. Global plastic surgery capitals. Designer babies, round three. He'd even stumbled upon and skimmed the Norwegian's old 2083 manifesto, a feast for grad students in Psych: "The reliable saviour of the intelligentsia is the common man and his common sense." Oh, right. "Q: Name your favourite eau de toilette. A: Chanel Platinum Egoiste." Lord. A worthy nugget to store away along with the fact that its author must have called himself a true believer in the Unabomber's *Weltanschauung*.

Information byte overload: one of the accidental benefits of procrastination.

Craving a post-allotment serving of chips, Marcus patted his belly.

Calisthenics? Maybe. That—those?—he could manage. He remembered Saturday morning TV—1975?—and women in nylons, ballet slippers, and belted mauve leotards stretching on a thick-carpeted set of three interlocking circles.

Had calisthenics weathered the upheavals in physical fitness? In the era of CardioCreatineCore regimes, did it—they?—even exist anymore?

Syb:

"The World Street Workout and Calisthenics Federation is based in Riga, Latvia, Marcus. According to Oxford Dictionaries the roots come from 'kallos,' meaning 'beauty' in Greek, plus 'sthenos,' which means strength, power, ability, might. The word's first known usage was 1827; it was thought to be coined by a Swiss physical culturalist.

"In 1956 Dorothy Parker claimed, 'There's a hell of a distance between wise-cracking and wit. Wit has truth in it; wise-cracking is simply calisthenics with words.'

"The form of physical education was popularized in the nineteenth century in North America by Catherine Stowe's *Physiology and Calisthenics for Schools and Families* of 1857. Stowe has also been identified as responsible for the word's coinage.

"Relatedly, another scholar has made the case that calisthenics takes its name after the ancient Greek historian and Pythian games expert Callisthenes of Olynthus, a relative of Aristotle who died in prison after he was accused of plotting the death of his former friend Alexander the Great.

"Stowe's sister, Harriet, published *Uncle Tom's Cabin* in 185—"

"Got it, thanks."

Marcus rocked in his desk chair, straightened papers, pressed some keys. Noting a threadbare cuff he began an order for new pajamas—striped light blue cotton, Brooks Brothers; he'd been wearing that model for years. XL or—? His finger hovered. Nothing worse than snug sleepwear.

His stomach grumbled. Would it be an irony to address Syb's mic to find out why science people still had not come up with tasty junk food that could dispense with the warning label about socially awkward side-effects caused by lab-doctored fat molecules?

Flab pressed against his waistband. "More cushion . . . ," he thought. Did profile writers attempt to merchandise a few excess pounds as a perk, or take "I Am What I Am"—which Benjamin had embraced as a theme song for an interminable period of years—as a triumphant warts-and-all personal motto?

Also, what ever happened to "I Love You Just the Way You Are"?

Marcus typed as Syb emitted her factory-set glow. His eye passed along screen results.

The song would pass its fiftieth in 2027. In the previous century the singer-songwriter had stopped performing it after a costly, shaming divorce. Scandalous claims and counter-claims: the stuff of money-maker newspaper headlines. "I said I love you and that's forever": temporary and false, a myopic lyric printed on tens of millions of cardboard record sleeves and embraced as gospel truth by entire demographics of the population. From a comments page: "My dad worked for CBS Records & Tapes as a Promo Man in the 70s and said that the Ex had a Butch haircut and she didnt have a decent bone in her body, I hope she gets HERS in Hell."

So much for love songs.

11:38 on the desktop screen. Sunday night. I'll knock my head against this wall of a problem for another 22 minutes, Marcus vowed.

A sample question from an *Online Dating for Dummies* chapter had stumped him. *Please share key aspects of your relationship history.*

Jeez, how about saving that revelation for a face-to-face setting? Or better yet for a shadowy confessional. He'd never been, but saw the appeal. Like pillow talk, but anonymous and formalized into ritual within a polished wood enclosure. At least in movies.

Then again, why not a Tom Ripley strategy, where history's an occasion for bogus, audience-specific pseudo-autobiographical vignettes?

Maybe: "My wife and I had a good run of it, right, but we gradually drifted—it happens—and decided 'Let's call it a day.' You know, as divorces go, it was pretty much by the book. Final but necessary, like closing the lid of a coffin." Common-law would make fudging easier. Less of a paper trail.

Another possibility flashed—hospitalization, a dramatic opioid drip, and a devastated widower's retreat from matters of the heart. No. Any background check request uttered to any gadget would reveal that fabrication in an instant. Plus, he'd have to take to the virtual stage wearing a virtual black arm band for every imaginary birthday and anniversary. Madness.

Unlike other lifetime misdemeanors—"I voted for X," "I used to wear Y," "I never reached goal Z"—that could be held aloft and then batted away for the purposes of a mutual chuckle or worldweary shrug, "key aspects" disclosures registered differently. The more you took off and the more skin you displayed, the worse. What's the term for a strip-tease in a horror movie? Strip-torment? Strip-afflict?

How could a person—anyone—bundle something so complex, so freighted, so . . . exposing into an enticing package of thirty or ninety terms without shooting himself in the foot? Or, sounding as though he'd accepted a job as a speechwriting hack tasked with spinning famine as prosperity and oppression as freedom for the latest news banner dictator?

Nothing much to say or *At least buy me a drink first* would come across as evasive or coy, each a red flag.

How many of these aspects the question blandly requested would the serial monogamist include? What about the thrice-divorced? The sexagenarian virgin, assuming such a beast trod the earth? Certainly, information-wise, the more would not be the merrier. Screen readers with profiles crammed with mirroring characteristics might conclude *alotta work*, or *tainted goods*, or *asking for trouble*, or *impending disaster*, and *avoid at all costs*. They'd do so—hypocrites!—even while intuiting that the between-the-lines-conscious viewer of their own surgically-worded profile would judge them and the telling words of their relationship history as too high risk, as a survey of a blighted past that predicted a similar future.

Although ridiculous and merely a placeholder, Marcus' Joe Lunchbucket frontrunner—*I'm single currently and would like to get back in the saddle*—avoided the request altogether. Better, the attractive vagueness of "currently" would allow any reader to think whatever she chose, but nudged her toward concluding both *market fresh* and *the attractive owner of a palatably temperate history void of worrisome drought and flood*. As for the folksy "saddle," he figured it could help undermine the ivory tower stigma.

What Marcus wanted was to pound the keys to spell out *Married to my work*. Measured by steps taken together or emotional investment, the relationship surely counted as a marriage, right down to *for better, for worse, for richer, for poorer, in sickness and in health, until death do us part*.

But typing those four words, talk about self-sabotage.

Sure, he might attract an unhinged woman who'd otherwise end up in a cult's bunker. If her passivity and self-denial registered as catnip to Supreme Leader types, it struck him as clingy and adolescent. A woman-child requiring parenting, or who answered "What would you like to do?" with "I dunno, whatever you want, you choose," held no allure for him.

The Stepford Wife scenario had always struck him as perverse, more or less. The *occasional* fantasy of a subservient robot did appeal universally, he supposed. As did murder or other lesser crimes. All that compulsive bubbling? Neural business as usual: ladies and gentlemen, it's a pleasure to introduce the human genome, whose contradictions and complexities have beguiled reason since the Bronze Age!

(Eureka. He jotted "self-directed" on a stickie. He remembered that Venerati's supposed brain trust posed another question that asked about what qualities he admired in a romantic partner.)

Then again, Marcus considered, *I'm married to my work* could mistakenly convey a status as Type A, a CEO in the making, all vise-jawed ambition, second-nature networking, and constant workweeks of feral, kill-or-be-killed rivalries. Predator-eyed, Ms. Type A would echo him, and they'd become a power couple. Or, she'd exchange her assets (beauty, social graces) for the prestige and equity he embodied.

Marcus realized he'd picked up these ideas from TV programs. Though influential, he doubted their local veracity.

Tap, tap, tap, delete. How did jobseekers with résumé sinkhole gaps fix the issue?

He asked Syb. "The top answers, Marcus, are 'Do make sure you fill in the gaps with something active' and 'Don't say you have no explanation.'"

Further information with limited application. An explanation? "Easier said than done." "Time flies." "It's over before you know it." Any salient platitude would serve. Was "That's the way the cookie crumbles" an *explanation*? "That's the way it goes"?

Fingers brooding, poised for the flurry of letters, he thought of *marriage of convenience*. When had his begun, at what anniversary date should he raise a glass? Obviously one-sided, the marriage felt real, felt complete. Sometimes, anyhow. Needless to say: the optics. Less a meeting of minds or a grand passion than a pestilent species of narcissism. But what had Wilde quipped? "To love oneself is the beginning of a lifelong romance." Marcus wondered if that witticism had passed through the man's mind at the Hôtel d'Alsace's Room 16 on a sullen Friday at the end of November in 1900. Had the turn of phrase consoled him?

Maybe, then, an extramarital affair would cure what ailed him. Marcus wondered about the pretzeled logic.

Marcus doubted this late start, his last-ditch effort.

He queried Syb, heard—"Marcus, etymologists have traced the origins . . ."—circa early 1800s, from the military sense of last ditch, the geographic last line of defence. Used now figuratively: the last possible attempt.

Marcus replied with "Thank you."

Speaking to a technically inanimate object, a difficult habit to break. The machine required no manners, no kindness, no encouragement. No pronoun, either, only electricity. He might perhaps limit Syb's name-use frequency to every third response. Maybe altering the voice to ungendered would help too. No sane individual called a mechanism a friend, though he could recall news bytes about legal challenges about marrying a model of Geminoid 3. Or maybe Nadine 6. For him, though, the intelligent personal assistant would revert to being a tool, a mechanism; nobody ought to bond with an autovac or smartfridge.

The osmotic information he'd picked up about Integrated Humanities pairings over the decades led him to understand that nearly all the married faculty had met their spouses in university over the grad school years. The marriages, then, suggested companionate temperaments, stresses, and schedules, if not like minds; the marrying window was not categorically different from religious closed societies that eschewed outside influences in the name of scriptural Tradition.

As for the not insignificant remainder, their status as single—so far as he ever heard from a people scrupulously tightlipped about sharing personal-life details—went without comment, without complaint. No rom-com bestie set up blind dates that turned into next-day punchlines ("Oh. My God."). And no meddlesome parents trotted onstage with tone-deaf picks or better-something-than-nothing outlooks. Simply, confirmed bachelor and bachelorette status drew no attention. Like bibliophilia, it too was part and parcel.

And they, a nation whose borders extended to him, filled the Aristophanean void with routine: research, hobbies, and the monastic quietude offered by text. They might pine—who doesn't?—but that sentiment they locked up tight.

Over decades of conversations, Marcus had observed seamless marriages that other eras would have generated as encomiastic poetry. Adversarial other ones could be viewed as divorce depositions—file under: Mental Cruelty—in the making. A big pie chart slice appeared to depict the mercurial nature of the human character as somehow more than doubling upon "I do."

As for the Institution of Marriage, he felt no special animosity. Whatever inequalities and transactional politics its history exposed and kept as tradition, the exchanging of vows didn't cause anything bad or good by virtue of the contract. He'd have given it a whirl, but for this, but for that.

And now his activity at midnight was fashioning himself as a lure. A mature lure carrying a few extra pounds and who knew what baggage. What a catch.

As a fact sent out into the world, *widower* or *divorcee at* 65 possessed a distinct set of connotations. Like a hunchback or the mark of the Antichrist in movies, *single and not married once* marked him as discount bin inventory.

The words he'd prefer not to write, the reveal his every fibre yearned to postpone indefinitely: "Single, never married, and when I write 'nothing serious in the last little while' the truer statement would be 'the last time I went on a date—exactly one date, in fact, that concluded with a *Nice to meet you* and a literally frigid professional handshake—transpired in 2018; and as for something serious, I'd have to look back to the killing of bin Laden.' Those, dear viewer, are the key aspects of my relationship history."

Warm bare feet in plaid slippers, Marcus shuffled to the kitchen, refilled the bowl with a fat camp portion. Ha, another retirement idea: start Fat Chance, a wilderness camp where chubby kids could laze away whole weeks.

He'd chew over the question for another hour. A grey '65 to sell. With luck the craze for retrofitted vintage models had continued. Mileage, under the hood needs a little work, plenty of get up and go. He'd come across that approach to profiles, wondered who it attracted. Extending the metaphor he could chuck in "rust-free" as well.

Applied to a person, though, what traits would that even represent?

Political and religious views (firm, flexible, non-applicable)?

During my junior high years, my father began a series of sit-down conversations in his den. He started off talking to both of his sons together, but quickly realized that one per session would operate better. "It was turning into a goddamned three-ring circus," he told my mother with a wink when she asked at dinner.

As you can guess, the general category was "the birds and the bees" and, to a lesser degree, "passing the torch." After a few clearings of the throat and imploring glances at the den's closed door, he began with "You remember when Pierre [the white Standard Poodle next door, eight then and a holy terror] started humping everyone's legs and they had to take him to the vet . . . ?" So began my introduction to The Body and Soul of the Adolescent Male.

At subsequent low-volume meetings in the den, my father moved on from biology.

He touched on dating. On hygiene. On responsibility. On communication. He wound up at love, which he called a "real handful." Also, marriage: a "complicated, ongoing bout of negotiation" and "a devilish institution." "Your uncle can tell you all about that," he added unhelpfully, as my uncle remained unhitched.

Under the broad category "keeping the peace," he spoke in favour of a shared bedroom but separate beds. He mentioned the importance of togetherness as well as the value of spouse-free socializing.

When this series concluded, my father searched his mind for any remaining nuggets of wisdom. "Oh yes," he exclaimed, "who you vote for and what you pray to, that's no one's business but your own."

Of course I came to roll my eyes at some of my father's old-fashioned views, but still respect his notion of the inherent privacy and sanctity of certain subjects.

ACVQ 16

How often do you exercise?

Define exercise.

How old do you feel/behave?

~~If I answer "sixtysomething," how does that get translated, what does it signify?~~
~~If I say "Age is only a number," what does that suggest?~~
~~If I write evasively, "You're only as old as you feel," what does that even mean?~~
~~What if I choose "50"? "35"? What then?~~
~~Depending on the time of day, the answer varies.~~
~~Until I catch sight of myself in a mirror, I feel more or less the same age I've always felt.~~
~~What does a "retirement-age male" feel like? How does he behave?~~
~~Some parts of myself feel older than others.~~
~~It seems that with this question there's no answer that's unproblematic.~~
~~How about let's change the subject with some comic relief here: "Age is an issue of mind over matter. If you don't mind, it doesn't matter" or "The secret of staying young is to live honestly, eat slowly, and lie about your age."~~
~~-~~

Years ago I took a tour inside an abandoned coal mine located in a former company town. Beneath ground and inside the shaft—an absolute darkness illuminated by head lamps—the tour guide told us about his career there.

He limped as a result of a cave-in. He was stooped because the mine shaft's height forced the miners to dig while crouched. He described hardship: long hours, appalling working conditions, truly brutal labour, draughty shack housing owned by the coal company, regular accidents, ailments and employment that began for men when they were still boys who'd dropped out of school. Then, he was the same age I am now. I believe I will never feel as old as he must have.

Marcus envisioned a gritty science fiction script.

The establishing pan zeroed in on his office long after a rogue synthetic intelligence program (named P.A.N.D.O.R.A. or the like) had initiated a hellfire of intercontinental neutron missiles designed to eradicate the living while keeping infrastructure intact.

Dust insulated, his glassy desk and Syb on it persisted without so much as a bird chirp to break the output. Though he'd perished there from radioactive fallout, Syb's unperturbed voice—awaiting his answer-terminating prompt of "Thank you" or "Got it" or "Yes, that's enough"—continued to siphon endless strings of phrases from automated server battalions clustered across the depopulated globe: "production theory," "*ceteris paribus*," "individual production functions," "marginal incremental output," "successive diminishment of real output to the decreasing quality of the real inputs," "total return on investment as a proportion of the total investment (the average product or return) decreases," "taking into account the costs of true equity in addition to miscellaneous costs included in the profit and loss statement as usual. . . ."

Maybe the scenario would come from an ad pitch instead. One rejected by execs as "sending the wrong message."

Pulling back from the faint glow behind Syb's black speaker grille, the camera reveals Marcus' slumped form across the desk, grey desiccated mouth an eternity from having posed its final question.

The ad's tagline would appear then: "Syb. Available even when you're not."

On a Sunday night of pacing at the apartment Marcus had merely queried about the law of diminishing returns. He felt nagged by the sense that his understanding of it and the actual definition corresponded only roughly. The thought had been prompted by the freshly read and red-annotated ("Chk yr facts") opening hook of a student essay: "As Dr. Einstein's dictum about relativity made quite famous, for every action there is an equal and opposite reaction."

Syb's maker allowed a setting range for answers. In Marcus' experience his choice of "expert" invited a species of AI logor-rhoea, with one source flipping domino-like to another, potentially forever.

He'd cut her off with "Understood, thanks" and mentally crossed out law of diminishing returns. If he misused the term, chances were she—the eligible woman, the reason for all the words, all the acrobatics—would as well.

Marcus fully anticipated a query—soft or blunt—about his Relationship History. Something with notarized references maybe, affidavits. Authentication.

He'd predict it, in fact, just as when he bumped into Mrs. C on an overcast day he knew he'd hear a reminder to carry an umbrella. Mrs. C's barometric hip throbbed complaint and that meant downpours sooner rather than later.

After the gruelling initial round of questions, perhaps Venerati reserved another set. Advanced. The preliminary twenty would weed out the half-hearted, the time-wasting dabblers. After them: the Everest of queries, the *primum movens*. If not, then surely Profile #2135, his choice who'd also taken the plunge and selected him, would tiptoe around the room's elephant as she sawed through a grilled scallop or stood at a balcony railing and admired steep mountains in silhouette across the wide flat bay. Marcus had already decided on that restaurant with the expansive view and tomato-poblano relish praised in reviews. Factors like those could only bolster his chances.

At the keyboard (at the front window, at the open fridge, stretched flat on the too-short sofa), he'd thought about giving

it—romantic personal historiography—purposeful narrative
shape. In telling the potted history, which neat but evocative
phrase could relate the essence, which punchy figure? Crash and
burn? Loved not wisely, but too well? No, hardly. Catch and
release? Feast and famine? Limping along? Boom and bust? Firing
on two cylinders? Cruising on empty? Scorched earth? Dustbowl
farming? Drought? The slow decline? Flatlining? None fit, not
really. And not one enticed, absolutely.

What was the opposite of "an embarrassment of riches,"
but still sounded okay? Could anybody rejig the equivalent of
"Initial long range low yield productivity that gave way to a
lengthy fallow period," and have its sorry implications unwind
instead as an attractive or intriguing line, something to capti-
vate? Sure, technically. Maybe. Still, the agricultural metaphors
didn't suggest Wordsworth so much as a Resource Economics
thesis.

Sheen, allure, mystique: he'd need to spin gold from what
amounted to a stockpile of straw.

The story of his romances—if the word fit—featured no
episodes of melodrama of the hurled vase and slammed door variety. One had never shat in the other's bed or hacked up a
wardrobe with a cleaver. Commonplaces—overturned tables,
restraining orders, strangled pets, revenge porn, lawyering up,
devastating words that couldn't be unsaid, and police knocks after
inebriated nights of bellowed disturbances—remained completely within the frame of his 32" screen.

Stripped of kinetic conflict, the tale hardly registered.
Mostly . . . what? A failure to thrive, a promising, nutrient-
dense seed that sprouted, grew spindly and yellow, and keeled
over in nature-authored defeat.

Introduction to Biology, Figure 1. Not Meant To Be.

No *histoire romantique* in a phrase, then, nothing pithy. No
suave lady's man line that captured it all.

How about a concise framework, something science-hued?
The progressive ages of a male citizen, cut into whatever spans
the state defined as legitimate. Yes, that had potential.

He'd ask Syb, then strive for alchemy.

Marcus tapped "0–5?" and addressed his desktop machine.

0–4: Everything and nothing. Object permanence. His mother as primary caregiver: alert, alert. She'd read Benjamin Spock decades before the man decided "circumcision of males is traumatic, painful, and of questionable value." Later family joking about potty training that went on and on. Cue more wisecracks, trot out Freud for searing insights! Gruesome Bluebeard and Aschenputtel tales for years at bedtime. What would Marina Warner and the former director of the Orthogenic School for Disturbed Children surmise? A dart gun for a transitional object. Oh, boy. Independence and insular bookishness accepted without much intervention, uh–oh. Parents as authorities, as reinforcers (positive? negative?) inside that neat but by no means obsessively neat Skinner Box eventually listed as a centrally located mid–century rancher. Ambivalent attachment style? Wayward apperception? Stunted higher order functions? The flamboyant brother, that fierce rival for attention. The weedy root of a Competitive Personality Syndrome?

No matter, evidently the base subjectivity of little Marcus O was a done deal, neural aspic that had more or less set ages ago. Whatever happened, happened. You can't make an omelette without breaking eggs. You're stuck with who you become: time and again, lab coat types had proven that an individual can change but to a degree that's small at best.

5–9: In movies, the easily summoned memory triggers an aftershock of pain—the stuff of utility–grade poetry—that never quite subsides. Regal Sally Buttermeyer marches across the gravel playground at recess, all assured beauty, and informs the boy she's picked him. At the 3:30 bell, the epochal sentence that means "It's over, I'm just not feeling any spark" and a brutally truncated reunion.

In grade 3 or 4, such a waif existed for Marcus. Her name escaped him. Carole. Maybe Karen. Carly. If shown the class photo, he guessed he'd be able to narrow her down to two or three. A willowy girl with twin plastic barrettes holding straight centre-parted hair in place—and enrolled in a class where three handfuls of similar willowy girls modelled themselves after cola and shampoo commercials.

Near the end of the school year the risk-taker dared him to go on a walk through the wooded trails behind the school's chainlink perimeter, a zone every teacher forbade. Rabid dogs, kids reported, a hobo camp. Only later did parental litigation dawn on him. The deed accomplished at recess, Marcus returned to his boys-only group. They decided he was now going steady with her; after guarding little Carole or Karen or Carly, trying to finger her fell to him as a primary duty. Proud but confused, Marcus smiled and affected a wizened look. He sensed that if spoken aloud the questions on his tongue would lead to ribbing for possessing a toddler's foolish ignorance.

With a literal push at 3:32 he approached this girl's clustered friends. Mercurial, she'd moved on, heart smitten by the secret admirer who'd left a braided leather bracelet inside her desk. Instantly protective, his gang began calling her a lez. (Time would wait until a leaden November afternoon in 1984 before Marcus actually heard "It's not you, it's me"; he returned the favour with a generous—he told himself—twist about a year later: "It's not you or me, it's us.")

A tell-tale episode in an origin story, both scarring and decisive? Nah, a hill of beans, his parents would have declared. A stubbed toe. He'd have to agree.

Marcus had virtually forgotten the going steady experience by his arrival home. A finicky pull cord mower demanded his attention, as did Old Lady Temperley's yard, dollar bills to cram in a pocket, and a model airplane to choose and snap into pieces for assembly.

Later, as a striving grad student and earnest TA piecing together a lecture segment about American lit's 'revolt from the village' phase, he ran across "And the earliest wound, when a little mate / Leaves you alone for another." He'd thought of his own parade of little mates and decided that Edgar Lee Masters had really taken artistic liberties. Tears!?! What melodrama.

10-14: The basic picture: a scrapbook sampling of experiences that could belong to any North American teen—the 1970s white middle class male subtype, dressed in the standard uniform of sneakers, cords, and a striped pullover. A show-off kid learns to pop a wheelie, aims for notoriety with a Knievel stunt, and snaps a forearm before his specially invited audience; Agatha's "No comments from the peanut gallery back there" as she concentrated on learning—white-knuckled, translucent scarf over sprayed hair—to drive the Riviera; his father passing on wisdom of the ages: buffed shoes, cufflinks, and a knock-out tie announced a man's success to the world, truth be damned; compulsive mid-row whispering and illustrated notes in classrooms where teachers smeared interminable facts across blackboards; summers at once too short and too long.

If his lo-res picture of that past selfhood could also be a puzzle with most pieces missing—whole seasons evaporated—the dominant visual, a film clip series set at school, starred a tight group of boys and him often close to its nucleus. Near exit doors, adjacent to gym doors, on a second floor landing or the steps leading to the sports oval, they dared, jostled, pushed, and swatted each other fraternally. Roving from one building corner to another, second-stringers also competed for higher status through swapped insults about the pathologically dry or stretched or droopy or malodorous body parts belonging to Mrs. Mc or Miss B. Boys could point to girls' favoured parts, as though they were the Cuts of Beef chart at the butcher's and in Home Ec. But the huddled gang's internal exchanges typically seethed with claims of mounting scurrilousness about the girls' sexual how fars, wheres, and how oftens—as well as with whom (boy A or teacher B) or what (pets, vegetables, household utensils). "No way!" and "Yes way!" the gold standard for debate and forerunner to eventual adult drinking bonding exercises.

By having the quickest access to the grossest jokes, or firing them the loudest, or owning an enviable iron fist, the succession of leaders rallied this army of marauders to their feats of conquest.

The blue moon occasion of an admired teacher passing by instigated a zealous recounting of the man's epic (if fabled) past, and unflagging (although never eye-witnessed) talent for *getting some*. He became the sung hero not because of his stupid job but because he'd scored so many goals even while looking not demonstrably better than everyone's humdrum dad. For the contemptible rest: as-good-as-true reports of public nose picking, underwear stained yellow and brown flapping on the back yard line, a flickering, blue-lit bachelor's existence of TV dinners and drained bottles, or a storied shame (split trousers during class, growing a boner while teaching Health, left in the lurch at the altar). Also, routinely, possessing just one testicle.

At home, post-group: nondisclosure or selective revelations. "She's quite nice," a truth about a Language Arts teacher otherwise reputed to spread peanut butter on her naked crotch for a neighbouring German Shepherd to devour. "They're okay," also apt, but applied to Social Studies and Music classes headed by a pair who'd been seen cheating—all the way—on their spouses with each other right in the staff parking lot.

Asked to protect his brother, Marcus agreed while sure he'd renege. Benj could navigate the hive's corridors himself. He had to. That fell into law of nature territory. The consequences of coddling or a big brother's interference: weakness, that sin. A long rite of passage, school couldn't be cheated or circumscribed. Besides, placed in his brother's shoes, Benj would reach the identical conclusion.

Other than asking a girl classmate for a loan of paper, pencil, or eraser, Marcus recalled only himself in the boy chorus sounding off—words, barks, whistles, howls—in the direction of an ambulatory cluster of girls. Holding their own, the girls would retaliate with jabs about puny body parts, appalling lack of maturity, or the family secrets of Scotts, Brians, or Darrens.

Boys were beyond the pale, Bonnies and Cheryls announced. Marcus, who'd presented on Catherine the Great's Pale of Settlement, didn't bother correcting boys who claimed the backward parents of offending girls still pissed in pails at home. Egghead, brainiac: the only tag worse had to be queer.

For compliments, flattening judgements, or declarations of love; for like, hate, interest, or attraction: hallway groups hurled words. Always.

Leaning against library shelves Marcus spoke to a few girls tête-à-tête. "I really liked *The Chrysalids*," "Me too," etc. After a beat, the pubescent version of "I've got . . . a thing . . . I need to be at."

At the home office, Syb's two cents: "Oxytocin can also intensify memories of bonding gone bad, such as in cases where men have poor relationships with their mothers."

15-19: The neural-testicular sucker punch of radical peak testosterone production scarcely equated to readiness for dating or long-term anything.

Deep into the imagined lyricism and pageantry of medieval history, Marcus continued to feel astonished by the bygone practice of teen marriage. Learning that at best his father, forty-nine when Marcus graduated, would have been steeling himself to meet his maker in the fourteenth century, he realized that schooling either created or artificially extended adolescence. Marcus saw that if he'd managed to survive childhood hundreds of years ago, he'd have been a working adult since about twelve; or, closer on the time line but still comfortably far off, an ideal candidate for one of those wards in lunatic asylums reserved for enfeebled patients verging on masturbatory insanity. Later, as a History-English double major (with a Political Science minor; he reserved the right to choose a career in politics and accepted the value of a CV and looking good on paper), Marcus submitted minor-variation-on-a-theme essays conceptualizing the adolescent-adult divide. Professors recognized his clarity, his focus, his intuiting where he was going. They advised, "Read more Foucault."

Still, randy as an afflicted baboon, in a state of constant self-consciousness about oily hair, the lodgepole silhouette, pimples no different than an on again, off again plague, and a burdensome blurting mouth that *lectured*, or spoke nonsense, crudity, or loudly when within earshot of an attractive girl, Marcus crept back and back, ultimately standing at position 8 or 9 in the juvenile male bowling pin rack. To a mind that resented mirrors and fretted about the affliction of a clumsy gait and paltry social skills, gravitating toward being just slightly visible and in the foreground only when the lead pins had been knocked aside felt logical. Or at least safe. In libraries, his unadvertised respite, he muttered Hi to girls he'd earlier mocked or deigned as dogs that would barely do in a pinch. They responded with understandable wariness. Dates did not result, nor did cloakroom blow jobs, the girls' widely reputed expertise.

Now hairier and more pungent, boy-man groupings came and went, gained a tenser atmosphere of competition, rivalry, and urgency. Plus: tight bonds that could easily turn to feuding, shunning, or "Okay you two, break it up and take it outside." With no provocation they carpet bombed the word "Loser." Still clustered, they entertained each other while maintaining dominance with the insult-sneeze—"Pork-chop!" instead of "Ach-oo"—when a C- or D-ranked girl walked by. Like the paper bag over her head joke, everyone knew this one.

At home, support that sounded like indifference: "It's biology's little joke, son." "Have patience." "A girl looks past those surface things." "This too shall pass." In turn, him mouthing a thousand variations of "You don't understand!"

Marcus skipped grad, making an open and shut case for the empty ritual of it all, and at the belated age of nineteen woke alone and luxuriating in the ache of a Saturday morning hangover after Halloween. Incapable of recollecting stumbling back to 79 Tolmie Place (his first rental unit: "studio garden view w/ attached bath") he held absolute—and scented—knowledge that his first fully sexual experience had turned out to be a semi-naked 69 + 6 skirmish with two international students (Spain? Columbia?) dressed as EPCOT robots while "Let the Good Times Roll" actually blared on repeat from the house party's living room above. He never saw the girls again or fully mapped how they'd all wound up—praise be, tequila—in a basement bedroom. For good luck Marcus kept a shred of tinfoil from one of their costumes tucked in his wallet.

Despite willingness and desperation, further good times did not roll that school sophomore year.

Easy to achieve, success in classes buoyed his weeks. Relieving constant groinal pressure by taking care of business twice a day sabotaged annoying biological urges and the appalling compulsive scheming that accompanied them. With sex as taskmaster and goal, he figured he'd be able to rationalize pretty much anything.

Before discovering the orgasm management system (aka the OMS, spoken of to no one but himself), he'd dialled and hung up on escort services a few times. Aside from a cost that would necessitate additional shifts at the Student Union Building's information kiosk—an impossibility—he felt sure that hiring one of the ladies would somehow leave a mark or reveal a permanent flaw within his very core. The sultry women described in phone book and newspaper ads must view the work as work, he guessed, the necessary evil anyone agrees to in order to fill wallets. The university paid him five dollars each hour to answer inane questions. In far less time those women earned quadruple that.

His parents' calls from a couple of hours away passed forward the expected mixture of worry and pride. And news. Hardly a surprise, Benjamin's dinnertime *Get used to it!* announcement about his sexuality distracted them from the abject studiousness of their eldest. Benj had discovered punk eyeliner at sixteen and peacock hair dye a year before that. Bringing a girlfriend home would have been the real shocker. On a weekend call to Marcus, Henry confided that Benj's tomcatting kept them up at night. Who could say what went bump in the night. Their elder boy's safety caused them no worry.

"You know, there is too much of a good thing," Marcus heard on subsequent Sundays. "Let your hair down," his mother joked, rubbing his brush cut.

20-24: Heyday #1. The Golden Age passed in a quiet basement suite away from hometown buddies and family watchfulness. As for the former persona defined by an unreliable mouth and skin and a towering height, Marcus felt thrilled to bid it adieu.

Golden meant the relative sense, Marcus saw, not categorical. Examining the twentysomething's impending Silver Age a sports star would detect austerity measures, if not outright abstinence.

When an undergraduate paper—"The Structure of Belief (re: Classic Looney Tunes Animation)"—won a prize, profs assured him of a place in top-tier graduate programs, all the while warning him—hopeless nods, pursed lips, finger wags, Nostradamic tones—about contracting job markets, eternal budget cuts, and a fate of pursuing tenure in newly-accredited Bush League schools with industrial smokestack views. The uphill battle of it all, in short. He heard the encouragement, not the caveats. Inspired, he even flashed on an idea that, almost nine years later, became his first book, *Learning 'History' From Hollywood*.

Swept up, Marcus indulged in fantastical sketches of a contented future: deeply stimulating classroom discussion stretching into the twenty-first century, fruitful cross-campus idea exchanges that—somehow—turned to further conversation over brunches that culminated in another overnight stay and satiating physical closeness. He wanted orgasm after orgasm for both parties, he decided, but also the companionship of like-minded equals. A shared address, eventually, and a pet. Even immersed in what-ifs, Marcus never conjured kids.

When word of the prize passed from mouth to mouth he detected a distinct positive change in his status. His eligibility, he felt, became visible. The readiness inside him, he thought, would be met with open arms.

But the dates, not unplentiful, fell into the set pattern: event → talk.

Following whichever venue—the Fassbinder and Italian neorealism retrospectives, the Wertmüller double bill, the Russ Meyer and John Waters matinee series, anything David Lynch touched; opera and chamber music; the plays where Freud, Lizzie Borden, WW I, family dysfunction, or womanhood in the 1950s drew applause; student productions, student performances, student rallies, student poetry; gallery shows;

concerts—a slow, thoughtful walk, a coffee shop booth, a restaurant for tea and dessert. And then talk: analytic, assessing, politicized, clinically attentive. The typical closer: "Oh, wow, it's gotten so late. I'm going to have to pull another all-nighter to get that damned assignment ready for class." A handshake in spirit if not fact. The preferred contact—a quick hug perfumed by patchouli, sandalwood, ylang ylang, or some signature blend—transmitted the identical message. He prayed for mind-reader capabilities but remained baffled, nodding empathetically within the security of his own skull when a playwright had ol' aggravated Sigmund exclaiming, "Vhat does a voman vant?" before a mirror.

Either settled down and complaining or equally perplexed and single, Marcus' MA-tier buddies helped only in the peas in a pod sense.

He'd go home, take care of business, and sleep until morning's tumescence. Up next: another *Groundhog Day* of learning experiences.

True, the universe did offer his monkishness the treat of occasional breaks. A few of the dates evolved into a semester of "hanging out." A smaller portion proceeded directly to Go: "Let's skip dessert" or "If I spend one more second immersed in discourse, I'll go bonkers. I mean what's the deal with mind-body dualism?!?" The dates calcified as talking with passable, intermittent sex; the one-off messing around at her place or his came with a clear expiration date: an hour after mutual throes. For the dates, eventual proactivity: a polite declaration (by her, by him) about preventing hurt feelings. "Yeah, I see your point," the standard reply from the opposite side.

No direct queries from home about "someone serious" reached his ears. On visits his mother would mention grandkids wistfully, with Benjamin's loud political raging about *breeders making one more baby on this overcrowded planet* and *don't assume we're the same as you* pushing all that maternal longing toward the avowed heterosexual child at the table. Marcus wished for a third child, preferably a wide-hipped sister with a cottontail's high-output uterus.

Apparently indifferent to family line continuance, Henry, still "Dad" half the time, mentioned *settling down* delicately at a holiday meal or two, as though the touchy subject might explode in his face. "It reminds you about what's important," Marcus heard.

Syb:
"Studies show that most men experience a 2% drop-off in testosterone production each year after they turn thirty, Marcus."
"Thank you, Syb."

25-34: During graduate school's long haul: the plusses, the minuses of singledom, along with reassuring interludes named Janine, Cynthia, and Astrid. Also, Mena, who refused Philomena, her legal designation, as evoking—she'd crack—a suburban goth gone to seed who still wore cameo chokers and wove her parents' hair into mourning jewellery. For reasons she never explained, Mena later dropped the pet name and gave witchiness, startling orange hair, and sphinx-like villanelles a whirl.

Brunette, brunette, brunette, auburn. Marcus could recall their particularities by the handful: Mena's collection of fragrance bottles on a floral cloisonné tray, organized by season, Cynthia's ankh wrist tattoo and her embarrassment about it, Astrid's tan gloves that matched a fondness for Bond film driving and parking lot quickies. Janine had nibbled and toyed with her food, a habit endearing at first and then not.

How they'd paid the bills since and how they'd picture him, he couldn't guess.

Ordinary casual dating situations, none of them ended with flaming arrow acrimony. They'd all petered out. After a half year, give or take, read/write/teach schedules became suddenly demanding. The dry-eyed post-mortem: whatever *it* had been, its course had run. Organically, pre-ordained, like any stable cycle. No one pleaded for second chances or the guidance of paid experts. Marcus never pondered sonnets in the territory of "I know what my heart is like / Since your love died"; he assumed the same for the women, freshly reconstituted as colleagues. Mena might have, just for effect. After a few weeks, temperate

Hellos in hallways and rooms where graduate students hung out. Business as usual. Friendly, not friends.

Before landing the miracle job and returning home, grey-flecked Marcus dwelled a semester here, a one-year contract there. In Bellingham, Calgary, and a serious misstep in Halifax (that dire January), employer and employee both understood his temporary status; the institution required teaching labour, he needed an income and CV-worthy experiences until prayed-for tenured permanence in a locale with winters where lawns never browned. In any of those outposts he'd have bedded a local happily, with gratitude. But with the routine—settling, teaching, research, and, always, securing future employment—making dates happen struck him as onerous, another item on a list that already appeared daunting.

The monkish trait that emerged as the path of least resistance: abstinence, celibacy . . .

Syb:

"The specificity of definition changes from church to church, Marcus. Popular opinion varies considerably too. For example, on the Daily Strength website's Abstinence and Celibacy Support Group message board, a commentator identified as 'deleted underscore user' writes, 'I think the Bible is against masturbation . . . it actually says to flee from any type of sexual impurity. I mean, if you really think about it, why would God ask you to hold off on sex with someone else but let sex with yourself slide?' I have corrected ungrammatical constructions, Marcus. Another remarks, 'I actually like to say a little prayer before pleasuring myself. Something like, "Please forgive me beforehand, God. I'm weak. I'm stupid. I'm only human. I'm sorry." And just get it over with.' A third states, 'According to Biblical scripture the only reason masturbation would be wrong is because of the lust of the flesh created . . . but if you can masturbate without a single thought of lust or sexual impurity in your mind, nothing, zilch, then I don't see what's wrong with it.' On an archived website called Waiting Till Marriage, for instance—"

"Thanks, Syb."

At points—numerous, actually—in the pre-tenure Assistant Professor's *learning curve*, that phrase then in constant usage, Marcus took stock of the smattering of available faculty, beginning with his department and moving up floor by floor. Measuring for liveliness and attractiveness, both spreads of points rather than adamant musts, he noted stern aged veterans, the too self-possessed and fully occupied, and various others who raised flags of varying colours.

After class hours, the campus turned into a faculty ghost town.

If he cannot pinpoint the exact moment he decided to adjust focus, he's certain he must have. Rationalizing phrases he'd have generated: career first, better to, less hassle, for now, cross that bridge when.

He should have known better.

Marcus had read how the average marrying age increased as a result of measurable external factors, but when he passed right by that national average without a prospect in sight—and, in truth, lacking in any recreational contact, or any of the terms then used to describe casual sex—consciousness of this unwanted status as exceptional troubled him. Justification, that balm, worked wonders, though. "I've got so much going on with work" sounded convincing inside his own skeptical brain, just as, in hindsight, he realized that "Just this once" reflected perfect reasoning to the addict in denial. Others: national averages mean nothing; educationally, he'd painted himself into a corner, an exclusive corner, but a corner nonetheless; pining for mating or a mate is either just cultural conditioning or Darwinian biological imperative compelling him; "I actually enjoy—nay, prefer—my own company"; there's a kind of courage in bucking a trend, a philosophical respectability in breaking with convention.

He externalized a few of these to an audience, Henry and Agatha over calls and weekend meals. Henry: "I smell bullshit." Henry kept an eye on single gals in the Warfield and alerted his son to potential keepers. Marcus declined, lighthearted but firm.

Agatha's outlook ranged from vague ("You should go out more") to vaguely optimistic ("It'll happen when it happens").

With the prepping-lecturing-meetings-reading-marking grind of labour by the semester and the demands of book #2, *Euphemism / Discourse / Mass Culture*—a bid at immortality, he joked—Marcus' open weeks transformed into a schedule. It tightened after he agreed to help out Henry with managing the Warfield. Still, he couldn't discern any shortage or lessening of testosterone, or sense himself easing into peacefulness about the state of things, which he'd muttered to himself as a halfhearted promise or wish.

On free nights, he found himself pensive, scheming. Figuring out the solution, though. Wow. Turning back the clock on Climate Change seemed easier. He took to watching *Who's Afraid of Virginia Woolf* and found pleasure of a sort in newsworthy marital scandals and TV programs that dismantled notions of romance, love, and marriage as habitats of absolute pleasure and fulfillment. Suckers! Why bother if, etc, etc. Ignoring the foregone conclusion at the 90-minute mark, he considered the inevitable montage of execrable rom-com dates as a meta-cautionary tale: spare yourself, you're better off without, the world's teeming with malformed psyches. Catching sight of dutiful, if last-minute, guys double-parked in front of corner stores for obligatory fifteen-dollar floral emblems on February 14, he'd think "Meh, they can have it." Calloused, he told himself, but not callous. The line between the two he wouldn't cross.

In retrospect, right. Trying a bit harder couldn't have hurt. Making more of an effort. What's the worst that would have happened? So you get burned a few times, big deal. He might have gotten creative about options, looked further afield. Once upon a time women had crossed a whole continent by stagecoach to marry bachelors they knew only by correspondence. Surely, a show of backbone on his part would have produced results.

All these, the constant companions of regret.

35-44: As Dick Deadeye in grade 12 Marcus had betrayed the fair lovers in singsong while gripping a mop—his tasseled waltzing partner five scenes later—like a staff and adopting a lowdown pirate's growl. He pushed throaty lines—"They are foiled – foiled – foiled!"—from the side of his mouth. "A scurvy wench," his ad lib, passed through dress rehearsal and ran for the production's four nights.

Since so many of the *Pinafore*'s crew of characters felt internal conflicts, the inspired drama teacher scattered Buttercup, Ralph, Josephine, and Dick throughout the auditorium ("front of house," in Mr. R's words) while Captain Coracan sang "Fair moon, to thee I sing, bright regent of the heavens, say, why is everything either at sixes or at sevens?" Lanterns in hand, each accompanist eventually hum-sang and circled their assigned gym corner, distracting those ticket buyers in stackable wooden chairs from the volleyball team captain's deck plank of a performance on stage.

The upsides of Marcus' sixes-and-sevens era (part 1) included a perfect record of attendance at departmental meetings, prodigious committee do-goodism, a top-notch credit rating, files, emails, and folders managed with assembly line efficiency, and weekly meal-planning any Home Ec teacher would assign a gold star. Taking a sick day then seemed less likely than palatable basement-vinted wine; he swallowed omega-3s like a champ. Home dust bunnies knew to quake at the sounds of his keys.

But the creature moulded from those components, what a repelling figure. He'd crow about numeric matters that turned listeners' eyes into fidgets, readied their minds for pouncing on the skimpiest of exit lines.

Hardly blind to social cues, Marcus knew better than to bother directing conversations toward pension figures, investment rates of return, or tips for organizing documents. He kept the insights under wraps and opted for standard campus shop talk.

Returning from libraries, a keyboard or television ate up his leisure at the Warfield.

Already unreliable, dating sputtered further. Unaccountably, his specs failed to jibe with his performance. Though a notable prospect on paper and an owner of commanding height and Samsonian hair (Darwinian characteristics that, he'd read, women couldn't help but respond to), his cup didn't runneth over on weekends and workday evenings. Stymied, Marcus persisted. Before sensing a burgeoning reputation—the desperado—he took the initiative with occasional dates with like-minded career builders, to him a calculation that appeared to promise far better results than hotel lounge, opera intermission, coffee shop, or bus ride pick-ups. Collectively, the dates went down in history as dreary and rushed, matter-of-fact. Networking and rivalry combined. Clipped, contract negotiation tones along with complaints and tetchy droning about workplace banalities: these emerged as constants. Or, as oxygen-deprived as though they'd met in La Paz. The exceptions: Dater 1 offering "We should do this again" while Dater 2's brain worked overtime to generate a suitably polite excuse. The ratio, he'd estimate: 1:1.

Marcus stopped taking supplements as part 2 began. He felt good enough, and, besides, he sprayed most into the toilet bowl. He bought bagged oranges and fish sticks instead. An earlier passion—so he'd told himself—for travel waned with tidal certainty. Wandering museums in storied cities hadn't come to bore him. But booking flights for one ("Aisle, please"), being handed a single room card at the front desk, and reading first editions during café meals drew steady sighs.

Numerically credible because of the guarantee of at least 40% heterosexual women, conference mixers did begin to bore him. Then conferences themselves. The quickest cost-benefit analysis revealed only deficits. Self-sequestering, aka work, became his habit of choice.

Agatha and Henry died without grandchildren or seeing their own children settle down into the standard coupledoms. Feeling guilt and guilt again about being a disappointing bachelor and an indifferent, occasionally dismissive and judging brother (to drifting Benjamin, also revealed as a disappointing son who ought to have outgrown shirtless weekends in Palm Springs and Montreal for what amounted to DJ'd orgies filtered through a narcotic haze), Marcus thought of making peace with the facts. Nothing could be done now, not really.

He took a crumb of solace from the fact of quick, painless ends while pushing away thoughts of his own fate due to mechanical failure. He'd inherited a heart and blood vessels, after all.

Revived, if at a slower rate, the OMS attracted deeper thought than in its first iteration, when, culturally-speaking, it had belonged to the can't-help-himself red-blooded young man's profile. He thought of Mark Twain's advice to not "play a Lone Hand too much" and felt glad for the man's ingrained facetiousness.

The necessity, that Marcus didn't challenge. Without release, he could find himself bearish, impatient, or adversarial just because.

Plus, he rationalized, why not? Upkeep: one pared toenails regularly, cleaned ears, emptied bladder and bowel.

But the gap between what could be and what was brought to mind plays he ordered and asked questions about during lectures. That tragic gallery: befuddled and deluded figures from David Mamet, from August Wilson, and of course from Arthur Miller. Students considered those protagonists as either "totally pathetic" or victims: "Why don't they just *deal with* their issues and *get on* with it?" What did these pups know? At the first obstacle, a 63 say, they crumpled, sprouted tears, or tantrum-typed on rate-my-prof sites.

Even fantasizing—narratives of getting lucky (with some extending to date scenarios and the majority directly to the beast with two backs, a means to an end) developed a sour aftertaste. *In the prime of life and here you are.* That voice. The nag that had turned Francis Sinatra, singing waiter at The Rustic Cabin roadhouse in New Jersey, into the Rat Pack's maestro. The voice that evolution had summoned into existence in order to make humans change their lousy circumstances and assure themselves of genetic continuance. Or, mysteriously, to feel awful. Or for some damned reason.

As the era's second part wound down, rigid order struck him as a lost cause—counter-intuitive and, cosmologically speaking, unnatural. A book left splayed on a table, spoons and forks unwashed, balled black socks thrown into corners, crusts of pizza on plates. What difference did it make? He took to thinking of his waist in European sizes. Schoolmaster grey in sizes 52 and 54, please, just in case.

45-54: [For this, Marcus thought, he could cut and paste lines from some Eliotan poem that likens middle age to an idling, sputtering engine. Or intones, "Tinned soup *pour un*, eros an island in a remote sea / Behold, the harbingers of a personal ice age."

His disgruntled era.

The irritation years.

The time of discontent.]

55-64: No last hurrah here. Just pathetic, by all but purely elastic standards. On par with those off-campus buffoons who felt obliged to exclaim "With the wild and crazy life I've led, I really should write a book" whenever they met him. And yet never lifting a finger.

For him: Not acting but thinking, speculating, postulating as the airtight philosopher in the comfort of his own brain pan: "I really ought to . . . ," "Perhaps I could . . . ," "Surely, if I make myself available something's bound to happen . . . ," "What's the worse that will happen if . . . ?" as his body aged, social capital shrank, and erections felt closer and closer to the sound of one hand clapping.

Or was that a tree falling in an empty forest?

Syb: "Marcus, the question 'When a tree falls in a lonely forest, and no animal is near by to hear it, does it make a sound? Why?' dates from a 1910 book entitled *Physics* written by Charles Riborg Mann and George Ransom Twiss. In sections 23 and 45 of the 1710 work, *A Treatise Concerning the Principles of Human Knowledge*, George Berkeley posed the earliest known variant of the thought experiment. Dating back to the ancient Greek deiknymi, the concept of a thought experiment predates Euclidean mathematics—"

"All right, Syb, thank you."

Where were the lovable jerks in his life who barked "Shit or get off the pot, man" and set him up on comically awful dates in a domino series that ended—at the very moment he'd decided to throw in the towel—with The One? Romantic comedy scripts promoted hope like evangelists promise salvation, he'd read. Messages of salvation, all for the price of a ticket or TV content bundle.

Even when no colleagues probed with "How do you like to spend your free time, Marcus?" or "Seeing anyone special these days?" Marcus found himself volunteering preemptive misdirection in the form of information underscoring production deadlines, travel-for-work itineraries, and the typical rest.

If asked, he might say he'd grown too busy to even think of the work-life balance. Get real. After, he'd feel no better than a playwright's character reassuring his buddies that, yessiree, things were on the upswing, coming up roses. Salesman of the month, any week now.

From this vantage point, former dry spells transformed into plenitude. Student years—the dates, long walks, and libidinal if chaste exchanges over tea—began to look like the repository of good times.

65-74: In the ad versions: counting pills, regaining mobility thanks to revolutionary Product X, beaming gratitude as young but able hired hands install a safety tub, pensive about a frantic outside world with few and far between pitstop toilets. Also, the inevitable long shot: a beach figure with a freighted glimpse of a looming and beckoning coastal horizon. Or else: medium shot, diffuse golden-lit carefree luncheons (at the 0:20 mark: "The Queen's Guard Group, Retirement Savings Specialists. Our investment guarantees can help you achieve your financial goals. With confidence.") and majestic holes-in-one at Leisureland (at 0:25: "In rare instances, Celebrian H's side effects include increased risk of suicide, stroke, depression, and/or ulcers. Do not use if you have preexisting conditions related to blood pressure, immunosuppression, or diabetes"). Comfort with close-ups? That had ended a demographic segment or two ago.

In quotidian fact, though, a pacing Poe story night ghoul counting calories while figuring out how to best merchandise himself as an eligible if long in the tooth bachelor.

75+: Enough already. Right?

Bones creaking and testosterone, vasopressin, and oxytocin nearly dry wells, but those carrot-before-a-workhorse testimonials in perennial circulation. So tantalizing.

"Granddad found love again at 80! At that age we never expected it, but then . . ."

"I'd spent my life alone until she strode into the room."

"Lottery ticket odds, sure, but, Oh! the thrill when you win!"

Would Marcus—in 2038 a toddler step from grotesque, a Hausmannian assemblage with prosthetic augments, power cells, and bionic replacement parts—show up for dates at Letheview Estates, the senior living community and retirement residence formerly known as an old age home? Perhaps he'd lease a unit there, dress in billowy yellow guayaberas, keep a robotic dachshund for company, and charm widows with his achromatic white dental implants over afternoon pinochle in the games room? He'd noticed those characters in movies.

Maybe. Still, he couldn't help doubt—everyone retired from jobs, so why not quests for love, sex, and companionship? Yet he heard his mother's voice just the same: "How do you know you don't like it if you haven't tried it?" Agatha, kindly, had tackled his prejudices with that question in the case of cauliflower, spinach, liver, sausage, gravy, sauerkraut, rye bread, wedged raw tomato, cream of wheat, hockey, Beaver Scouts, ocean swimming, and canoeing. Also, as he'd sat unbudging inside the station wagon while outside the imposing brick school building on kindergarten's first morning.

What ever happens at the end of the Sisyphus story? For believers, Marcus supposed, the chump's still there; at the base of the mountain or spying the peak, it doesn't matter. The conditions—the boulder, the obligation to push it, gravity—never change. Hardly the forgive and forget type, that Zeus.

Syb: "—an eternity of useless efforts and unending frustration, Marcus."

Understood.

No, absolutely not, Marcus thought. The profile-fill's distancing third person made no sense and snuck in an off-putting, mentally unwell tone.

But so much worse: the sheer paltriness of the figure, the deficiency his very cells radiated! If set up on a date with that, he'd run for the hills. Pathetic indeed. Serving the whole enchilada would choke a psychiatrist, so imagine anyone lacking the credentials. Over time, he'd offer morsels, bites instead.

He'd venture one in a family of clichés, a kind of 'I stopped to pause' line: I'd been *so busy* that I overlooked *me*; I realized that in pursuing my career I'd let other parts of my life slide and that it was time—high time—to nurture those neglected areas.

That'd work. In whatever form, people loved salvation and renovation stories. Also, late realization looked better than none at all.

He almost believed it himself.

PEDAGOGY

Monday 9:23 AM –

Work email:

Dear Professor Marcus,

Although we have never met, I hope you will forgive my informality. My eldest daughter (you may know her as Haoyu, a student in one of your freshman classes) has informed me of your preferences in regard to addressing. If she is mistaken, I beg you to accept my apology; the young do not always grasp the importance of decorum.

In the interests of concision, please let me proceed to business.

A growing portion of my weekly schedule as the Chief Executive Office of Lanyard Holdings involves airports, intercontinental flights, and meetings. While not necessary *sensu stricto*, over the years I have discovered the limitations of virtual communication as well as the virtues of face-to-face exchanges. Clients respect the effort, I've learned. As for employees at the managerial level . . . well, when Machiavelli wrote "in wanting to be obeyed, it is necessary to know how to command" on his meditation about classical Rome, he could well have been addressing the corporate environment of today. *She* who wishes to be obeyed has also come to accept the inestimable utility of speaking in person.

With that said, final negotiations regarding two projects on your west coast currently require my attention. Following the second, in Oakland, I have set aside time for my daughter. Admittedly, I have pencilled in a spate of business matters in your city during her class hours.

If it is appropriate, I will now request a meeting with you about Haoyu. Her adaptation and performance trouble me and, to be candid, I'm seeking guidance.

Additionally, you are no doubt aware of the interest expressed by one of my residential property development analysts. Lanyard is seeking a permanent foothold in the region. For such access circumstances occasionally dictate expenditures above market value. Perhaps we could meet off campus to discuss what is, after all, a concern unrelated to your profession.

My assistant tells me of an esteemed seafood restaurant near my accommodation. Perhaps an exchange of ideas benefits from the setting of a shared meal?

I look forward to receiving your response.

Most sincerely,

Lanying Zhang
Lanyard Holdings, CEO
Central Area, Singapore

Never, Marcus thought, not once. And despite expectations. He'd never met a single parent of one student. Over decades of workweeks, hundreds of classes, and afternoons of tapped keyboard squares that cemented the final grade standings—some damning—of thousands of tuition payers.

No Concerned Parent united front had ever shown up at his office with faces set at Hope or Expectation or We Will Not Leave Without Results. Nor had any thought to blast an accusatory email toward him. No demands or pleas had been uttered. Not a shaking fist raised. No sly references to quid pro quo or bombastic ones about a ferocious lawyer on retainer.

If little Maxwell flunked out or little Serena slunk home with a 67 when familial expectations had pegged her for a 90, well, so be it. Whatever belief prompted distraught moms and dads to bully, question, or yell at K-12 teachers—an occupational hazard, according to TV—apparently ceased to operate higher up the ladder.

In his career's budding days, before the PhD and right after, well-wishers—long in the game, bruised but veteran—had thrown advice his way, *be wary* the takeaway.

The Boschian canvas—

When in trouble students instinctively dropped the facade of innocence and turned to wiliness. Helplessness? One sly pose of many. Teary outbursts? Signalling only the beginning. Punitive and averse to self-restraint, these corrupt judges networked, firing off tremulous emails to Deans and Heads, showing up in Admin offices to mouth litigious complaints sopped with implication. Having absorbed useful ideas from antique plays still on high school curricula, the willful, guileful so-and-sos led university representatives to fill in the blanks. Harm causing! Trust betraying! Innocence tampering! Inappropriateness! Or else, Marcus had been warned, foxily pursuing a first-class grade, they hinted at material offers in exchange for a 5% hike. With crossed legs in a short skirt and cleavage creating siren's magic, they reshaped themselves into career-annihilating temptations.

Accept nothing, he heard, not even a cookie in a bag, any item that ostensibly impartial—Ha!—administrative officers might construe as ethically compromising.

So Marcus had pondered over a series of low-volume between-you-me-and-the-fencepost disclosures. He noticed too a presumption: he wouldn't need to concern himself with male students. Thanks to genetics or training, they didn't resort to tactics.

The fingers wagged about student malice and prognostications about its inevitable surfacing had, Marcus thought, added a gust of sensation to a job where make-or-break decisions—which bomb wire to snip, what step to take on the dirt road scattered with anti-personnel mines—seemed so remote as to not exist in any real sense.

So much for forecasts. Other than the sporadic coffee shop gift card valued at a single beverage and taped to a Thank You! note, nada.

The undercurrents of Ms. CEO's email flustered and intrigued him, especially the ridiculous lack of proportion. Unless he'd misread her intent: above market value to the tune of millions in exchange for a piddling grade change. He wondered about "*She* who wishes to be obeyed" too. A taste of her imperiousness, slip of the tongue. Indication of *menace voilée*?

Along with everyone else, Marcus knew Admin's directives advised the communique's immediate forwarding. Faculty and staff: wash your hands of the matter. Immediately, thoroughly. A moment's hesitation raises doubt.

Kick the matter up the chain of command, pass responsibility to workplace ethics personnel and their numbered protocols in virtual binders: Section 9c: In the Case of Attempted Bribery . . .

No, he'd mull over the ins and outs of Lanying Zhang's sentences first.

In class, end-of-term listlessness and the thousand indicators of boredom (adolescent edition) but nothing out of the ordinary.

Mid-classroom with an aisle seat: L'Oréal. Slouched, a loden cape across her shoulders. Not one to leave well enough alone she'd added what might be a marching band jacket in ivory with brass buttons in twin rows, a flowing skirt of silver pleats, plastic saddle shoes. Ladies and gentlemen, the thankless offspring of go-getters. Bothered by a bit of paper stuck to her left shoe's platform sole, the conundrums of split ends, an unsightly cuff thread, flaking nail paint.

Outside that fatuous bubble? Cluelessness. Would a gap year of volunteering at a desalinization plant in San Diego or aboard a maintenance vessel roaming the Great Pacific Garbage Patch have made a difference? Who could say. Perhaps gawping overboard at a colossal jellyfish bloom would inspire only another weekend shopping excursion, this one in Los Angeles.

A lurching trolley bus, for the sake of change. He traded the palpably compressed bodies of the accordion express for quiet and stops increased by a factor of five. In place of an interior climate made of coffee vapour and marijuana residue intermingled with human breath and sweat, fine saltings of beached sea kelp along with traffic emissions.

As for ads: ongoing and emergent medical conditions of the mildly to moderately severe types, outreach for students with sexual questions, study programs from rival institutions, a poem excerpt.

Neck pivoted downward, Marcus typed: Lanyard Holdings wiki. In public he disliked addressing Syb.

What a tale. Rags to riches, against the odds, secret shame, a double life, and Faustian, all in one.

Born in garbage-heaped Tondo to a teenage single mother, a *Sekundarya* school drop out christened Mark Anthony scrounges up a job sweeping construction site debris. Luck and a quick learner's work ethic assure his fast climb up the ranks. He eventually strikes out on his own. The business thrives, bypasses one downturn, then another. Mark Anthony secures a questionable, shady financial associate, is dogged by rumours (cut corners, greased palms, underworld dealings with thugs bearing tattoos, scars, and machetes), but begins a noteworthy run of successful bids.

Though a screenplay would add firearms, cocaine, and occupational paranoia, the man's rise to business prominence checked every Hollywood box. And yet. Well before his exposure as either hopelessly compromised or a *bosyo* whose official story of success through *harte Arbeit*, street smarts, and fortunate timing existed only a cover, fate nudged him in an unexpected direction. Following a late night meeting the entrepreneur collapsed over his office desk and expired. A congenital heart condition, no less.

Soon after, Lanyard suffered a sea-change.

Marcus listened to engine noises, doors folding open and closed, and "Jesus fuck, that bèn dàn couldn't even bother to lift a finger and look at the bloody Excel file before he went off on me like a rabid mutt" from a loud standing guy evidently mired in a Joe Job.

Nearby aerosolized motes of coffee, alcohol, armpit, feet, and hamburger (beef fat, mustard, ketchup, salt) set off Marcus' nasal receptors. He pictured the airborne molecules on eventual paths to terminal run-ins with O_3. Wondering if he gave off 'old man smell'—where was the ad for that medication?—he pretend-rubbed his nose with the meat of his palm. He detected no scent, appealing or otherwise. With an electron microscope they'd find molecules of chalk and ink, no doubt about that.

Marcus realized he'd been hearing strangers yell at mobile phone receivers off and on for thirty years.

The outside passed by—intersections, sidewalks, businesses. The city's millions of vehicles and inhabitants in a sliver fraction. A minute later Marcus pointed his nose toward the phone screen.

Whereabouts was Lanying Zhang? He wanted to put a face to a name.

Images in rows of the replacement CEO divulged scant details via generic poses. Her publicist favoured benign corporate photo ops: the illustrious leader seated behind a white modular desk; studious in a glassy, sky-high office; hands-on, a key player on the executive team; capable of dirty work while on site and going over plans with a hard-hatted client. Scrubbed of personal quirks—of character—only entrepreneurial acuity remained.

The few others watermarked by a Manileño photojournalist depicted sunglasses and attire for court date and funeral. Shot from a medium distance sixteen years in the past, Lanying Zhang registered as perfectly, acceptably ordinary, a cipher for normali-ty. Behind the trim figure and professional veil? Virtually any-thing.

He could guess about age, of course. But screen information revealed she'd already crossed into eligibility for pharmacy, rental car, and budget hotel discounts: fifty-five.

Marcus read that Mark Anthony's widow had relinquished assets but somehow retained the company name. Across the patchy collection of articles he noticed "closed-door meetings," a repeating phrase, as though freelancers had latched on to the same unnamed source and dug up nothing further.

Soon after, Lanying, a London Business School graduate, sold the family home and relocated four hours away in Singapore.

While touching on the alleged criminal family ties of Lanyard Holdings, the pieces mostly quoted platitudinous comments to reporters. The time was right to "turn over a new leaf." With a "fresh start" and a "clean slate" she'd focus on rebuilding. A column-length profile in *Singapore Report on Business* sustained the mood by noting the CEO's preference for "a notional drop of milk in her Earl Grey" and relayed her—"no *tai tai*, she"—desire to "capitalize on opportunities in an inviting, business-friendly environment."

The woman's choice of phrases telegraphed a desire for onlookers to join her in addressing the future. The past? Dead to her. In print, anyhow.

During the ritual tenant news update from Mrs C and before her freely offered weather outlook, Marcus foresaw an awkward "Oh, by the way" conversation.

If accepting Lanying's incentive, he'd have to follow up by distributing a governmental form with a basic message that could only trigger anger and panic: vacate by such-and-such date.

Those official announcements must get delivered by the score in a demolish-and-rebuild metropolis whose founding mayor had sold real estate, Marcus supposed. Since the remote era of sawmills, brick-making, orchard farming, and panning for gold nuggets, the city's byways, offices, concourses, and parlours had been abuzz with land speculation.

Expropriation, for progress. In the name of enterprise and wealth accumulation. For the sake of doing what one does. Having supplanted a rooming house, the Warfield had already played its role in the grand tradition.

Careful to minimize the resentful looks proclaiming him heartless, a reprehensible landlord who'd sell his own mother for pocket change, he'd maybe dawdle on campus. Or keep to himself at home, skulking about only when Mrs C needed his input.

Feet slippered in the penthouse, Marcus returned to Lanying Zhang's implied offer.

Refusing was his call, of course, but why should he?

Selling the Warfield, liquidating it: a foregone conclusion, at least within the next several years. If he keeled over and ceased to exist in the manner of Mark Anthony, his brother wouldn't hesitate to arrange the sale. With the proceeds, Benjamin would likely buy a vacation pad in Palm Springs or Puerto Vallarta. Both, why not?

Selling was inevitable, like death. Only stalling presented an option, and for what purpose? Was that merely him raving at close of day?

Giving is a thing, Marcus thought. Half of 40 million dollars for his own use post-retirement, or bequeathing the old dear to the city for use as . . . what? A legacy. Housing for scholarship students? Whatever social workers had decided to call wayward mothers or the down and out?

If he could ask his parents they'd say "Do whatever makes you happiest." Marcus felt sure of that because they'd spoken the phrase to him into his early forties. Along with "Do what you think is right," the advice only raised additional questions.

At the stove watching red soup in the saucepan nearing the Do Not Boil recommended by the label, Marcus closed his eyes. As with those old word-association test therapists used, he thought of a handful of letter-shaped balloons that spelled H A P P I E S T and then waited to see what would appear.

A boy flying a kite.

A living room at Christmas with a garlanded tree in the corner.

A girl in a princess gown serving tea to dolls.

A grey-haired couple clinking cocktail vessels of cored pineapple on a cruise.

Lord. The stock nature of the images dawned on him. They originated in ads on television, greeting cards, holiday programming. Happiness as sold by American Greetings Corporation, LLC, The Coca-Cola Company, and the Hallmark Channel.

Marcus realized as well that he might have mixed up word-association with a Rorschach test. What the analysand discerned in the inkblot series and interpreted in the word choice, were the revelations one and the same?

Syb:

"The disputed polymath Sir Francis Galton has been credited with inventing the word-association test. He utilized the Free Association Test for the International Health Exhibition of 1884 as part of an experiment to measure national purity and individual normality. 9337 participants paid 3 pennies each to be measured.

"Galton also used the test at his short-lived anthropometric laboratory at Cambridge University. With the test Galton studied the relationship between stimulus words and response words and sought insights into the unconscious . . ."

Digging around for cracker packages, Marcus let Syb's reply unfurl.

"A biographer described Galton as one of the Victorian era's chief exponents of the scientific folly.

"While visiting Vichy, France, Galton classified women into six size categories, from thin to prize fat.

"He subsequently devised a project to define a beauty map of Great Britain and publish his observations about women as attractive, indifferent, or repellent. Galton's methodology involved using a needle to mark one end of a cardboard rectangle attached to a glove to register an attractive girl, the middle for an indifferent girl, and the opposite end for the repellent specimens.

"Men were not recorded.

"In *Gregariousness in Cattle and in Men* of 1871 Galton argued that slavishness in the mass of humans is a hereditary taint that will need to be bred out before true political freedom can be attained.

"In 1873 Galton proposed that Africa should be resettled by the Chinese because he believed the Chinese people's natural capacities would displace a population with inferior intelligence, with resultant benefits for other civilizations.

"Galton regularly observed patients in the Earlswood and Darenth Asylums for Idiots to test hypotheses.

"An argument in *Inquiries into Human Faculty and Its Development* of 1883 was that criminal nature tends to be inherited and that the typical criminal is marked by peculiarities of character. Galton wrote, 'his conscience is almost deficient, his instincts are vicious, his power of self-control is very weak, and he usually detests continuous labour'.

"Galton's influential 1869 study *Hereditary Genius* has been called the first systematic attempt to investigate the effect of heredity on intellectual abilities.

"He is popularly associated with eugenics advocacy.

"Knighted in 1909, he died of tuberculosis in 1911 . . ."

Far more misses than hits, Marcus decided.

Eminent Victorian Nutbars: students would have a field day with a course like that. Nothing better than outraged bafflement over the wrongheaded beliefs of the long deceased.

Seated at the kitchen table and facing the delicate blush streaks of Monday's diminuendo outside, Marcus wondered if Syb would now return to the subject of his query. The accurate prediction of her turns eluded him continuously.

The soup tasted vaguely scorched. He always forgot that cream of tomato demanded milder heat.

"As a measure of psychiatric evaluation Carl Jung theorized that the delay between stimulus and response in word-association testing indicated a block in self-expression.

"In *Structure of the Psyche*, Jung claimed that we make slips of the tongue and slips in writing and unconsciously do things that betray our most closely guarded secrets—which are sometimes unknown even to ourselves. These phenomena can be demonstrated experimentally by the association tests, which are very useful for finding out things that people cannot or will not speak about.

"His Word-Association Experiment consists of a list of one hundred words. The list is the basis for ferreting out these unspeakable things.

"During the 1970s association tests became a common procedure in psychoanalysis.

"They have been used to investigate personality and its pathology. In the latter the subject's reaction to emotionally charged memories and ideas provoked by certain of the test stimuli may produce atypical or revealing associations or, more often, unusually long or short reaction times.

"Marcus, a Word Association Thesaurus indicates stable patterns for word-association in test subjects—"

"Thank you, Syb."

Self-administered, a word association test looked little better than folly. He'd need to know how to measure the lag time in responses. And, following that, a method of understanding the significance of the lag itself.

What closely guarded secrets did he still have, what unknowns to himself? None, nothing, off the top of his head. He was an open book, or would be once he posted his ACQV.

Selling the old place, residence and nest. No, "happiness" was not the word that instantly sprang to mind. Instead, "hassle" rocketed up. "Inopportune." Brokers, lawyers, bankers, and notaries public in a carousel of dull meetings.

Sorting, packing boxes, scouting out a palatable real estate agent, and getting driven far and wide for a *retirement-appropriate location*. He could hear the placating tones now. Perhaps away from the city, following the migratory pattern of other snowbirds.

Restful, he'd hear. Restful views, walls in a restful hue to comfort him as he settled into restful new hobbies. After so many years on the go, why not put up your feet and rest awhile? Standard unit features include clocks on countdown embedded into every surface, sedative gas piped in through vents. *Go to sleep.*

Marcus slid the empty bowl out of the way and brought his elbows to the table. A habit of pensiveness that stretched back to adolescence, he steepled his hands, chin resting on outstretched thumbs. Nose tucked inside, he savoured the humid warmth of breath.

Selling could wait. Ms. Zhang would wait. Yes and yes.

If the Warfield truly meant a foothold for Lanyard, she'd have to.

Once the undeniable pleasure brought by the prospect of a suitcase of cash had coursed through him, he'd grown lukewarm about the offer.

Besides, the bother of what to do with it. Spend, spend, spend. He had no taste for the supposed good life—yachts, gems, private jets, casinos, perpetual vacationing, a fleet of Bentleys, a retinue of beauties. Nor for, as yet, philanthropic do-goodism. While an assurance, an investment portfolio flooded with seven extra zeros meant little to him. He felt comfortable. *As is*, in the way stores tagged slightly damaged items.

Nor would he be bought. The idea offended him: following this transaction, with this seduction, I'll own you.

She'd offered an unbalanced quid pro quo, too much for too little. The proffered exchange induced scenes of follow-up requests, subsequent obligations. *Godfather*-y stuff.

Besides, assuming he'd read the letter correctly, L'Oréal deserved accurate evaluation. Her mother's backstage ministrations? Infantilizing, if well-intended.

He'd agree to dinner, however, and skip the alert to any institutional officers. Marcus couldn't deny his interest in the exotic chapters of Lanying's story, in the determination and iron will immediately below the professionalism. Also, she'd flattered him with the pretence of helplessness, of seeking guidance. What man didn't respond with an I-can-help! grin to that. Who knew what neuronal cluster that posture activated?

Perhaps she'd let the living character—so little accessible to reasonable arguments and so entirely governed by instinctual wishes, as old Sigmund had written—seep out from the public guise of stolidity. He'd do the same.

Roused by the coastal ambience, they'd talk. To start, fill the space between them with agreeability. The weather, the menu, the difference between there and here. Shop talk in limited bursts. Before the entwined business of a flailing child and desirable real estate, the conversation might falter. Or, thrive: successes, failures, hardships, disappointments, satisfactions. The remaining ambitions.

It wouldn't be a date, although in retrospect they might decide it had been. If he came to understand over skewered prawns and poached salmon that the agreed-upon meeting was exactly that, or noted how Lanying Zhang appeared captivated by him in no way—or vice versa—then he'd write off the hours not as a failure but as practice, a test-run.

From the experience he'd learn what to include on his list of post-career pursuits.

In the summer of my sixty-fifth year, Marcus thought. Though technically inaccurate, it could be the title of a sun-dappled French comedy. *The Summer of My Sixty-Sixth Year*.

The premise sounded ready-made, a TV listing service's thumbnail description. *After retiring, a _____ professor embarks on _____. _____ and _____ ensue.*

Adjectives, nouns, conjunctions, and the rest.

Within reason, counting limitations, the blanks were his to fill.

In the animal kingdom you would be . . . ?

~~Toast.~~
~~A pile of bones.~~
~~Fearful of the watering hole.~~
~~Nothing with hooves or wings. Nothing too predatory or scav-~~
~~enging. Annie Dillard's weasel: "That is, I don't think I can learn~~
~~from a wild animal how to live in particular—shall I suck warm~~
~~blood, hold my tail high, walk with my footprints precisely over~~
~~the prints of my hands?—but I might learn something of mind-~~
~~lessness, something of the purity of living in the physical sense~~
~~and the dignity of living without bias or motive. The weasel lives~~
~~in necessity and we live in choice, hating necessity and dying at~~
~~the last ignobly in its talons."~~
~~A fox. A seal. A dolphin. A whale. A tortoise.~~
~~A chimpanzee (if my character aligned with the class divisions of~~
~~*Planet of the Apes*).~~
~~A blue whale.~~
~~A black panther in body, but a raven in temperament.~~
~~A raccoon.~~

A bull elephant. Make of that what you will.

Fate: who is in charge?

~~Really?~~
~~Ha, that's one for the ages.~~
~~'God's Plan' is either a mass delusion or evidence of a creator with less common sense than a puppy.~~
~~Depends where you live. A person in Caracas and another in Oslo cannot truthfully answer in the same way.~~
~~No one.~~
~~We all have some small degree of control over select parts of our fate. After that? Chance, the machinations of others, the strength of social norms, unknowable historical developments.~~
~~By virtue of genetics we are fated to ask that question and produce only soggy, half-baked answers and then treat them like manna.~~
~~For the sake of expedience, I'll say I pretty much align with Freud: "Religion is an illusion and it derives its strength from the fact that it falls in with our instinctual desires."~~
~~The afterlife is a consolatory fiction for our consciousness.~~
~~-~~

An interesting question. One perhaps best saved for a conversation in real time . . .

ACVQ 20

The scariest words are:

~~Pain, death, loss, emptiness. Aren't everyone's in the same vicinity??~~
~~Death / oblivion / the end of consciousness~~
~~Concentration camp / gulag / super-max~~
~~"Sir, I regret to inform you that you're the victim of identity theft."~~
~~Buried alive.~~
~~"The act of birth is the first experience of anxiety, and thus the source and prototype of the affect of anxiety."~~
~~There are no scary words, just the facts or actions they describe~~
~~"I'm afraid I have some bad news about that pain in your lung"~~
~~"If an alert is broadcast, it's time to act. This is not a test."~~
~~"Dear Sir, The pension fund has incurred catastrophic losses due to mismanagement."~~
~~Hell is real.~~
~~"You have laboured in vain."~~
~~Life's shape—from cruelty and disease to joy and beauty—represents the efforts of 'intelligent design' or the unfolding of a divine plan.~~
~~"Okay, so here's the deal: No one values or respects you or your work."~~
~~-~~

Alphabetically: death, emptiness, loss, pain, shame.

MTL—MoL Post Factum
(Here and There)

The fucking salad.
　　　Why that, why now?
In view of all the calories he'd burned through!

Syb:
"Marcus, if a sample adult person's total daily calorie usage is 2000, then approximately 20 per cent of those calories consumed results from brain activity. Research findings are inconclusive or contradictory about the relationship between kinds of neural activity—reading, daydreaming, or recalling memories, for example—and caloric usage."

"Got it, thank you."
Earlier that week Marcus had been nudged by "Decisions, An Annual Budget," a mini think piece column in a giveaway transit newspaper.
The article's facetious author had calculated how calorie-reliant everyday choices—"Walk or drive?" "Cruller, apple fritter, or bran muffin?" "Recycling or garbage bin?" and the rest—added up over the year.
With "I wonder . . . ?" as well as an equivalent arithmetical sloppiness and a ticklish awareness of "Idle hands are the devil's workshop," Marcus had applied the premise to the Judaea problem.
Though an inarguably moronic pursuit, he set about determining the hits to his bank account for channeling anger. Directing and expressing its manifestations, at what cost? How high a fee for attaining a semblance of commensurability while simultaneously imbibing the fragrant wafts of holy righteous air

when he passed by his defeated, wrongdoing foe—prostrate in essence if not in practice.

If he spent X dollars on food and Y minutes experiencing Judaea-related, food-fuelled anger *per mensis* and multiplied the number by 12, and multiplied that number by 5 point x, then . . .

Marcus thought of self-sabotage when, days after arriving at a dollar-value (a cheese, bread, and wine vacation in Burgundy, the specious tally informed him) and helping himself a final time to Judaea's salad, he noticed the steady foggy drifts of a turbulent frame of mind. A sudden funk, in short.

He associated the distinct sensation with the singular adolescent experience of getting caught in a wrongdoing while living under his parents' roof. Not the chin-jutted, unapologetic variant—"He deserved it" (some run-in or other involving Benjamin) or "Department stores over-inflate their prices and have insurance anyhow" (the keychain he'd shoplifted). No, the slumped shoulders assailing him corresponded with the blue mood caused by misbehaviour of the unjustifiable sort: ignoring rules or laws because, as he had to explain once found out, he'd felt like it.

Those dinner table hearings had unmasked Marcus as a Disappointing Child, a letdown unaccountably festering with selfishness and worrisome apathy about the consequences of impulsive actions.

And for a youth largely untouched by material hardship or personal loss, what could be worse than getting pointed out as a source of pain for kind, caring, and hopeful parents, as being recognized as a thankless miscreant who squandered opportunities while also failing to live up to his stellar potential? No one yearned for the reputation as blight on the family name.

Now, fifty years forward, the salad offence gnawed at Marcus' . . . he couldn't say.

Soul?

No, a species-flattering and quaint—if poetic—fable.

His humanity?

No more than a piece of rhetoric politicians and sentimental writers and moralists wielded as standing for altruism, generosity, compassion, self-sacrifice, and the heroic rest that somehow always overlooked the breathtaking history of egotism as a core operating principle, cruelty for its own sake, and genocidal zealotry. As though these traits swept under the rug somehow represented qualities alien to anatomically modern humans.

His preconscious ethical faculty, where that makeshift psyche-mechanism sorted clearly right, clearly wrong, and the myriad grey in-betweens operated?

He'd wait before ruling out that possibility

Door shut in his office, Marcus wondered too if instead and unbeknownst to his everyday awareness he'd stumbled over the end point. Simultaneously, he pictured the eruption of a craze founded on the belief that through the burned calories that thought alone required an ideal weight could be attained. Yes, *The Mind Over Matter Diet*. It'd sell oodles of copies. Perfect for sloths everywhere.

At intervals between home and campus, Marcus reflected on the likelihood of his happening upon satisfaction vis-à-vis Judaea. That some deep logical thought structure, a spongy iota of frontal lobe—if that applied—monitoring or regulating or brooding over longterm psycho-judicial processes had reached a verdict: "Okay, I'm satisfied, we're done, it's over." At last. After sixty or so months the gavel had resolved to swing down: the aggregate of Judaea-directed punishments—correctives, really—finally corresponded to the crime's severity. And acceptable restitu-tion—not material, of course, but psychological—had been . . . accomplished? Enacted? Achieved? Whatever word fit, that's where he stood.

Yes, yes, a fait accompli. The injured party felt contented while assured too that the wrongdoer had come to understand—profoundly—the toll of a hurtful action.

Gaze unfocused on the transit route, Marcus nodded inter-nally, in agreement with his own findings. As for cognitive bias, he pooh-poohed the notion. He knew what he knew.

Or, perhaps his mind's gavel had walloped his mind's sound block exactly a single episode before he'd scarfed down the sec-ond of Judaea's refrigerated lunches—tartly dressed rice and quinoa grains that, laughably, had turned out to be seeds of doubt. And the ruling had taken a circuitous path before reaching his self-awareness. By overstepping, by assigning Judaea a fractionally harsher sentence than strictly required, he'd begun to feel low. That guess merited attention.

Then again, maybe not. After a bus stop CMT notification about phytonutrients (microscopic underdogs, according to the contracted copywriter) and a subsequent information dump from Syb about the physiology of moodiness, Marcus bet that his B6 and zinc might need topping up. He ought to check the CMT for numbers. Perhaps swap cookies for pumpkin seeds, resume purchasing wholemeal bread. Buy lamb chops too: evidently, those little critters were zinc on hooves.

The decision-reached hypothesis made a certain kind of sense, Marcus believed, especially since he'd never pictured equitable retaliation rolling on endlessly in the manner of legendary family vendettas (criminals, aristocrats, vampires) that refused to expire.

Just the spectacle of a lively feud with staying power, a juggernaut until he wore the emeritus crown, had struck him as dubious.

On the days and weeks immediately following the Incident, even though rigid with ire and furious at unpredictable intervals, Marcus had held firm to confidence about the eventual termination date. One memorable campus morning in the visible future, he'd expected to find in-his-face Judaea turning ghostly somehow. She'd reconstitute overnight as a kind of persona non grata that he might pass by or listen to during a meeting—of necessity—but regard with utter yet sincere indifference. A return to the old routine; he wouldn't even have to try. Judaea could as well be an empty office chair: visible, naturally, but a quotidian object without much significance. And certainly nothing threatening enough to raise his hackles. Meritless.

That vision might be fantasy, he'd gathered; expectations aren't reasonable, not always chained to earthly cause and effect. Witness lottery ticket booth habitués, for years on end: "This time, for sure. I've got a good feeling. It's my turn now!"

In another ameliorative scenario, a forecast Marcus had seen as iffy at best, Judaea either apologized or directly acknowledged—wearing a convincingly bowed penitent's face—that not only had her action been unnecessary, thoughtless, and cruel but the base assessment entirely incorrect. "I was unspeakably petty, brash, and such a troublemaker, please forgive me": that mode of hindsight-inspired realization and disavowal common to politicians and film scripts that excuses the person for the asinine upstart they'd formerly been. He'd be on board with the outcome even if he couldn't fully accept the woman's radical about-face, the underlying premise.

Marcus allowed for the positive outcome of a disappearance too.

Not the atrocious sort that Latin America had been bringing to the world's attention for decades but, far more probably, a professional one. News would worm into his ear that Judaea had accepted a position—a boast-worthy address, naturally, all cobbled walkways and ivy-latticed brick—near the Atlantic coastline. Or on another affluent continent. Later, by grapevine, further details about the latest career peak she'd connived. With that, the bête noire would become a memory activated only by her name's appearance in print. Or a donkey's braying, should he encounter one. And he'd march toward retirement, as calm and pleasant as a brook.

(Alternately, but fat chance: *he* would have grown, become a bigger person radiant with Gospel of Luke-level forgiveness: "To err is human, blah blah . . ." She needn't lift a finger. The storybook version might offer a last-minute change of heart, a redemptive budding of personal enlightenment or legitimate late-onset moral evolution in the direction of the Dalai Lama rather than the latest magnate, politician, or religious leader coached to verbalize manufactured outrage—"I've been falsely maligned"—before a crowd of proffered mics.)

Cycles end organically, after all, Marcus thought, processes reach completion, fevers run their course. The solar system does its thing.

Ever-negotiating, participants shape and reshape marital relationships along the way, so why not romance's ill-tempered opposite? Surely, that added up. If grief—or: happiness, depression, wellbeing, fury, contentment—could last seconds, days, months, or a lifetime, then obviously anger or the sense of being wronged could take on any of a number of permutations. And in many of them, perhaps all, the best before date wouldn't be categorically different than those stamped on the soup cans in his cupboard: the contents held their integrity until they didn't. Plus, after the date—2 Oct 2027 or 23 Feb 2028—passed, who knew what breakdowns occurred, what unhealthy muck resulted. Better to use it up and continue forward.

Yes, in theory, retribution *had to* come packaged with a built-in deadline, a cap. A conclusion. The person failed to get even or succeeded, one or the other.

Infinite retribution could no longer claim to be retribution. He'd label that state of mind pathological, unhinged.

When the culprit stole one hundred dollars from you and you recouped every cent, plus whatever interest and processing fees you'd calculated: voilà, the show was over.

Easy peasy, right? As elegant as a bloodless coup.

If his own situation with Judaea had run into overtime by a smidgen, he could feel at peace with the calculation error. Within acceptable parameters, as business titans said.

The meals, rides, and walking accompanied by specialized calorie usage—the moral quaking (tremoring, perhaps) and intermittent neural wrist-slapping—halted alongside the moodiness one sodden Friday morning when several colleagues in succession let Marcus know that Judaea had secured a pre-nomination for unit Head. An email confirmed the woman's ambition later that afternoon.

Whose arm did she twist, Marcus asked no one, after silently exclaiming *Of course, of fucking course* and *Didn't need a clairvoyant for that one.*

In the very same faculty lounge where he'd righteously stolen Judaea's food and the main office where he'd committed to blameless acts of gossip, Marcus soon began to overhear guarded and sotto voce conversations that signalled the dawning, mid-morning, and high noon of informal pre-election campaigning and voter inducements. His division of the unit, formerly the English Department, would presently nominate its representative for Chair of Integrated Humanities.

Per usual, for a few weeks the building's whisperings would bring to mind Vatican passageways in the hours leading up to the papal conclave's locked doors.

Under the grand causes of What, Going Forward, is Optimal for the Unit? and Who Can Best Speak for the Stockpiled Needs of the Electorate? he caught typical exchanges, often in the form of any number of rhetorical sins faculty outlined as such year after year before students handed in essays. Ad hominem ("He just rubs me the wrong way, I don't trust him"). Ad baculum ("Choose her if you wish, but trust me we'll all pay"). Dicto simpliciter ("Some new blood will get things accomplished"). Ad misericordiam ("It's got to be her turn, look at what she's been through"). Ad populum ("The smart money's on her"). Argumentum ad verecundiam ("She is, I suppose, certainly . . . popular . . . with students").

As with the outside world, the old disputes and gut feelings of ad hominem dominated the corridors.

In glassy passages, airy stairwells, newly-minted door frames, and red cedar-faced pockets of the main office, secondhand word about what Judaea promised (the world, naturally) and how she characterized other rumoured-to-be nominees drifted his way. Among the woman's terms: "fossil," directed not at him but Simone R., a Medievalist hired two years after Marcus.

Out of habit Marcus fumed while seated and standing in routine locations before realizing his stingy heart—or whatever—refused to feed his head the desire for prompt, merciless, and decisive action.

His final spring semester, meanwhile, passed from week five to six.

Marcus felt unsurprised when his first instinct, practically a reflex, involved the generation of shorthand lifted from six decades of books, films, and television. The chess master weighing the necessary opening strategy with a wily upstart opponent two feet distant. The lawyer marshalling inner resources for the decisive closing argument that alone could free the innocent victim on trial. Stern Prussian-moustached generals in wartime sweating over maps cluttered with battalion icons and awaiting their own Austerlitz; their descendants, in spacecrafts, doing much the same with holographic representations of the quadrant.

The situation demanded response, no?

He saw himself mentioning to Associate Prof T or Associate Prof C that he would not be opposed to a nomination. Or perhaps something off-the-cuff to Senior Office Administrator L, that busybody. From there, a campaign of reeling in a career's worth of favours, of drawing attention to his exemplary record of service and the essential rightness—rightfulness—of him over Judaea. If those failed to persuade, he'd opt for underhanded ploys. Surely, a millennia or so of precedent established an abiding tradition.

Syb:

"As an observational commonplace, Marcus, 'All is fair in love and war' can be traced to authors of Rome's antiquity. Not until 1850, though, does the exact phrasing that is now used appear, in Frank Smedley's forgotten 1850 novel, *Frank Fairlegh: Scenes from the Life of a Private Pupil*.

"The earliest known familial origin of the aphorism 'All's fair in love and war' is found in English poet John Lyly's prose romance *Euphues: The Anatomy of Wit*, published in 1578. The book recounts the amatory adventures of a handsome Athenian gentleman, and includes the statement 'the rules of fair play do not apply in love and war.'

"*Euphues* helped make Lyly the most fashionable English writer of the 1580s, but the Londoner died impoverished and embittered in 1606.

"In November 1605, the English Catholic mercenary Guido Fawkes—"

"Yes, yes, understood. Thank you, Syb."

At the prospect of the actual meetings and diplomacy to ensue, though, Marcus retracted. The unrealizable promises. The glad-handing. Worse, if chosen, on a daily basis for a two-year stint he'd sit and listen to voices complaining and watch stabbed fingers asserting, hands defending, eyes questioning, and mouths requesting. Nodding and nodding, meeting after meeting. A magnet for arterial plaque and visceral fat and a bleeping CMT all the while, he'd face pleas or demands in his office or similarly-furnished rectangular spaces belonging to deans, Finance reps, or Enrolment Services officers. All Kafka, no whimsy. For him, then, a textbook Pyrrhic victory. A career cap he'd happily live without.

A first cousin of an idea, to sponsor Judaea's loss or assure the victory of someone—anyone—else, floated up agleam with possibility. With a defeat he'd catalyze, that he'd author, he could wash his hands of her. Slow-learner Judaea would comprehend and feel the hyperinflation of her self-estimations. You are not well liked or respected, she'd recognize; people have insufficient faith in your credentials; no one trusts you; know your place.

Bah, Marcus thought on the usual buses and homeward sidewalks. That serpentine villainy, all cool calculation, belonged to—had appeared on—stage and screen. He'd only need a side-kick, a cavernous lair as a headquarters. The old furnace room in the Warfield, maybe. That cad's insinuating, power-hungry machinations behind closed doors belonged in the profile of a weak character, aspects he did not discern in himself. Cardboard stuff. It lacked nuance.

For part of a late night route to corner store snacks Marcus favoured a narrow residential street dwarfed by a canopy of leafy trees.

Along its root-heaved sidewalks, trimmed boxwood and cherry laurel hedges—tranquil in appearance but poison-veined—fronted what looked to be quaint Edwardian family homes. In the post-nuclear family decades, these relics with room for six kids, a servant, and visiting relatives in droves had out-grown their usefulness. Developers bought and razed them.

Gutting the interiors while retaining crusts of historical facade, they engineered each residence into six or eight, with a laneway house to boot.

Just past a stand of them at 8:45 PM on an inauspicious Monday of heavy clouds and damp air, Marcus stopped before an eyesore-yellow '40s duplex as yet untouched, like the Warfield, by any developer's transformative vision.

Inside, mirror image men perched on couch edges while watching a game (hockey left, basketball right). Further back, seated women shuffled papers and tapped screens at rectangular dining room tables.

Marcus kept an unaccountable soft spot for the twin rental addresses; if the building stood empty, he'd consider inquiring. Following a successful bid, hired painters could restore the white exterior.

The spare, modern lines suggested a back turned to another era's fussy pieties. Also, the picture windows lacked drapes and served as a diorama of a kind. Unaware of passersby, complete strangers in two sets opted to illustrate everyday life.

With a certainty that induced an involuntary nod, Marcus knew what to do. Poof, he thought, *and the waters were divided.*

As he'd walked by the latest historical luxury refit, this one's signboard—Belgravia Mews—spelled in filigreed letters, Marcus hadn't been aware of percolating about anything especially.

No, in fact, he had flitted from idea to idea. A foil package of parmesan crackers in hand, he'd wondered about opening them en route. Plus, about the duration and severity of the rain to come, about what immuno-mechanism prevented the city's fecund stucco mold from growing on skin, whether the pumpkin seeds on the crackers were sufficient in number to count as nutritious, about how much he could improve his eating habits without the change registering as deprivation, and about if, food-wise, going cold turkey could shock his system adversely, as when alcoholics expire from *delirium tremens* after a vow to pour out bottles, lock doors, and battle demons.

Amid the patternless firings of these thoughts the realization hatched nevertheless.

As he always had, Marcus saw he would cast a ballot with what he imagined as a typical complex of feelings, hope and futility chief among them.

For anyone but her, of course. Professor B, perhaps, habitually bureaucratic to his last chromosome. Or S, that gruff, tweed-girded prima donna. Even young whatshisname, with the quick smile and earnest promises to every faction he'd never keep.

Save for voting, though, Marcus understood he'd commit to doing nothing. If asked beforehand, he'd answer who he favoured and why. Or his reservations. But he wouldn't go out of his way to disparage Judaea. Nor would he concoct any laughable plan to discredit, humiliate, or undo the wearisome arriviste.

In significant ways, the matter belonged to him no longer. Shortly, with a virtual click in a Payroll server his salary would change into pension. He'd keep an emeritus mailbox for a couple of years. Maybe pick up a course, leave a toe on campus. And toil—at no great pace—on a few articles and the next book. Or not. He might find better things to do. Swab oil-soaked birds and dig holes for tree seedlings, say. Summit a granite peak.

Otherwise he'd subside, relinquish, and evaporate as a campus presence, the ever-renewing institution continuing on to future enormity. New construction, satellite campuses, wider brand recognition. Promotions would continue. Elections, hirings, terminations, resignations, setbacks, retirements, input grades, scholarships and prizes, evaluations and grade appeals and service and assignments and exams and plagiarism and letters of reference, semester after semester ongoing and expanding, an assured pocket universe operating upon a foundation of first, second, and third laws.

Amid all that, if Judaea managed to fool or manipulate or charm voters intelligent enough to recognize or sense bad faith, then maybe she deserved the win.

Besides, Marcus hazarded, out there somewhere another him had already been born as well as another her. All of them and their character profiles, which would bind with some, orbit others, repel others, and collide (mildly, disastrously, haplessly) with still others even as their own replacements in diapers or preschool forged ahead, in the perpetual, eternal, absurd Pin Factory—

Whoa, Marcus thought, aware of himself now from an outsider's perspective, an old guy in a duffer cap and black woollen overcoat paused on a damp segment of sidewalk and apparently lost in thought. Or walloped by senility and just lost in the blanketing nighttime: "Excuse me, sir, are you in need of some assistance?"

Right past the elementary school and that aggressively ordinary beige condo on the corner, a few hundred paces, Marcus caught sight of the Warfield's rear corner.

He'd rip open that bag, with its temptation of chips—salt, fat, carbohydrate, flavour—and munch on a fistful before arriving home. Really, why deny yourself?

A lecturer of English literature at the University of British Columbia, Brett Josef Grubisic is the author of the novels *The Age of Cities*, *This Location of Unknown Possibilities* and *From Up River and for One Night Only*. He calls Salt Spring Island home.